Of Course I Love You..!
...Till I Find Someone Better

Other Books by Durjoy Datta

Now That You're Rich!
She Broke Up, I Didn't!
Ohh Yes, I Am Single!
You Were My Crush!
If It's Not Forever!

Of Course I Love You..!

...Till I Find Someone Better

Durjoy Datta
Maanvi Ahuja

GRAPEVINE INDIA

Grapevine India Publishers Pvt. Ltd.
Plot no.4, First Floor
Pandav Nagar,
Opposite Shadipur Metro Station,
Patel Nagar,
New Delhi - 110008
India
grapevineindiapublishers@gmail.com
contact@grapevineindia.in

First published in India by Grapevine India Publishers in 2012

Copyright © Durjoy Datta, 2008

Typeset and layout design: A & D. Co.

Based on real life incidents.

Acknowledgements

Were it not for these people whom we thank below (and an active God), this book would still be languishing in the *My Documents* folder of our computers. These people might not be literary super powers, but they always made us feel that our book was Booker material, often without reading the manuscript. Needless to say, we took them seriously.

To start the list with somebody who was dying to see his name in print just as we were, we would like to thank Sachin Garg, the first and the last, to think that we are small Rushdies in the making.

Stuti and Mayank, who are still in a state of shock upon hearing that we, can write. Worse, get published! There are others, most of who have led strange lives and ended up, willingly or unwillingly, contributing to the book:

Megha Sharma, Kanika Suri, Deepika Kapur, and Sheetal Shishodia - the four of them who thought it was a long joke until they realized we were not actually rolling on the floor laughing or as they say – ROFLing.

Nishit Bhatnagar, Neeti Rustagi, Archit Garg, Abhishek Sachdev (Thanks! You rock!), Nitin Verma, Nikita Singh, Naman Kapur, DVYRAS (partly) – who put up with our strange ways, and all of whom wanted a free copy until they knew they would be on the opening page. Now they want two.

All our fellow bloggers, and the people on Facebook for all the appreciation they showered on us – and still do – despite hating us for the mindless things we write.

Our batch mates at our alma mater(s) who unflinchingly provided us with proxy attendances whenever and wherever needed.

Our families, and especially our parents, who constantly supported and encouraged us, even as they grappled with nightmares of two of us, leaving all material pursuits (read careers) and end up as intellectual paupers. That is until they read the book and realised we were up to no good.

And finally our sisters, Rituparna Datta and Tanvi Ahuja, who have inspired us and made us believe that this was our calling in life – besides finding ourselves a job, pursuing a management degree, having kids, taking out the garbage, among others – and this is what we should continue doing.

We also thank Sri Sri Ravi Shankar, whose blessings were always with us.

We are glad to have come out this ordeal of writing a book together, with just a few bruises here and there. We thank ourselves.

Desperate Measures

This is perfect. This is perfect, I kept telling myself. It had been twelve hours on the trot. I had already spent my entire month's allowance on her and there were no signs of getting myself treated to any sort of guilty pleasures other than the expensive and the utterly fattening ones. The fact that Smriti looked fumingly hot in her floral spaghetti and the short pleated skirt that ended inches after her butt line did, wasn't doing any good to me either. The very purpose of the skirt's existence was being defeated that night. Easy accessibility and eventually *get rid*-ability.

It had been a long day and I had started ruing the moment I asked her out for a night-out. I had missed all my classes that day, all in vain.

'So, what next?' she asked.

What next? For starters, she could have fried my bloody head and chomped it down. Oh no, wait! That wouldn't have cost me *anything*. She, without doubt, would have ordered her third cocktail that evening to wash it down. Not that she would start seeing things in double and eventually be oblivious of me rendering her clothes useless. I might be a jerk, but many guys would agree with me on this - *Nudity suits girls*.

'I don't know,' I said with a dreamy look plastered across my face shouting that I was content doing nothing but to look at her. I hoped it would work this time though it was the millionth time that day and she had not even blown a kiss, let alone do it real time.

I wondered why I had decided to be in love with her. I could have lived with the tag of an ugly but *lucky* jerk with a one-track-mind. For a guy who looked as bad as I did, it was surprising that I had dated a *few* girls before Smriti. However, none of my relationships worked and every break up used to be my fault. This time I had decided to make it work.

Why?

Because I was just tired of the nonsense said about me and it was time to fall in *love*. They said I had no respect for women and it was not true at all. I was losing every bit of credibility on the dating scene. Soon, I knew no friend who would set me up with anybody, which itself happened very rarely in my world. Being a perennially on-loan, *struggling-to-save-money-for-dates* student of a nerdy engineering college, relationships where I was, were more than partying out each night and drinking oneself to sexual inability. People around me wanted love, care and long conversations, for *whatever* that meant.

I just *had to* find somebody to love. Or at least somebody I would not hate after the first few weeks. Smriti fit the bill. I was *lucky* I got her.

She was not too hard to handle and was low on maintenance. At least I had thought so when I started pursuing her. The *most* important thing – she was busy. As a medical student, she did not have much time to talk. She spent more time examining other people's things than mine. It meant that I was spared the agony of answering questions like *'Am I looking fat?' 'Is my ass too big?' 'You love me, right? 'She is horrible, isn't she?'* etc. I couldn't have asked for me.

She was a little too thin, a little too fair for my bulky five feet ten frame and consequently, a little less endowed at the places I would have liked. But what the hell, she was beautiful. Not like the ones you would stare at and shag until you are blue and frothing, but the one you would take home to your mom. Although in our case, I could never imagine the last part happening.

Something kept her from reaching the dizzying heights of dollish beauty. It was either her smile that extended from ear to ear giving her a slightly chimp-*ish* look. Or the slightly longish, crooked nose. Whatever it was, there was something wrong in her. I would find out in due time and find her not likeable, if the need arose. For now, I had to concentrate on getting her to kiss me.

I was not in a position to comment on something such as looks, anyway. The only redeeming feature on my face was the patch of unmanaged beard that covered my chin and took away attention from the below-average features I had managed to crowd my face with. The unmanaged mop of hair on the top of my head helped too. My basic idea was to hide as much of my face as possible. Okay, well, I had a dimple too.

It had been close to a month that Smriti and I had accepted that we loved each other, but until now, there was no physical proof to back it. We had not even kissed until then. However, a night out was *exactly* what I needed to weave my magic, and weave her off her clothes. Alternatively, even if I failed to do so, I would have told myself it was pure, untainted love that I was after. As 50 Cent preached in one of his songs – *Be a gentleman.* It was tough, though; she was not letting me be a *man.* Gentle, I never was.

Anyway, I had managed to put my hand around her and land a peck on her cheek during the wretched movie we watched, Gold Class plus popcorn. Moreover, the peck was so woefully devoid of passion, it could have graced a greeting card rather than a Cosmopolitan centrefold.

How was I supposed to know that *Chronicles of Narnia* would seem so interesting to her that she would fail to notice the peck? She was a doctor, all right. But not a vet! Definitely not Dr. Doolittle. Ideally, she shouldn't have been interested in a talking lion, let alone cry for the damned thing.

'It's closing down. Let's go to a place that will be open all night,' she said.

Nightlife in Delhi was pathetic, to say the least. I suspected even a tribal region in Sikkim showed up on the US military radar systems more than Delhi did. The deserted roads meant going to *Comesum*, the only all-night place that I could have afforded after the amount of money in my wallet had hit rock bottom on that boring, clothes-on night. Comesum was a place where all the inexpensive night outs invariably ended... amidst lots of pathetic food and mosquitoes. Nevertheless, its large and empty parking space and low *do-not-disturb* bribe rates excited me, and many others who spent the night romping away to glory behind tinted car windows.

Sex was engulfing every part of Delhi, having long replaced television as the favourite topic of discussion. People who were not doing it, refused to see. However, it was all around. The geeky girl in your class, the stud guy, the backbencher *sardar*, however incapable you might have thought them to be, morally or physically, they were all doing it. If you had a girl, then you would be doing it. It was everywhere – schools, office backrooms, movie halls and parking lots. Secluded places were paradise. Tinted car windows were *in*, illegal they might have been. In a few years, *not having* a girlfriend became as odd as *having* one was, a few years back. The DPS MMS of 2004 was just the tip of an iceberg.

'How about going to *Comesum?*' I asked a seemingly stupid question to a seemingly stupid suggestion.

Nevertheless, I did not blame her for her naivety. The girl I had dated before Smriti was so astonishingly boring when we weren't making out that I had to look for interesting places that one could go to in Delhi.

'We can go to AURA. It's in Hotel Ashoka, I guess. I heard its fine too. Lots of girls! I bet you will like it,' she said and nudged me. I could have leered at wiggly tits at a club, but an option like that is more luring when you are no longer trying to get inside your girl's shirt. It had been three months since I had broken up and it's not very easy convincing people to still be in contact, *especially physical.*

'I have been to AURA. It's not as good as people say it is. It just has a few drunken local brats dancing. That's it. And it's anyway not worth it driving that far,' I said.

'Your call... it is your treat. You decide.' *Thank god for that.*

I loved that place, AURA. Especially on evenings when stags weren't allowed, that place was heaven... and an expensive one at that. I had to shoot either the plan down or myself. *I loved myself.* We headed off to *Comesum*, driving off a drunken auto driver's directions. His breath was in no way different from what Smriti's mouth reeked off. It's amazing that *I paid for her bad breath.*

We had to take directions from whomever we came across, thanks to two of my most feminine attributes combined with a masculine one – I couldn't remember roads, was a terrible driver, and pretended to know it all.

After about a million detours and a zillion U-turns, we finally reached the place where I hoped all my hard work for the day and the few weeks preceding it would pay off. I told myself not to expect anything because I was so damn much in *love*, after all. Wasn't I? That was the time I realized how hard it was to be a good boyfriend who pays and is not on his knees *begging* for a kiss.

'Ice-cream?' she asked.

'Sure!'

The urge to kill her was now bursting out of my veins. I could feel it seeping out of my skin. I had started wondering what options she had if I were to abandon her in a desolate street at 3 a.m. in the night. She would probably be raped and I wouldn't be the one doing it. It wasn't a particularly clever idea but I did consider it when she looked the other way while I fuelled up the car! It costs money and I was barely above the poverty line. I wished someone would tell her that.

In the previous relationships, I was loaded with the advantage of being an engineering student. With better calculations, I always had things rounded off to my convenience. However, with Smriti, there were no calculations. All the bills went only one way. *My way.*

I wished I hadn't turned down Nitin, a college senior's invitation to his job treat. But then, girls and sex make the world go around, and I am no different. And like the rest, he would have expected my refusal.

My eyes started roving around the complex as we gulped down the slimy sweet thing she had ordered. It was a two-storied building and most of the people sat outside. It wasn't anything spectacular – in fact, it wasn't even air conditioned or heated – but then, you couldn't expect it to be. It opened primarily for railway passengers and not drunk party revellers. Every weekend it used to turn into a hot spot for *bird* watching! Whoever, who ran out of money, got thrown out of a club or got too drunk, landed up there. So we had there, a mix of short skirts and long flowing ones (Mostly short!) bought from anywhere from Janpath, the place where you can bargain till the time you get just too tired to continue or some swanky upscale mall in Vasant Kunj!

Delhi girls never dress up *conservatively*, making it a pleasure ogling at them. Especially, since I didn't give two hoots about the supposedly subtle/boring fashion trends. Anything that started after the navel and ended before mid-thigh was fine by me. Exposure is *always* in vogue! There is nothing more refreshing than a pair of freshly waxed legs. This is not objectifying women; it's just appreciating a certain fact about them a little more than others.

Suddenly, leggy beauties with pancaked faces were all around me, bitching about the girl wearing the shorter skirt, to their boyfriends in their crotch hugging jeans. Those girls could have fired up a power station to full capacity. It just worsened my already sky-high testosterone levels. I tried to finish off the ice cream quickly as it had been a pain watching her chew every atom down to its proton and neutron and then taking it down.

'Aren't you feeling cold?' I asked, as I rubbed my hands. Obviously, she wasn't. All girls have an internal heating system that is activated once they put on their halter-necks and short dresses!

'No. Are you?' she asked.

'No, I thought we will sit in the car; there is too much noise out here,' I said.

'Are you sure?' she asked and smirked at me.

Now, what was that supposed to mean? Was that a yes? If it is, why doesn't she bloody say so? Can we please cut the crap and make out? At least kiss, damn it! It's been three months since I have done that!

I guess she was getting some kind of a sadistic pleasure seeing me get robbed of my money, which was forever short and my mind, which had short-circuited, by then.

'Yes,' I said.

As I started walking towards the parked car, I hoped that she would follow. She had to! Girls like men who lead the way and know what they want, don't they? I definitely knew what *I* wanted. I wanted her to strip. Or somewhere around that.

I took the first few steps and paddled my hands around me to hold her by the waist. She wasn't there. She wasn't coming. She didn't follow. I looked back. She was standing right there. Right there, staring down at me.

'Deb?' she said.

'Um, err... yes,' I said as I paid.

'*Bhaiya, paise,*' said the vendor. Thank god for small mercies!

'Smriti, can we go now?' I said. Maybe pleaded. It was no

time to get angry on her for why she couldn't even pay for her own ice-cream. I had to stay focussed.

'Yeah, sure,' she said.

As we walked towards the car, I winked at the moustached security guard and he got the message – *Do not disturb*.

Another 100 bucks down. But then, it was an *investment*. I could already feel a twitch in my jeans, which was the only thing that held it in place. The problem with low waist jeans is that when you walk, it is always as if you have a helmet stuck right between your thighs... and if you have mammoth thighs like me, God help you. Yeah, I was a little *healthy*... and detestable.

'Deb, why did you get Vernita's car? This one guzzles up a lot of fuel, don't you think?' she asked as she walked ahead of me. I didn't stop her from doing that. Her skirt looked even shorter and more alluring from behind. Yeah, I acted like a cheap pervert. But then, every guy goes through this phase!

'My car wasn't serviced,' I said. *It didn't have tinted glasses.*

She was playing around. She couldn't possibly be concerned with the money I blew on fuel. Had she been concerned she wouldn't have ordered the ridiculously expensive Irish coffee at TGIFs'. It wasn't even worth the tax I paid for it!

As soon as we settled down in the car, I got the elementary step wrong. However, I didn't blame myself for it. It had been quite some time that I hadn't leered at a real naked girl and I was dying to do it that night. I had started to rub my nose against the nape of her neck, which was meant to send her in to throes of hormonal overdrive.

'Are you trying to seduce me, Deb?' she asked. Not that she didn't like it. She wanted me to say some mushy and nice before doing anything. Hypocrites as they are.

'Mmm... err... no.'

'Mmm, err, no,' she mocked me and I turned red, only to turn scarlet later. 'You might have had your way with girls in the past, but not this time,' she said. It was strange because I had *never* had my way with girls in the past.

'As in? What do you mean?'

'As in, I would initiate things whenever I feel like doing so, whenever I am comfortable with it.'

I was still hovering around the reddish red and the slightly mauvish red. *She was in control?* Something in that tone was incredibly inviting. I wanted her *bad* now. Only that I didn't know how to.

'Okay, whatever you say. I love you,' I said.

'I love you too,' she replied and I faked a smile, as an airhostess would at the ogling oldies. Without sleep, without rest, she would rather have them minced by the turbine blades. I sunk back into my seat, wondering if there was any porn left to download. I wished I were in Mumbai or Bangalore. Delhi girls are tough, Shrey once told me.

'Why do you love me?' she asked. She looked at me as if she was expecting me take out a pen and start listing things down on a mile long toilet paper roll.

'You are very *different* from others.' That was supposed to include everything on the list.

'How am I different from the others you have gone out with?'

I *resisted telling her she was no different; she had the same* questions to ask.

'I love you. With others, it just wasn't so. It wasn't love. Love is what I feel for you, pure and untainted. With you, I feel different, I feel special, I feel wanted, I feel loved and I long to make you feel the same. You make me feel so. You *complete* me Smriti. I love you. I really do.'

Whoa! I still had it in me. I paused and stuttered. It nearly sounded spontaneous!

'How sweet, Deb! I love you too. You are not as bad as my friends tell me. You are so sweet,' she said and ran her hand over my cheeks. *A little lower, a little lower, just a little lower, damn it!*

We then talked trash for what seemed like an entire eon. To be frank, it wasn't as if it was entirely boring, she was much more interesting than an average girl. It was just that I wasn't looking for the *interesting* conversation – that's what married people do. I was just an average bloke looking for some *extraordinary* sex. Sex was maybe too far-fetched (Obviously!), but I could have at least done with a little stripping, a little kissing and little groping. Not too much to ask for, I suppose. Of course, I *loved* her too.

Somewhere between the interesting conversations, I had slept off with my head resting on her shoulder. It had been a long and an expensive day. I slept thinking whether I would still be awake enough the next morning to attend the Mechanics of Solids class. The date wasn't worth missing it.

It had been a while when I felt something against my cheek, something nice and delightfully wet. Oh, man! She was kissing me. For real! I tried hard to stay still to see all that she was up to. I opened one eye and saw a bit of my cheek disappearing inside her mouth and be slathered over by her tongue. I woke up wondering what all I had missed.

'Deb, you look cuter when you are sleeping.'

'I am going right back to sleep, you don't dare stop.'

She started all the nice stuff, crossed one of legs over me and sat on my lap until her neck was within licking distance. Then it flowed, a few great kisses, some wild fondling and she grabbed for something hard in me. It had started to feel real good, as I tip toed my fingers up her back to what she was wearing inside and was just about to unhook the joys of being a man, when she stopped me.

'Nuh-huh… Not that quick, my boy…' she said as she pulled my hands out.

'Why not?' I asked, as I pulled my hand out and placed it

beneath her skirt, moving it up slowly, for something stupid inside me convinced me that she would not notice. I aimed for the stars. The twitch was getting twitchier but she was no longer interested in it.

Clothes can be a pain. Why the hell couldn't we just be dressed like prehistoric cave men with neither clothes nor any source of entertainment other than... you know...?

'No, not that fast... we will save the rest for later. It's not fun doing everything at once.'

'But—' I said dejectedly.

'I don't feel like doing anything else right now,' she said, as she grabbed my hand and pulled it out from its silken abode.

Now what was I to make of it? I had done reasonably well, to think of it. It was officially our first night out and the fifth date and to have managed all that I did till then, was commendable. It came at a price, but who cared? *I loved her.*

I took heart from the fact that she said that we would not do everything at once. And that probably meant we would do it but not at once.

It was getting easier to love her. She left me with some big mosquito bites on my neck. If mosquitoes ever grew up to the size of dogs, that is. The kisses were great, so I decided I would continue loving her. And I did. After all, it is easier to love a busy, smart girl – who's a good kisser – rather than loving somebody you love. Smriti was turning out to be amazing in all visual and tangible assets and I loved it.

I had to think of a reason to explain those love bites. Mom would have definitely asked for a reason for those marks. I tried my sister's concealers and they helped a bit. I roamed around in ancient turtlenecks for the next few days.

I was shallow and I knew that. I loved being so and I knew many who wanted to be me.

The Trio and The 'Break'ing (*up*) Ground

'How much did you score?' she asked. The fifth semester results were out. This was January 2007.

'52 percent,' I replied.

'That's not bad,' Smriti said.

'It's not bad? My class rank is eighty on hundred. It's not bad, it's terrible. I am done. I so screwed,' I said.

'You didn't study, so you couldn't have done any better,' she said.

'Thanks for the help. I could have done without that,' I said.

It's strange how people can't lie when they have to. I knew I didn't study, but I could have done without being reminded of that again. But she had always been like this, straightforward and ruthlessly un-diplomatic. It was fun when we had just started going around and she used to pamper the man in me saying things like that I was the *best guy she had ever kissed* (which is probably the same thing guys before me would have heard), but of late she had started saying pretty irritating stuff. Like, '*my friend Virangana, her boyfriend is so brilliant that he has got a 7 figure job.*' Or, '*you are not great looking but yes, I still love you very much.*'

Had I said anything remotely close to what she used to, I

would have been dead meat. And yes, it had been two months, and things were not the same anymore. Relationships deteriorate; mine just did a little faster. Every relationship has an expiry date.

We did do a lot of things but a lot of it fell short of my expectations. She wasn't as dreamlike as I had imagined her to be. She started acting like a little kid in a big city with no one else but me. We did have numerous night outs, thanks to Lady Hardinge Medical College's non-existent hostel rules. However, the charm was gone and consequently my classes became too important to miss. I hated her prolonged foreplay kisses that exhausted her beyond twenty orgasms. Yes, we had stamina problems. *From her side.*

Importantly, I managed a split in bills every time we went out. My dating costs were finally under control.

'Are we meeting tonight?' she asked.

'Are we? Yes, why *not*? Let us celebrate; I just blew up my semester exams. I may not get a job after DCE. Now that's something to celebrate about,' I replied, sarcasm dripping off every word that I said.

'Deb, we hardly talk for twenty minutes in day, can't we meet, at least?'

'Don't be stupid, Smriti. We talk a hell lot more than that. And what about the messages I send? The missed calls? We are on the phone the whole day, damn it,' I shouted.

'No, we never are. You never reply to my messages. You have time to talk to Vernita. You have time to reply to my friends' messages. *You* never call me; *I* do. You have time for everything in the world, but not for me,' she said, her voice shook. Her tear glands got ready to start working.

'Smriti, I am really pissed off right now and can do without your nonsense. You will *never* understand this. My college marks are important, damn it. I am close to being screwed and all you think about is *you*, your dates and your calls and the goddamned messages. Fuck man, I can't believe you can be so selfish. Bye… and please don't call back unless I call you,' I said agitatedly and disconnected the call. It is better to shift blame than try to fight it. It also meant a licence not to pick her calls for the next few hours.

As expected, my phone kept buzzing with her texts for the next half an hour and she apologized for things she wasn't responsible for. Most of the messages didn't make any sense, but they were long and that is what generally matters. Smriti was a sucker for these long messages and expected them to have the same effect on me. I hardly read those messages.

I knew I was being harsh on Smriti. But then, something had to be done. I couldn't have just walked out of her life, left her crying and be spat on again. If things were breaking down, she had to take blame for it too. She had to be bad in some way. The breakup had to result out of *mutual* frustration and incompatibility.

I mean it wasn't my fault that I didn't find anything interesting after all these months. It was a congenital disease. I couldn't help it. For heaven's sake, nothing changed for the better, it just became worse! I had to talk to her for four hours a day and give her the minut*est* details of everything I did in the day. It had started to get on my nerves. She had shut out all her friends and devoted every minute to me! Worse, she wanted me to do the same.

She wasn't even sexy anymore. Those glistening, marble-white thighs now seemed to have stretch marks marring them and her petite breasts seemed to have retreated into her body. I noticed all that. Too bad if nobody else did. And to top it all, she was supposedly wrecking my college performance too. The relationship was killing me.

Going on like this was against the very laws of nature… only the fittest and the *sexiest* survive (Don't ask how I did). She was neither. I couldn't have possibly gone against the laws of Darwin. I wasn't the church. I wasn't even a Christian.

'Hey… what's up? How was the result?' said a voice from behind. He had gone to the hostel to catch a nap between classes but had not returned for any.

It was Shrey, in his imposing six-foot frame, dressed in a Manchester United tee (he liked the colour, not the team), faded blue jeans that had been soiled to brown now, and *chappals*, not the jazzy ones, but the ones meant to be worn strictly within the confines of one's home. Shrey, with his tanned complexion, as he would put it and beehive-ish curly hair on top, which according to him were perennially in vogue since the 70's, though, did a good job of making me look better.

Shrey was the kind of guy who actually gets on your nerves the first few times for his theories about life, IQ, education, poverty, progress, engineering, even girl psychology! They were all bullshit.

Shrey had stopped caring about his semester marks long ago. To be precise, it was the day we took our first semester exams. The reason? *He had studied all he had to, in this birth.*

That was sad, as he had quite a few high powered processors embedded inside that noodle hair covered head. The big problem with him? He wanted to be everywhere and be everything. To make things worse he didn't think there was a scintilla of a chance of that not happening.

'Average, I guess,' I said.

'I flunked in two,' he said without a touch of sadness or regret. I think he even smiled. I *so* envied him. I would have shat in my pants had I scored like him.

'Marks are material things. They are not something that's going to affect our lives, man. We are on for bigger things. Are you going somewhere tonight?' he asked. Though a day scholar, he was often mistaken for a hosteller for he spent most of his time flitting from JCB (Jagdish Chandra Bose) to BMH (Barah Mihir Hostel) to others to find a better bed to crash on or a better computer to crash into. He had flunked two exams and had short attendance in the current semester, but that would change nothing in his schedule. He would still go out that night.

Not only did he manage to smile in the face of adversity, he had the balls to poke at it with alarming frequency and audacity.

'Naah... I'm a little busy tonight,' I said.

'Smriti?'

'I guess. Nothing is sure. I will surely come if it doesn't work out.'

'C'mon! Now is the time, man! The girls are waiting. You're still on with Smriti? That's great going, man. Is there somebody else too?'

'It's still *just* her.'

'Okay. We will go out some other time then... I have to rush. Vandana is waiting. We are going to the place I told you about with those great kebabs, man! I bet they are the best in Delhi.'

Vandana was his girlfriend of three years whom he loved dearly. But that certainly did not stop him from exploring newer, fresher vistas. He had dated a few girls on the side too while he was in a relationship with Vandana. It was a simple equation for him – *keep one constant, and vary the others*. Girls were his second love. His first love had always been big laboratories, engineering science and Wikipedia!

'I have been there once Shrey, nothing great,' I said and almost immediately pulled back my words.

'Not great? Are you nuts? The softness, the melt-in-the-mouth texture... mmm... it is awesome, man...you have to develop a taste for mutton kebabs... and that takes time.'

It had been barely three months that he had gone non-vegetarian whereas I was a hardcore non-vegetarian Bengali! Still, I needed to *develop* a taste for mutton.

'By the way, Vernita was looking for you,' he said and left for the place he thought had the best kebabs. Poor Vandana, she would have to agree too.

Vernita completed the core trio. All three of us were nerdy enough to drag ourselves to a decent engineering college but non-nerdy enough (by choice or by nature) to be suffocated by it. However, it helped that DCE (Delhi College of Engineering) wasn't loaded in favour of people who studied until their eyeballs popped out or in. All three of us perennially envied the lives of students in non-professional colleges. The grass is always greener, prettier and hotter on the other side of the fence.

The other side of the fence was Delhi University's north campus – the place with the highest number of pretty faces per square mile.

Vernita was the only female friend left who didn't mind my presence. Usually, I ended up dating or disgustfully hitting on my female friends – both of which always ended badly. Vernita and I had come close to doing it once but I realized it was just me! She never had those intentions. *Damn.*

Vernita was really short and good-looking. She had quite a horsey face with sharp, pointed features accentuated by her creamy white complexion. However, what stood out was her loud and overtly sexy sense of style. She was like those seductive girls from animated movies who dressed up in black dresses with *really* long slits.

Let's just say that nature had been very kind to her. Her voluptuous Indian curves and endowed features were the reasons why we became friends in the first place. Shrey, for the first few days in college, had stalked her like a maniac. She was excessively hot to be ignored. Eventually, both of us stammered and stuttered our way into her life. Though she had made it clear that neither of us would have any chance on her and that she thought we were jerks.

She had a history of boyfriends and a couple of pregnancy scares in the past. That's *why* I hit on her in the first year but she was too smart for my unpolished charms and unflattering looks. It is always easy being the second or the third boyfriend. Making the girl shed her inhibitions for the first time is such a pain! The *'it's okay, everybody does it! You're not a slut!'* routine takes a lot of effort and patience.

Nevertheless, I was forever charmed by her! Vernita had perfected the skill of abuses, which I still hadn't. Since I didn't drink, I just had to learn to abuse. Failing to do either of the two meant that you were socially ill equipped.

'Hey, going out somewhere, fucker?' she asked.

She wore a white Espirit T-shirt that clung to her best assets. A slight rip and the tee would have split all through. Her skinny Levi's showed off that ass, a million girls would kill for. She hadn't missed the gym for a single day in the last three years and it showed – not a speck of fat on her. I was lucky to see her every day and unlucky to have seen her only with the clothes on. An awesome girl is a scarce commodity in engineering colleges.

'Naah, no plans,' I said.

'Why so?'

'My attendance is a little short, so will attend classes. I am leaving for Mishra's class. Coming?'

'Obviously. You are not the only one fucking around doing nothing all day…'

Strangely enough, the most worthless kids found their way to the Mechanical department and in effect, they were tortured endlessly for the slightest mistakes, which they made in gay abandon. We attended all our classes while the students of other hallowed branches – IT, Computers and the like – wasted away their time at the nearest coffee shop. At the end of four years, they were the ones who used to get placed in the US and shit.

It was gut wrenching to see guys who didn't have to risk their body being incinerated at an induction furnace or having a limb sawed off on a lathe machine, end up as millionaires.

Just a few codes, a few chips were all that they needed.

No lathes, no welding shops, nothing.

No lecturers, even.

On the other hand, we were blessed with the most frustrated and sadistic lot of teachers, none of whom had completed their PhDs in less than a decade. They were the *dumbest* of the lot. Nevertheless, given their limited intelligence and knowledge, their urge to teach was exemplary. It takes a brave man to pretend that he is wise when he is not. Thanks to these teachers, the lack of girls (Vernita being the only one in our class!), and an uncertain future made us the most frustrated group of students. The heaviest drinkers, smokers and dopers of the lot! And when some of *us*, defeated by life, go on to become professors, the vicious circle goes on!

The class went as usual. The frontbenchers jotted everything down, middle benchers pretended to write something and the last benchers slept, talked, or texted/chatted on their phones.

'Any plans with Smriti tonight?' she asked.

'Not quite, things have been a little rocky. It's not going too well. We have some problems.'

'Don't give me that crap.'

'Seriously.'

'I know you better than that, shit face. You are playing, aren't you? It's your bullshit *let's breakup* trick again.'

Smriti and Vernita were one time school buddies but some time back somebody bitched about somebody to somebody, everybody came to know and things fell apart. I never went into the details. Both of them tried to make me understand but I never got it. It's very hard to understand why girls fight, even for the most intelligent of men. And well, I was just a dumb guy.

It suited me, though. Vernita, being a big mouth, would have certainly put me in to some kind of trouble, had they been friends.

'No, believe me, I am not. I really want to be with her but things are not going well.'

'Whatever. Don't you fucking hurt the poor girl. I don't think you ever loved her.'

'Of course, I love her. I won't hurt her.'

'Anyway, how much did you score this time? I got a damned 62. I think all the professors are just biased against me,' she said.

'69 percent,' I said, proudly.

Since Vernita and Smriti weren't friends any longer, I could afford to tell her the *truth*. Smriti would never know that I had *lied* about my marks. I had *improved* over last semester, with a good five-percentage increase.

'What the fuck? That's your best ever. Congratulations, Deb!'

'Yup. Thanks,' I beamed.

'I am sure you fucking study the whole night and don't tell us. You are taking tuitions, aren't you? Such an asshole,' she said and made no attempt whatsoever, to hide her displeasure.

Does Size Really Matter?

'Whoever goes to a place like that?' I asked, voicing the opinion of Viru and Yogi who were still swearing at us for dragging them out of their hostels. JCB hostel was the most notorious hostel that year because of these two. Every few days, they would catch some innocent guys, make them throw a big alcohol party and turn the washrooms of the hostel into a puke dump.

'It would be fun, trust me. And we can't let these free passes go waste!' Shrey said.

'Shut up, man! Let us go to a coffee shop or watch a movie. Why drive all the way to there? We have our bloody exams in a few days,' I suggested, not so politely.

'Deb, just because you scored 69 this time doesn't mean you will do all that exam bullshit in front of us. Are you coming along? Yes or no?' Vernita looked at Virender and Yogender.

They were small town guys – one from Ludhiana and the other from Jalandhar – and not quite the smoothest, but they complimented each other perfectly. The huge, muscled Virender and his stand-up acts and the thread-thin Yogender with his cutting one-liners, did pretty well together. It was hard to imagine them without each other. And just like every other guy I hanged around with, they were obsessed with...well...you know! Most of our lives – the engineers –

revolved around one focal point, girls.

Viru and Yogi usually tagged along with us whenever we went out somewhere.

'Yes, sure,' they echoed.

Arguing with Shrey and Vernita was something they couldn't do. Moreover, they knew as long as Vernita was in the scheme of things, there would also be free alcohol which was quite a change from their Iodex and cough syrup highs. For Vernita, it meant company, as I didn't drink and Shrey thought it was cool not to drink after he lost a beer challenge to Vernita way back in first year.

'But guys, seriously! There is nothing out there. It's defunct and nobody goes there these days, definitely not in this weather,' I said but it fell on deaf ears.

The only incentive of going to an amusement park cum Water Park was to see Vernita in her two-piece bikini. I knew she would not wear anything like that, but the one in a millionth chance was motivation enough to say yes. Even if she didn't, there was nothing to lose. The *wetter* she was, the *better* she was.

Moreover, amusement parks were places I could actually prove myself manlier than others. Big rides didn't scare me. All thanks to the extreme torture of jibes, my sister and my dad subjected me to every time I backed out from risking myself being flung out to hell from those huge rides! I got used to the rides. Now, it's fun to prod big guys who turn blue and puke on scary roller coaster rides.

It was February and it was getting warmer. However, not warm enough to be in *Splash*, the water park cum amusement park. But we still hauled our asses down there because Shrey wanted to do something *different*. Driving below 30km/hr on a highway, working as a server at *Kake Da Dhaba*, haggling at a women's lingerie store: were all his ideas.

We entered the amusement park section and saw that most

of the rides were hanging together just by a thread of rust. Both Shrey and I – weighed in the mid 80's – decided against subjecting the already crumbling rides to the unconquerable forces of our mammoth thighs and bulky asses. We chose the water rides instead.

We hired swimming costumes that were supposedly free sizes but were anything but *freeing*. They almost managed to merge my balls into one bigger one. I was getting tired of looking around every time to check if anybody was watching before I could pull out the costume, which kept burying itself deep inside the crevices of two huge masses of flesh that jutted out from my back. One could have studied human anatomy and reproductive organs of men by looking at me or Shrey. Yes, it was that tight!

We moved out from our washrooms and what greeted us wasn't actually unexpected but it still left us gaping in shock.

Our day-out had empty slides, water with spit and greenish-black algae floating on it, three guys with protruding crotches in undersized costumes and a couple of attendants, woken up from their slumber by a girl in hot pants and a delightfully tight white shirt that would have turned transparent if she had stepped into the water. An *amazing* thought.

'Now what, guys?' Vernita asked, as she looked around. If we were not to die of pneumonia, then we would certainly die of every water-borne disease possibly known to man.

'Let's look around. There must be a cleaner pool,' Yogender said and left with Virender. The quicker they found one, the sooner we would have moved out, the earlier we would have reached *Mocha* (a cheap drinking place), where they could have knocked themselves out silly.

'If you look at it in the broader sense, it's not as bad as it looks. The water below the upper surface shouldn't be that bad. The algae must be doing a great job keeping the water clean and healthy. Therefore, if we can just skim off the top surface, we have a great day at hand. At National Physical Laboratories, we do have such a...' Shrey said pulling his costume down from beneath his crotch.

'Do you even think before you open your mouth or even that is mechanically controlled by some guy in the "National Physical Laboratories"?' Vernita barked at Shrey who had gone into one of his ultra-hi-tech nonsensical talks.

Meanwhile all I could look at was the sun glistening off Vernita's legs. I seemed to have a fetish for legs. All kinds. How could somebody go on with some technological bullshit or look for cleaner water when you had an option of staring at a half-naked girl. It was not something that happened every day! Maybe they weren't just normal. I was *normal*.

'Nice, sexy, legs... Aren't you just the hottest?'

Vernita started staring at me as if she would gobble me up alive. I would have loved that look if it had been in a closed dark room, but not there. *Shit! How could I?* I mean everybody knew I was, let us say, a little *overt* with my sexual comments and references, but this was downright ridiculous. *I couldn't have just said that.*

I didn't.

He did.

There he stood, as if mocking Shrey and me. He was a little shorter than Shrey but had a body that seemed to be custom made. Huge biscuit like abs, big shoulders, rippled muscles and a great tan that would have Brad Pitt looking for cover. The same costume this time seemed to be made to his specifications. Not an ounce of fat on his body whereas we had oodles of it spilling out from all sides of our costume.

I hoped the good things about him ended at that, but they didn't.

He was an ultra-chic south Delhi guy who was friends with everybody who mattered. He was Vernita's boyfriend and that's what I hated about him the most. Not that I envied him, as I knew Vernita made for a lousy girlfriend, blaring and knocking the daylights out of him 24/7. She made life tough for her boyfriends when she left no stone unturned to freak out the guy every time she was late on her periods. She *never* trusted condoms. Or self-control. She was one of a kind.

'Hi *baby!*' he said as she hugged him in what seemed like the assembling of a high precision machine. Every curve of hers fitted into every muscle of his as if they were parts of a beautiful, curvaceous, sensual sculpture. It was so incredibly sexy that we almost started shifting in our places, embarrassed, as if caught watching porn.

Shrey and I had this peculiar habit of finding flaws in guys to offset the better things in them. Often non-existent flaws, but Shrey and I had found nothing wrong in him.

It was good that Tanmay was always busy managing college affairs, looking good, sculpting his body or trying to top his exams! The lesser time he spent with us, the better we felt about ourselves. He was every girl's dream come true — sincere, intelligent, hot and unbelievably soft spoken.

But Shrey and I weren't used to regarding anybody as competition and called this the '*nobody-is-a-stud-except-me*' phenomenon. Every guy in Delhi suffers from this. We think we are studs, though we are really not.

'Anybody game for suicide? Pneumonia, cholera, typhoid, tuberculosis? We found just the place to do that. A cleaner pool,' said Virender, rubbing his hands with obvious delight.

'We can all now die an excruciatingly slow death. The filth in that pool isn't as deadly as this one. Hi Tanmay!' Yogender answered with obvious sarcasm.

'Let's go honey. It will be fun,' Tanmay prodded her.

'Can't you see the water here? Are you fucking nuts?' Vernita shot back.

'*Frozen* fucking nuts, in a while,' Yogender butted in.

'At least let's go and check out the water. The tissues of our bodies are made of cellulose and proteins which actually store the sunlight and release its energy according to the Planck's law of irradiation where the wavelength is so controlled that maximum heat is released according to the Dasons' formulae and our body slowly adapts to the...' Shrey started again.

'Jump right in and stay in for an hour or stay shut,' Yogender interrupted thankfully.

'Fucking true, man! Great job, Yogi. Let's see you prove your National Physical Laboratories bullshit right here...' said Vernita and winked at Yogender.

'Let's do it then,' Shrey said.

'Let's do it? Are you serious? Are you serious?' Virender exclaimed, as he looked wide-eyed at Shrey.

'Yes, I am damn *serious*.'

'No, don't bullshit. Three years. Three damn years,' Virender said with a strangely accusing tone.

'*What?*'

'For three years I thought you were this really funny guy who can relate the colour of one's pee with the kind of rum he prefers. Tell me this is the only time you ever talked sense. Tell me the rest of them were still jokes!' Virender chuckled.

'Cut it out, guys! This isn't bad... one... two... three... just three floating blobs of spit,' I said as I fished out my costume before it threatened to disappear between the humungous blobs of fat.

'Heaven itself!' Yogender smirked.

'See there is nothing much in this place anyway, so rather than just standing here naked. Let's all jump in and make something at least of it,' Tanmay said with seriousness fit only for practical vivas.

The only slide that was working was a 50 feet tall slide that came vertically down. Quite visibly, everybody wetted their pants just at the thought of coming down through that one; I grabbed the opportunity to yet again mock the weak hearted.

After school ended, I never missed an opportunity to do that.

'So, are you sure?' Tanmay asked, almost nervously. *This is new.*

'Of course, I am sure. I have been doing this since I was a kid. I don't know why you guys are so afraid,' I said rubbing it in.

'Okay, see you on the other side.'

As I stepped out on the ledge, the first doubts crept in. There was no way this was 50 feet. I was so damn floating in the clouds. And all I could see of them were their tiny little heads. Nevertheless, egged on by their shouts – and more importantly, by my ego – I lay down at the ledge; one hand stuck to my thighs the other grabbing hold of the attendant, trying to streamline myself as much as I could. The attendant let go.

Bucssssuuuwaaaaaahh!

I was numbed. The ice-cold water gushed into my nostrils and lungs. It felt like a thousand hands had slapped me on my chest and legs. The impact had been terrible. The bump in the slide had unbalanced me and I splashed into the water, with my legs and hands wide open. I had gone side first into the water. It was surely not the most gracious of moves, and definitely not the kind that I expected from me. I could already hear their chuckles. *Make a great appearance out of water and it will just be fine*, I told myself.

So I sucked in my paunch and braced myself for a Casino Royale style emergence from water. I pulled myself up from the pool, helped only by my not-so-muscled hands and felt the water slip down my curves à La Daniel Craig. And seeing their eyes stuck on me, it seemed as if I had actually managed to do that. Their eyes were fixed on me as if they were too dumbfounded at my stupendously sexy achievement. They followed every step of mine as if to register whatever I did, so that they could replicate it when they go in next.

'So?' I broke the silence. 'How was it? Pretty great, huh?'

'Hmmm...' said Vernita, looking at me as if to check whether I managed to come out in one piece. 'Not that impressive! I had expected something... more. You know. It's just not enough.'

'Not that I am interested, but yes not impressive enough... maybe just enough,' said Yogender.

'Yes, but I still want to know Deb, with something like *that*, how do you get your girls to stick around you? They must be *really* in love with you,' Virender said barely concealing his laughter.

'It's a miracle, really. I told you guys, something *different*. I told you that Deb has something that we don't,' added Shrey.

'Talent, maybe? Not everybody has it,' I said, still confused at what they were getting at, but I decided to play along. 'I am thankful that I do.'

'Not many need it, but you do,' said Tanmay as they started laughing their brains out. Virender nearly fell into the water and as my eyes followed him, and that's when I saw *it* floating on the water.

My costume? MY COSTUME? Oh. Fuck. My Costume!

All this while, I was stark naked with my stomach pulled in, posed as a playboy bunny, and let them make a fool out of me. Not only that, I had joined in too. This will never pass, I thought, as I jumped into the water and with one fluid motion covered what wasn't *impressive* as per their standards. But the laughter wouldn't ever stop. This was just that kind of incident that tends to stick on for life. It will now forever be *Deb and the floating costume*.

As if it wasn't enough to bury my head in the sand and nuke my ass away, I was gripped by the question that would trouble me for a long time to come. *Was I small?* I kept telling myself that size doesn't matter. But then why did Vernita come out with the *not impressive* remark? And that she had expected *more*? My mind wandered to the time when Vernita got dumped once and she ended up going around telling everyone that the guy had a *miniscule* penis. I thought she was being revengeful.

To make things worse, they weren't the least bit interested in the water slides or the water park anymore. They now had an issue of national importance to discuss. Very minutely, indeed. How I wished to go back in time and settle for a coffee rather than the god damned *Splash*! Even the Mechanical canteen seemed to be a better option.

'So, Deb, we had fun, right? We got to see your talents. And something more! Or whatever,' said Yogender as he moved out of the washrooms wiping the non-existent water off him. He even smeared moisturizer on his f whole fucking body. Oh hell, was I irritated? The damned costume left an intricate design on my waist but couldn't hold on to me. Damn *Made in China*.

'Deb, it's not that bad, you know. These things can be corrected. Electric impulses in the ultrasonic range can elongate certain tissues in the body if delivered in conjunction with some microwaves. People are known to add a few inches in a matter of months. Don't feel depressed,' Shrey said.

'National Physical Laboratories?' asked Virender.

'No, my friend, it's all thanks to www.enlarge.com,' Shrey answered.

'What the hell were you doing there? www.enlarge.com?' I asked, trying to shift the focus off me.

'A friend in need is a friend indeed,' Yogender said and they all burst out laughing. It's never easy to be the butt of all jokes and certainly not when it pertains to the most sensitive of areas. Fortunately enough, we moved out of there as there wasn't much to do and the conversation shifted to other things.

'Hey, Tanmay how's mom and dad? Still minting money?' Virender asked as he killed the engine.

The plan to go to *Mocha* had been dropped. The sun had set. The car was parked on a deserted road. The doors flung open. A bottle of rum, roadside chicken, coke, a few cigarettes, a few plastic glasses, car speakers blaring out loud under the moonlight, and their party was complete. Who cared about the ambience!

'They are good there. Mom just got a promotion, so she might just hang around there a little longer than planned. Avantika is there too. She will be here in a few days,' Tanmay replied.

His parents had been living in Dubai for the last few years and had been earning quite a lot. That explained all the expensive labels on his clothes or maybe they just looked like labels when he wore them.

'So, what's *Avantika* up to these days?' Yogender asked as he rolled another joint.

'Nothing much, doing B.Com honours at SRCC and preparing for CAT. She has her vacations going on, so she took the flight out,' he said as he stretched out the car bonnet.

Now that fascinated me – '*she/he took the next flight out*'. As if it costs pocket change. Whatever happened to booking early and saving money?

However, what fascinated me more was the obvious mention of Tanmay's sister. Going by how Tanmay was and his mom – who on her few visits to Tanmay, really looked like his big sister – Avantika must be a definite possessor of some great genes.

'Now that Deb is a little preoccupied with some senseless *small* issues, I thought I would ask something on his behalf,' Yogender said, as he settled before the front tire and took a long drag in. 'Is she single?'

The expected giggles had now started to rankle. I mentally thanked Yogender for doing the needful.

'Yes, kind of. She has a boyfriend she has been trying to get rid of, for the last few months. Precisely from the time she said yes, but it's not working out.'

'So, Deb? Are you interested…? Oh maybe you won't take the chance. Now that we know your… ummm… err… *little* secret!' Vernita said, mocking me. She climbed up the bonnet and deposited her body into Tanmay's arms.

'Not interested,' I didn't strangle her. Or grab her breasts.

'That's good for you. She has a penchant for the beer swigging, fast driving, rich assholes, anyway. The kind of guys you wouldn't like to face unless you are on a death wish,' Vernita said.

'You have a girlfriend too, right Deb? Smriti? That cute medical student? Tanmay asked.

'We are kind of breaking up,' I said as I sat beside Shrey on the road.. Such answers were always a reflex action for me. I was always either single or in the process of being so.

There we were a bunch of aimless kids in the middle of a deserted road, half of them knocked out outside or inside the car. We were in a premier college that guaranteed a placement, and we cared about nothing else. We had four years at an engineering college to kill. And we were doing it, with a smile and a bottle of rum on our lips.

Killing it.

Of Arranged Books and Arranged Marriages

I saw them, my school mates, looking for me in my college armed with rulers and stretched, wet, twisted handkerchiefs, smoking like chimneys, one hand around their girlfriends, who found something immensely funny in their boys chasing down a fat, crying me. I stumbled on a step and fell headlong. I looked up at them, and they looked down at me — mocking, laughing at what lay between them.

I woke up, it was 6 p.m. *Fuck! Machine design, tomorrow.* I rushed to the bookshop.

Life at DCE had been quite the same for the last three years. We were supposed be studying in a college that oscillated between seventh and fifteenth rank when it came to countrywide engineering colleges rankings.

The DCE campus was a huge one, definitely not as big as IIT or Pilani, but big enough. Situated at the outskirts of Delhi and Haryana, the hostel students had the opportunity of counting *real* cows to bed. However, being close to the Haryana border meant guys could get sloshed like shit every night from cheap liquor and grass.

Beyond all the alcohol and the desperation to get laid, it was a college of IIT rejects, who were just short of genius material when they entered the college. But four years of mind numbing college dumbed most of them out.

'Hi! Which book, Pandey or Lahiri?' I asked Vernita when I called her from the bookshop. I hoped she would say Pandey as I was in no mood to shell out an extra three hundred bucks for a book that was to grace my table for less than eight hours. It was March and my sixth semester's mid-term exams had started.

'Lahiri is better. All the *ghissus* are doing it from that book.'

'But the other one is thinner... and cheaper.'

'Yes, I know. That's why the rest of the class is preparing from it.'

'Which book do you have?'

'Both. But I won't fucking do it from the heavy one,' she said

Of course, she had both. The seniors were extra generous when it came to Vernita. She had never a bought a book. *Ever.* Her investment in gorgeous bras always paid off.

While Shrey had his friends in IIT, who gave him their books, I was the only one buying them hours before the exam.

'Okay, I am taking Lahiri. Text me the tentative course,' I said as I kept the phone down.

There were predominantly three kinds of people I was studying with, the *ghissus,* who attended all the classes, regardless of how dumb the professor was. Their exam preparations began a month before the exams. These ones created the huge *tentative* course. The next group consisted of the ones who attended classes but never studied. These ones brainlessly copied what was written on the board just to remain in the good books of the Profs! They would generally start studying around ten days before exams. These guys created the final course. They used to slash and cut out the useless or tough stuff from the course that was either too hard or had not reared its head in the question papers in the last five years.

You can do without professors. You can do without classes. But life is tough without previous years' papers.

The final course would get finalized the night before the exams and this is what the last group waited for. We all belonged to the *last* group. Though the first group people invariably topped, that did not mean the people from the other groups couldn't do so. It always boiled down to the last day. However, it was more likely that someone who had been studying for the last month or ten days would put in more effort than the non-serious ones who bought the book the previous day. It was all about the person who ran the last mile faster.

'How much have you done? I asked Shrey on a conference call.

'I haven't started. Was out for football match, came and slept off.'

'Shrey, are you fucking crazy? Eleven chapters. And its Machine Design, not some bloody elective,' Vernita barked, as expected. Girls generally panic more in exam situations. How often had we seen Vernita begging for an increase in marks even for copying the questions down! She could afford to do that. She was hot and if I were a professor, I would have loved to have Vernita down on her knees, *begging*.

'How much have you done? Shrey asked as if it mattered to him.

'Three chapters and will sleep for a little now. I will get up at four and do the rest of it. The exam is anyway at two. You, Vernita?'

'You have done three? I am still stuck at the fucking second chapter. Okay bye.'

The conference call ended, in the usual abrupt manner. Shrey showed no signs of concern to whatever had just happened. He would probably play FIFA on his PlayStation for a while. I was happy that I had finished more chapters than Vernita and she, as usual, panicked. I knew Vernita would crack any question if it comes from the portion she had studied. She was way more intelligent than I. I just used to memorize whatever I couldn't understand… and not many things got a coveted place in my miniscule brain.

Shrey did nothing of the two. He waited until two hours before the exams and asked people to say out loud whatever they had studied and that's where his preparations ended. It was nothing short of a miracle that he managed to pass in a few subjects.

'Get up, you stinking ass hole. It's eight.'

Vernita had been saying the same thing for the last minute or so and all I was doing was breathing heavily on her. This time I had to react. And fast. I quickly did my mental calculation and checked if I could still pass with no major glitches if I slept for another half an hour. I couldn't.

'Hmmm... I am up.' I wasn't. 'How much have you done?' I croaked.

'I am totally screwed. Just done five chapters. Fucking feel like crashing right now. Wake me in ten minutes. I am leaving the last three chapters. Are you doing them?' she asked.

'Obviously, I am.'

'And keep calling up Shrey too. He has just done one and is sleeping. Bye.'

Being a day scholar was a tough job. You have nobody to shake you until you wake up, nobody to give you an idea about things to be studied and nobody to copy *farras* from. You miss out on exam time bonding and you miss out on great friendships. But then you have a life outside the four walls of the college and crappy hostel food ceases to be your main concern. I had a *life* outside college. I had been too busy for most of the *could*-be-friends in college.

Coming back to exams, Vernita always relied on *quality* and I on *quantity*. I knew my pea-sized brain wouldn't stand me in good stead if the questions were a little twisted. It happened again as it did on every single exam day, Vernita snoozed her alarms and me and I skimmed through the course in a tearing hurry.

Though I dutifully took time out to rebuke Smriti for her irresponsible behaviour – calling me up just twice to wake me up when Vernita, who was *just* a friend, called up some fifteen times. Finally, Smriti was giving me valid reasons to be pissed with her.

However, there was no trace whatsoever of Shrey, till he

finally called to say he had left his cell phone home and was out for a jog. It was ten, he had still done just one chapter, which according to him was disconnected from real life machine problems, and hence he left it midway. *Same old story.*

I ended up finishing the course half an hour before time and sulking about the slipshod way I had done the course. *Same old story.*

On the other hand, Vernita's preparations ended as they always did, with a few chapters left out, 15 minutes into exam time. She was always the last person to move into the exam hall. Once in, she used to be this goddess of concentration, never looking up for one moment.

Exactly one and half hour into the exam, the inevitable churning started in the restless bowels of the third group. That's when the people from the third group were most inclined to use the washroom. Going by the time they took to relieve themselves, it felt as if after all these years they had finally discovered that they had a rectum.

Vernita and I used to do that too, what was called *Toilet-isation of Notes,* but we restricted it to desperate situations. For Shrey, it was a way of life.

'You did this question? I did this and seems like fucking nobody else did. I wonder if I did this right,' Vernita said.

'No, I did not,' I said.

It was the time, which I never looked forward to – the after exam time. Vernita was used to cracking the toughest questions in the exam and flaunted that all day long or until the time you acknowledged her genius. I doubt whether I had ever scored outside the theory questions in the four years of college. All I did in the exams were to look for the short notes questions, the *why* and *how* questions and try to fill up pages writing about them.

Shrey did nothing of the two. He just managed to find a new answer, a new theory for the age-old concepts based on some experience of his at the National Physical Laboratory.

He spent the most part of his time after the exam, engrossed in explaining his theories to the dumbest person of the class or some junior or sometimes even the canteen boy. He had a life. Without marks, though.

But his businessmen parents hardly cared. Neither did he. Not that my parents were too interested in how I did in my exams. They had bigger troubles. My sister wanted to get married to someone from a different community. My marks could wait. So could the long due appreciation for my hard earned 69. Marks, of course.

'Hurry up! *Orra kintu esshe jaabe je kono shomoy* (They will be here any moment),' Dad shouted as he started stacking at least twenty utensils with some dish or the other in neat piles. Did I not tell you? Yes, I am a Bengali. We talk a lot, we shout a lot, and we argue a lot... and we are a perennially hyper-vocal community.

'They have just left. They will still take two hours to get here,' my sister said irritably.

But dads know all and dads are always right. My dad too, like all other dads in the universe and beyond, was just too paranoid about being on time. It was my elder sister's *aashirwad*. That's the Bengali equivalent to the Punjabi *roka*. Unlike the Punjabis, it's a homebound affair. In Delhi, it was treated as yet another opportunity to flaunt their immensely *hard earned* money.

Anyway, it was hard for me to imagine my sister (Sonali) getting married. I mean, she still hadn't got out of talking to her imaginary friend and shouting at me in loud guttural Hindi, till the time mom and dad got riled out of their wits. But I guess those things were not meant to stop ever.

Also, my sister was twenty-four. That wasn't late and definitely not late by bong standards, but delaying it would mean risking suitable Bengali grooms. Bengali men have these strange tendencies to either fall in love and get married or decide not to get married at all.

Bengalis, as a rule, fall in love way too often. My sister had too, that too with a Haryanvi *jaat*, who was by no standards the dream groom my parents had pictured. Not only did his *jaat* image not go down well with my dad's academic outlook and my mom's kohl lined eyes and the big, forehead covering *bindi*, he earned less than my sister did... and that was a cardinal sin. Moreover, my other elder sister, Moushmi got a husband that every girl in this country dreams of – an IIM graduate. They were settled in London and spent their free time by going sailing in Alaska.

'Advertising?' Dad exclaimed when Sonali put forward the proposal for the first time.

'Why is he not an engineer? Who on earth does advertising?' My exasperated mum said as if my sister had just decided to marry a last stage leprosy patient. Or maybe that would have been better.

'Mom, I do. And so did *didi!*'

'Yes, you do. But you are a girl. And I wasn't keen on you doing it either. But Moushmi did find someone who didn't! He is from IIM Ahmadabad. What would people say if you get married to a boy in advertising? Why would a sane guy ever do advertising? What kind of parents would allow that?'

Apparently, for my parents, the world was run by just four kinds of people – engineers, doctors, lecturers and lately MBAs. All other professions ranging from lawyers to IAS officers were for *stupid* people, who either couldn't clear entrance examinations or had the perseverance to stick around for ages till they made it to the civil services list.

'Why not? my sister shot back.

'How can you even think of marrying someone who earns less than you? There is no money in advertising and neither is it a respectable field to work in. All kinds of strange things go on there.'

'Dad, I work there, and I know better.'

'No, you don't. You were just fooled by this *jaat*. I am sure he is after our property. You haven't told him about our houses in Vasant Kunj and Gurgaon. Have you? I am sure you have.'

'No mom, he is richer than our whole clan combined. He owns a lot of property in Gurgaon,' I tried to help.

'Ohh! I get it. You are after his *money!*' I regretted as soon as I had said this. It would have been a great joke; I just chose the wrong time to say it. All of them started staring at me, as if I had disrespected Rabindranath Tagore or Saurav Ganguly. No, that would have been probably much *worse*.

'So are you trying to say, we will let you marry a good for nothing man just because his father happens to wallow in gold. What does his dad do?'

'He worked with the customs department and now he has his own business in import export,' she said.

Silly I thought, keeping in mind what my parents thought about customs and import-export. Both these professions topped my parents' list of the most hated professions, giving stiff competition to pot-bellied property dealers and auto spare parts suppliers. I just knew it was over for 'her. Rich people cannot be only rich. They have to be corrupt too.

'Oh, so now you want to marry a good for nothing son of a smuggler who is in advertising,' my mom said and glanced at dad to take it from there.

'Why would anyone quit a government job and start a business? And where did he get all that money to start his smuggling business? He is a swindler and a smuggler. One raid from the vigilance department and both he and his father will be behind bars,' dad said.

It had been 30 years since my dad was working in a PSU (Public Sector Undertaking, in short – semi-government) and quite understandably, he saw no reason for someone to quit a low paying but a comfortable government job.

'It's not that. His father had acquired acres of farmland and he sold them off.'

'Okay, so now he is a good for nothing son of a smuggler, farmer and a drunkard and who is into advertising,' mom said.

'A drunkard? Sonali asked dejectedly, not wanting to fight his case anymore.

'I am sure he drinks... and beats up his wife too. Would you like to marry someone like that?'

'Mom!'

'*Ar kicchu bolte hobe naa.* (No discussions anymore.) It is decided. From now on, you will never talk to that guy again. I will not let an uneducated smuggler marry my daughter,' Dad said.

This, along with similar numerous conversations, catastrophic astrology predictions and examples how love marriages had failed around them sounded the death knell for Paresh Ahlawat. My sister finally relented. Slowly, she began to see the upsides of getting married the conventional way. She realized that with her cute looks she was a sought after commodity in the Bengali marriage scene! That worked better than my parents' incessant hard talk.

What followed was my sister's spree of trying out and rejecting different guys on grounds varying from 'strange teeth' to 'un-matching footwear'. Every possible attribute was scrutinized in detail. She had some high standards to match up to. She would by no means get someone who was in any way inferior to Moushmi's husband – the suave IIM guy. So it was bye-bye for the strange named, rich *jaat* guy. Though I didn't quite mind the rich part.

Abhishek weds Sonali. That sounded nice.

Yes. Abhishek, was an electronic engineer with a hefty package and lived alone in Delhi. The last part made him extremely desirable. Constant bickering of your in-laws is the last thing you would want after a hard day's work.

Therefore, things fell in place in a jiffy. The guy was a little dumb or that's how I perceived him to be, as he didn't speak much. But the whole deal was nice overall. Cute, geeky looking, hardly a problem handling such a wimp, my sister would have thought.

Trrrinnngg...the bell rang

They had reached. Hugs, hugs, hugs. Nobody touches feet nowadays, it's considered regressive. And middle class.

'You are looking fabulous, Sonali,' her mom-in-law said. She was this small dark complexioned lady with curly hair and the all-pervasive kohl and a huge *bindi*.

'Thank you!' my sister said and faked a shy expression. That could have very much translated into *of course I am, I spent twenty minutes on it, and you saved your life by saying that.*

Suitable pleasantries were exchanged and everybody sat down for the ceremony where the pundit asked everybody to repeat some incomprehensible Sanskrit words. It was over in fifteen minutes giving way to the photography session wherein Sonali and Abhishek posed as a couple who had just found love. As soon as the elders got out of sight to look after the eating arrangements, I had my camera out and Sonali, her antics, flashing peace signs and other metal poses. Sonali and I loved the look of bewilderment on Abhishek's face. Moushmi wasn't there or she would have added tremendously to the overall craziness quotient. We missed her.

The eating arrangements were done. Mom was a great cook and eating anywhere else always seemed like an insult to my taste buds and my gastronomical faculties. We had on the table – two kinds of *paneer*, three other vegetarian dishes, two kinds of pulses, three kinds of fish and a kind each of chicken and mutton. I was born lucky and destined to be *healthy*.

Just as we were eating, Somali's mum-in-law looked at her hand and made a peculiar semi- angry, semi- shocked face. 'Show me your hand,' she said and almost *politely* grabbed my sister's hand. 'Isn't that *Asur*?' she asked, looking at her hand.

Obviously, I had no idea. I learned about it later – There are said to be three *gans* in Hindu astrology, *Dev gan*, *Nar gan* and *Asur gan*. Although they are determined by a careful study of horoscopes but a quick estimation can be made by looking if the little finger is below the topmost line of the adjoining finger. Though not accurate, this is relied upon by many who believe in it. For our family, it was all French.

'Yes the fingers... below the line. It's *Asur gan*. My son is *Dev gan*.'

And that meant it was not a suitable match. Out of all possible matches between the *gans, this* combination was not recommended. By some quirk of nature, if the match was still considered, the groom was bound to die.

'But the horoscopes don't show that,' Sonali's dad-in-law added and continued, 'anyway, the finger checking method is not that accurate, you see.'

'No, it is. It is something that we have followed for years now. Maybe the horoscopes had some flaw in it,' she shot back.

Now that was an outright insult. Was she suggesting we had fudged the horoscope to hook her son up? That geeky, dumb guy? I could see the expressions change on everyone's faces.

All we did for the next few seconds were to exchange glances. Mom was visibly worried, dad seemed a little confused. Sonali and I looked at each other and tried hard to conceal a smile at whatever was happening around us. I always felt Sonali never took the marriage thing seriously. For her, it was just another day, another joke to smile through.

'We've got to check with the astrologer. Please excuse us,' Sonali's mum-in-law said tugging at her husband's shirt.

They walked a little away from us dialled a few numbers and had a few discussions in hushed voices. Mom would have fainted had they taken any longer. Dad was his usual composed self.

'I am very sorry. My wife made a terrible judgment,' he said. 'I told you these things are not very accurate.' He looked at his wife.

Somehow, the tension on my mom's face had not eased. Dad didn't flinch either. I could notice a sense of disappointment on Sonali's face. She had expected more drama and I am sure she'd hoped for it to continue a bit longer. Unfortunately, that was not to be. Abhishek had been quiet all this while. Everything was wrapped up and they left after some gifts were exchanged.

As we sat down after winding up everything, my mom announced, '*Ami eta hote debo naa.* (I will not let this happen.) I am calling off the wedding.'

That was quite an overtly dramatic statement considering that nobody except the two immediate families knew about the wedding until then. But then it sounded good and my mom was quite used inducing drama in boring situations! Dad didn't react and I guessed they would have discussed it.

'Does that mean we have to return this? Sonali said as she started fiddling with a Mont Blanc set they had gifted her and immediately realized that was not the most appropriate thing to say and added as if she was worried. 'I mean, *why?* What happened?'

'Did you look at the way they behaved? If tomorrow something happens to the guy, they will outright blame you. This won't do. And the guy? He didn't even take the slightest interest. Momma's boy. That's why he doesn't speak much. His mother must have asked him not to. I am sure she will forever bind him to her *pallu*. There is no way this is going ahead... and you stop fiddling with that pen. We are giving it back.'

'But it's a Mont Blanc limited India edition, 2005, only 200 pieces exist.'

'Shut up, and take these glasses away.'

'As you say, but do rethink before giving these back,' she said as we laughed aloud.

I had expected some tension in the house, but it was hardly so. Sonali obviously didn't give a damn about the wedding per se. And I realized mom and dad were happier seeing their daughter fool around rather than see her get married off. They were content as they had weaned Sonali off her *jaat* boyfriend and so her wedding could wait now.

The wedding was called off a week later. All the gifts went back. The Mont Blanc didn't. We couldn't *find* it.

Smriti was sad about the wedding being called off.

Her displeasure at my parents turning down someone from a different community was evident. Though it gave me another chance for banging the phone down on her and be unavailable for a day. She had called my parents *stupidly conservative* and it was not a very clever thing to do.

'I am sorry for the wedding,' Smriti said dejectedly.

'I am not. Nobody is. It's as if nothing ever happened. Sonali is doing okay.'

'So does that open up any doors for Sonali's boyfriend?'

'No, it doesn't. My parents won't ever allow me or Sonali to marry outside our caste. They are totally against it.'

I had to say that. I had been building up for the break up since the last few weeks. My apparently bad scores in semesters, dipping performance at CAT coaching centres – I had planned to blame *her* for everything. Had those not worked, I had always exaggerated the resistance my parents put up against Sonali going for a love marriage. I used to do that to drive home the fact that we had no future together. And as she would know better, it's always easier to break up sooner than later.

'Smriti, I will hang up now. Vernita is calling me up,' I said as I looked at my cell phone to swap my call.

1:03:27. One minute was all I could bear her for. I would have faked a call waiting and put her hold until the time she would have hanged up had Vernita not called. But this time she had.

Dumb, Ugly... and Almost Dead

'Hey, Vernita! Need to show you something. Where are you?'

'See you in ten minutes at the Pitampura, metro station,' she said.

'Why? Where are you going?'

'Where are *we* going, not where am *I* going. *We* are going to Greater Kailash. I need company.'

'Fine,' I said and kept the phone down.

'To his flat?' I asked her as I got into her car.

Tanmay's sister had just landed and lately Vernita and she had become bitching partners.

'Naah! Not today, will just meet him. I did an assignment for him, so got to drop that too,' she said.

It was strange to see Vernita behave like a quintessential girlfriend. She always made us believe that she used guys as her personal toilet paper.

'Assignments? I thought all your assignments are done at his place, behind closed doors,' I mocked.

'Shut up, fucker. I don't make out as often as you make it sound. Can you fucking stop saying things like that in the future? I don't like it,' she said.

She didn't sound convincing. She knew her libido and

malleable morals were unmatched. I loved her for that, if only she didn't tell me once that, 'I was too good a friend to sleep with'. Damn, my *good*ness.

'Yes, you are the queen of chastity. You *never* make out. Period.'

We didn't exchange anything for the next few minutes.

'You wanted to show me something? she asked what I wanted her to.

I wiggled my wrist in front of her.

'What on earth is that? That must be worth a million fucking rupees.'

I liked that. It didn't happen that often. Money was never an issue for her. Her father was the most hardworking man there ever could be. He would be free on days when he worked for eighteen hours. Those long hours at a college, bookshop and grocery centre meant a lot of easy money for Vernita.

'I found it in my bag. Mom and dad, the gift they had promised on getting me if I get 65%. Haven't yet told them that I found it.'

We drove on and I just kept talking about my newly acquired asset. She was pretty bugged by the time we reached Greater Kailash. Greater Kailash was the most posh area in Delhi where an average looking girl would be conspicuous because of her *average*ness. Skinny jeans, great asses, stilettos, side brushed hairstyle et al, there was no way anyone could tell one from the other. And, you thought people in Chinese movies were indistinguishable.

A house there meant something worth upwards of three crores, but for Tanmay it wasn't a big deal. He had two, one where he lived with his uncle and the other where he frequently made out with Vernita. I envied his life.

We finally met him outside his uncle's house. Guys like him never had an off day. With Short-cropped hair, ripped jeans, he had an expensive looking light pink shirt on, half of which was tucked in while the rest hung out, carefully done. *Bloody metro sexual.*

'Where is Avantika?' Vernita asked.

'She is coming in a moment. She is unpacking everything. And she is looking forward to meeting you.'

'Who? Me?' I was taken by surprise.

'Yeah,' he said, as he flicked out his expensively framed spectacles and put them on. Perfect. The humiliation was complete. Now, he looked hot and *intelligent*.

'And why is that?'

'I told her that you were this stud who could hook up with any girl,' Tanmay said.

Bloody asshole. I was no stud, not even close. Guys like Tanmay are studs. We're just every day guys who girls go out with because they don't have better options. And such descriptions – stud who can hook up with anyone – do nothing other than ensure failure... and looking forward sounded more like *I-will-see-him*. Avantika had been to rehab for her drugs and alcohol problem but that was more than a year back. This is how Vernita first described her as. I had already started imagining Avantika as leather jacketed rock chic with metal piercing in every visible and non-visible part of her body. Not to forget the hideous black nail polish. Such a girl would kick the daylights out of me, I thought.

'Here she comes,' Vernita said.

That could have been the last thing I remembered from that day had I had a weak heart. I had passed out for a few seconds for sure. I skipped a beat or two. Or maybe my heart had just stopped beating altogether, I was choking. There was a strange churning in my bowels. I felt the blood rush down to the ends of my arteries and burst out. I could feel my brain imploding. *I am going to die, I am sure.*

She was breathtakingly beautiful. I guess unrealistically beautiful was more appropriate! All the things that I used to say to score with my ex-girlfriends had just come true. She was a dream. Even better, you wouldn't even dream of something so perfect. Plastic surgeons still can't rival god, I thought.

She was so hard to describe. Those limpid, constantly wet black eyes screamed for love. There is nothing better than a melancholic beautiful face. The moonlight reflected off her perfectly sculpted face, and that seemed the only light illuminating the place. Somebody stood nearby with a blower to get her streaked hair to cover her face so that she could look sexier managing it. She had the eyes of a month old child, big and screaming for attention. That perfectly drafted nose, flawless bright pink lips and a milky white complexion that would have put Photoshop to shame. Oh hell, she was way out of my league. She was a goddamn goddess. Or was she the *devil?* She couldn't possibly be human.

I just couldn't look beyond her face. It was strange, as it had never happened that way. Things were generally the other way around. Cup size didn't make the first impression this time.

'Hi Vernita! How are you? she said or rather sang. Something I would never know. They hugged. Vernita was half a foot shorter than her. Avantika had turned out in a simple dull brown *kurta* and jeans, without even a hint of make-up. I passed out for sure, as I couldn't make out anything that they talked about. I wasn't seeing right, I wasn't hearing right. *Maybe I will just wake up in a while.*

'Hi! How are you Debashish?' she serenaded with a big golden harp as I spotted her with a halo and two big white wings fluttering behind her, somewhere up in the clouds. Drugs? Alcohol? Leather? She wouldn't even know all that. However, I saw the remnants of a piercing just above her left eyebrow, and a tattoo peeked out from her sleeve. A red swastika sign.

Okay, relax, it's just a dream. It will be over in a while.

'Hello?' Vernita pinched me and brought me to life.

'Are you fine? Avantika asked.

'I am okay.' I said in what seemed like my fourth attempt at speaking after the first three ended in soundless flapping of my tongue.

Was I fine? I was sure she was mocking me. Wasn't she aware that half of the people she meets either slip into a coma or end up thinking the meeting never happened, believing it was just a figment of their imagination. I was lucky I was breathing, damn it.

'You guys talk, we will just take a walk.' Tanmay said as he and Vernita turned away from us.

Talk? I was barely alive. I looked at her and smiled stupidly. I wondered if her dog looked cuter than I.

'They look good. Don't they?' she asked.

Look good? *Only you look good! You beautiful angelic faced cherub. Go away! Don't make me fall in love!*

'Yes.' I said. I tried not to stare into death.

'I didn't quite like Vernita when I first met her. I kind of like her now. She is a little too brash, isn't she?'

'Yes.' *I like your nose, can I touch it?*

'What do you think? Are they serious?'

'Yes.' *I like your lips, are they for real?*

'Do you ever say anything more than that?'

'Yes.' *I like your eyes, do they ever close?*

Was she kidding? Was I not trying? I could have said a million things, mostly stupid, but my senses had still not recovered from the temporary paralysis she had just subjected me to. I tried hard not to make eye contact and stay alive and there she was mocking me for my dumbness. *She is here to mock you to death.*

'And why are you constantly looking down? I hope I am not that bad to look at? she said, her voluminous eyelashes fluttered over her big eyes.

That was it. I was right. She was the *devil*. She derived a sadistic pleasure out of pushing people off the edge to an unending pit of inferiority complex. I was not in any mood to relent and let this drop dead gorgeous witch have her way. I finally looked up.

'No. It's just that I have a slight sprain in my neck,' I said and mentally patted myself, as it happened to be the smartest answer ever under near fatal conditions.

'So tell me. How is Smriti? You're dating her, right?' she asked.

'She is fine,' I squeaked. *You are the finest. I love the way your hands clutch that handbag. Can I be the handbag? Can you turn me into one?*

'She has her exams going on, if I am not wrong?'

'How do you know?' *Silly question, you are obviously a witch. You know everything.*

'A friend, she is studying in the same college as her.'

'Okay,' I said.

I was getting progressively uninterested in her. It was of no use talking to her. I couldn't get her in my wildest dreams. And she couldn't have made a good friend. It was hard not to fall in love with her. I knew I had to *not like* her. At least show that I did not like her. I was sure she wouldn't be too impressed with me either. I was just a dumb, average looking bloke.

Also, *she was a witch.*

'So how is it going with her?'

'Not so fine. I guess we are moving apart,' I said.

She had started to sound more non-witch like. Maybe she was human after all. Or a goddess.

'And why is that? I have heard she is a nice girl.'

'She says I am a little too distracting for her. That's why. You tell me, how is it going with your boyfriend?' *Can you turn me into your boyfriend? A friend? The fly buzzing across your nose?*

'Who? Shawar? Oh, you wouldn't want to know. I have been begging him to break up. But I guess he would have nothing else to do in life if we broke up. For now, he just irritates me,' she said. Her voice had more force and more bass than mine did. Every word seemed measured and rehearsed. Her style was unmatched, sophistication personified. She had the grace of a 50-year-old cocktail-ed with the naughtiness of a 15 year old.

'So you have started all over again? Give him a break; he is still your boyfriend,' Tanmay said as he approached us. 'I guess you should leave now, it's getting late.'

I had not expected them to be back so soon. Maybe they did go out for a walk. Or that Tanmay didn't want me around his sister.

'Yes, I guess so, bye guys. It was nice to meet you Debashish. Jai Sri Guru,' she said as we shook hands. She turned around and left, leaving all of us in darkness... and I was still in the dream world the touch of her skin had transported me to. I had never thought a handshake could be so overwhelming.

'What was this Jai Sri Guru thing she did when she left us?' I asked Vernita as we got into the car. I had taken well over fifteen minutes to realize that I had a stupid *take-me-home- I-am-your-puppy* smile on my face. I wiped it off.

'Nothing. Didn't I tell you once about Tanmay's belief in something called the *Spirit of Living*? Sri Guru heads it. She is quite into all that; it helped her to get out of all the shit she was in. So did you like her?' she asked as we fastened our seat belts.

'Nay, not much.' I lied.

'You did *not*?'

'No, I did not!' I lied.

'*Don't tell me!* Why so?'

'She is pretty dumb,' I lied.

'Dumb? Are you out of your *fucking* mind?'

'Anyway, I had expected her to be better looking than what she turned out to be.' I lied again.

That's it, now I was certainly on my way to hell. But I couldn't have raved about her when I knew I wouldn't be a patch on the image Tanmay had brainlessly created. I could have boxed Tanmay's teeth in if he wasn't Avantika's brother... and strong.

'That's strange. I haven't seen such a beautiful girl in a long time, Deb.'

'Anyway, where did she have to go?'

'She had a date.'

'With Shawar? I thought she hated him.'

'No. With Paritosh. Her ex-boyfriend and Shawar's best friend before they broke up. He is back from the States for a week. Didn't you notice the tears? She *still* loves him. That's the reason why she started dating Shawar in the first place. To make Paritosh jealous.'

'Why did he dump her?'

'No idea, nobody knows. That's the way those rich bastards are.'

Now Avantika started to sound more human. Somebody had dumped her. The guy had to be a freak. Vernita and I talked a lot more about her on the way back. Avantika had wanted to take up engineering but her parents wanted something else for her. They wanted her to get married as soon as possible. She had fought her way through the years after she turned eighteen. Through rough relationships, hostile parents, drugs and alcohol. Her parents knew nothing about it. They had gotten used to the snubbing and vice versa.

It was strange to see how little they cared about her. They knew everything about what Tanmay did, but shockingly, they had no idea about Avantika's drug problem. She was addicted to Methamphetamine. Ice, we called it. The first and only time Yogi and Viru used it, the high lasted twelve hours, and that is more than cocaine and LSD combined. They wisely stayed away from that ever since.

This was the 7th of April 2007.

'Don't tell me!' I exclaimed. 'I always knew it was *you*. It had to be *you*. This isn't real.'

'Yes, it is,' Smriti said.

It couldn't be Smriti. It was a shimmering Tissot watch a huge blue dial. The watch must have cost her a fortune! I always wanted one of those. Or more.

'Do you like it?'

'Do I like it? Are you crazy? I am already in love with it.'

She hugged me as soon as I said this.

'Aww... My sweet darling,' she kissed me. 'Happy six months anniversary!'

Six months anniversary? What?

It was the first time I was celebrating such a thing. It was only April and I felt like I had been with her since puberty. Good old days. Now even if she dressed up in leather, it would hardly make me unzip. Mannequins aroused me more. She had been around all these months despite me giving her a torrid time. I had ignored her on grounds of illness/depression/bickering mom/friend troubles blah...

'Same to you, sorry I couldn't get you anything,' I said. I thanked god I didn't. A hundred rupee coffee mug wouldn't have appealed to her for sure.

'It's okay; it's not for the anniversary. I just felt like buying it for you, for you have been a great boyfriend.'

'And you have been a great girlfriend,' I said. If only I could tell her how much I wanted her hands off me while driving. One scratch and dad would kill me.

'Thanks, there was something you wanted to tell me Deb, what was it?'

'Was I? I don't think so.'

Now what was I supposed to *tell* her? That I really wanted to break up? Tell her that she had been clingy for the last few months and I couldn't take it anymore... and that too with that devil of a watch on my hand. Of course breaking up that day would have meant losing that too.

'Love you.' She rested her head on my shoulder.

'Love you too.'

Now that was getting scary. I never thought she would ever be like those girlfriends who save for months together to surprise their boyfriends with gifts such as these. I loved her, I thought. I could. *I had to*, at least for a while. She wasn't bad.

The watch was beautiful.

'Hi Deb, guess what?' Vernita blared on the phone.

'Not interested. Let me sleep, witch.'

'Yup... you got it. She isn't *interested*. She found you really dumb... and ugly too as far as I could make out.'

'Same here. Go tell *her*.' Click.

I hoped she would not. I was right, she didn't like me. I hated it. She knew me exactly as I was - *dumb and ugly*.

I didn't let that bother me as I had my placement interviews coming up and I was not in position to waste my time on girls I found desperately short on grey matter and the ability to judge great guys. I tried hard but Shrey didn't buy *this* explanation.

Placements is the one thing that is always on the minds of engineering students right from the time they enter college to when they leave it.

What after college? Where are you placed?

These questions needed to be answered. Sooner the better. It is why we all took up engineering for.

Though I must mention here, Shrey was more worried about whether management schools in India had a better sex life or engineering colleges abroad. He had to make sure he made the *right* decision after college.

Not Having a Job Sucks... So Does a French Girl

It was May and it was my first on-campus job interview. Four years of hard work or fucking around came to this very moment. The tension in the Training and Placement department was palpable. There was a presentation of which I heard nothing. Nobody asked the question I wanted them to ask – what will the crowd be like? Everyone was busy counting how much would they get to spend, trying to find their way out of the winding lanes of CTC (Cost To Company), which sometimes even accounted for the space you occupied in their office. Or the toilet paper you used. Anything to keep you poor.

There was a written exam, which people found rather easy. Those who didn't have their friends sitting on their behalf.

'Best of luck, ass. Do well,' Vernita said.

I texted Smriti that I was busy in the presentation and will not be available for the next few hours or so. She had forgotten about my interview and I was not going to accept an explanation that we had not talked about *it* in over a month. She had not wished me luck. She was not serious about the relationship. I, of course loved her and she was letting me down repeatedly. Bad for her. It couldn't have gone on like this.

'And we need a treat when you get through!' Shrey added.

'Shrey, I am telling you, there is still time. Why don't you fucking try to sit for it? They take everybody. Could you not at least try?' Vernita asked.

For Shrey, it was the best shot at getting a job. With a percentage like his, this was the only company that would take him. However, apparently, his formals weren't ironed and he didn't want to take the pain. His laxity was not only weird and baseless, but often looked self-destructive.

'I don't want to. It is not about my formals or anything. I just don't want to sit for it. I am not interested,' he said. All three of us knew it was about *the formals*.

'Whatever, Shrey. I don't know why you act so smart.'

'I act smart? Why don't you sit for it, then?' Shrey retorted.

'I have better options. I have a better percentage and unlike you I don't have any back papers, get it?'

The HR guy came out and called out some names, I was the third person to go in.

'How do you know I don't have any options? You should just shut up about things you don't know,' Shrey said.

'Fuck yeah! You know things? 52 percent? That is how you know things?' Vernita asked. As usual, she was saying a lot more than she should have.

'Yeah, why not? You know everything about everything? At least I don't go around with guys thinking it is *true* love. What about Varun? Did you know he wasn't in love with you?' Shrey asked. He had won round one and was talking nonsense.

'I don't want to talk about it. At least I don't say I love Tanmay and sleep around with *others*. You will tell me what love is? Go try and explain that to Vandana.'

Round two was still open.

They were doing a good job of keeping my nervousness at bay. I was called in. They left.

'Okay Debashish, which computer languages do you know?' the bald headed interviewer asked.

'I am afraid none, sir,' I answered, trying to sound confident.

'Why do you then expect an opportunity to work with us? Why should we prefer you to the students from the IT department? They are better suited for the job, don't you think?'

'Yes sir.'

'See, you understand. Then why you?' he leant on to the table and stared at me. I felt like squeezing the biggish blackish mole on his right cheek, which had a few strands of hair jutting out. Moles are such fascinatingly disgusting things that you can never take your eyes off them. Especially if they come with hair, like that one did.

'I believe I can learn languages and as long as I have the conviction to learn and the enthusiasm to contribute to the company I admire, I am sure I will prove to be an asset to the company.'

Was I not dying to work in a company that would require me to sit for fourteen hours a day in front of a blank screen typing out some brainless codes with another twenty thousand non-descript people with me?

'But that's nothing different from the other aspirants that have applied. Why should we take you?'

Because I have a fucked up percentage and a company like yours takes everybody?

'Sir, I am hard working and am always willing to put in my 100 percent in everything I do. I have the urge to learn and apply. I will be asset to any organisation I work for.'

'Your exam results don't show that.'

I know that, you dimwit.

'Yes, I know that, sir. However, I wasn't interested in Mechanical. It was a mistake to have taken it up. That's why my grades dipped.'

'Yes, I know. It can be a pain. Mechanical is not a very interesting field, you see. It's a very theoretical field and tends to get very monotonous. It's a languishing field. Don't you think?'

Fuck you.

'Yes sir.'

It seemed the only notable thing he did after being born was taking up IT as a subject. The presumptuousness of IT people never ceased to amaze me.

'See, you understand Mechanical engineers in India are no good. What made you take it up?'

'Sir, my dad is a Mechanical engineer and is working with BHEL.'

'A PSU? All these Mechanical PSUs are just sick industries with no work culture and absolutely no sense of ambition. Anyway, the IT guys have better percentages than you have despite IT being a tougher course. It would not be fair choosing you over them. They have worked harder. Don't you think?'

Oh wow. You're a fucking genius!

'Yes sir.'

I presumed sitting in the OAT lawns with the best junior chics college had to offer was indeed very tough. Juniors are always sexier, hornier and more *open* to stuff than the previous batch. While people in my batch were losing it in their 20's, our juniors were doing it before they left their teens! We just chose the wrong decade to be born in... More sex in the latter, no fucking IT in the former.

'See, you understand. What makes you think that you are interested in software, Debashish?'

Because it gets people jobs.

'Sir, it really intrigues me how certain codes can make things happen,' I said, still not giving up and trying to make something happen.

'It intrigues you and still you didn't make an effort to learn any of that. You know it's not very easy. In Mechanical, things haven't changed in the two decades or so. But the IT sector has grown. You constantly have to be on your toes to be competitive. You can't just sit and let things happen the way they are. IT and electronics are changing the world. Don't you think?'

If it changes the world, why are you still an asshole?

'Yes sir.' I would have loved to see his brain splattered against the wall behind him.

'See, you understand that too. People in Mechanical and Civil really have to start working hard if they want to make an impact. But they make lousy students and that's the root of the problem. Services still constitute 52 percent of the GDP. So we are doing pretty well, unlike you, don't you think?'

I fully agreed... to write a program for electronically wiping off Bill Gates' ass each morning because he is busy doing other important things. That's services all right.

'Coming back to the question, why didn't you try to learn anything about languages?'

Are you kidding me? They are fucking boring.

'Sir, I did not get time.'

'Why? Were you studying for your semester?' he barely suppressed a chuckle. I just got a feeling I was in for some special treatment. He had just laid his hands on a below average student with no special talent to speak of.

'No sir, I was involved in extracurricular activities.'

'What kind?'

Oh. Shit.

'Sir, I have been an active member of the Students Council and have organized fests. I have been working with *The Society of Automotive Engineers* for the last three years...'

'Despite having no interest in Mechanical?'

Oh. No.

'Yes sir.' This was getting tiring and frustrating. Even staring at the grotesque mole had become boring.

'Okay. But I don't see any certificates for any of them?' the bald guy added gleefully. He would have clapped and done a little jig had he been invisible.

'Sir, I didn't collect the certificates.'

'Why, didn't you get the *time* or you had no *interest*?' he smiled.

Will you shut the fuck up?

That was it and I knew I was not going to get it.

'Debashish? Any answers? See you have to be a quick thinker to give an answer but then Mechanical...'

'No sir. I think I am not fit for the company nor is the company right for me. Thank you, sir. For the exposure I wanted before I sit for other *Mechanical* companies. It was nice meeting you,' I said condescendingly and walked off fuming.

It wasn't the wisest thing to do, but it felt so bloody good. How not-so-good it was, I was still to realize. Until then, the huge two-storied Mechanical canteen beckoned me.

Thanks for the wishes. I had a terrible interview. You obviously don't care. Please don't call and irritate me right now.

The text would have reached Smriti as I stepped in to the Mechanical canteen.

'Heard you had a pretty interesting interview?' Shrey said.

He was the one who came up with the idea of cutting the water supply to the electrical canteen in a bid to divert the crowd to the newer Mechanical canteen. It worked like a dream. College authorities took two months to rectify the problem, by which time the students had already got used to the new canteen. He was the godfather of this place. Every Mechanical student knew him and the story. Never did he spend a single paisa there. He fed off what others ordered.

'I don't want to talk about it. You tell me, how are the formalities going?'

'I went to the French embassy yesterday. You have to see it to believe it. It's heaven. All those girls in short skirts. I wonder what Paris would be like. I talked to my professor in France. She sounded sexy too,' he said.

Heaven for sure. He was soon to be in a place where people would listen to him and not bludgeon him for they won't understand the language he would speak in. And where those people would be short-skirted university girls. I knew getting all those things fixed with a foreign university and running around wasn't my cup of tea, but I still envied him. If hard work pays in hot, French girls, then why not?

'Have you managed all the money?' I asked.

'I am getting a scholarship from the French embassy,' he said.

'What the *hell*? With that fucked up percentage of yours? What did you do?'

'I forged the mark sheet. There is this mammoth machine called exxaccopier at the National Laboratory which charges...'

'Fuck that. What about the signatures?'

'I forged that too. That's what I am telling you. That machine with its meta stable lasers...'

'Are you crazy? What if you get caught?'

'I will either be resting in my grave or be too old to be jailed. So chill.'

'Are you sure?' I asked.

'Yes, I am sure.'

For a few seconds I hoped he is caught sooner. I felt I was missing out on something. I was tired of heart wrenching stories of successes around me anyway. But realized soon enough it was useless to envy him. The Paris internship would do nothing great to him. With a percentage like his, he would find it difficult to get placed. Or get into a good university for his masters.

Moreover, doing masters wasn't really my thing... since the very thought of opening the bonnet and looking at an engine made me queasy enough to take a bus back home. But a foreign internship in the midst of French girls would have done no harm whatsoever to my burgeoning health.

'What does Vandana have to say about it? Is the cool with it? You haven't been apart for this long, have you?'

'Were she to discover I had cancer, the only reaction might be a frown. She is taking it easy,' he said.

'And you? Won't you miss her?'

'Naah, will concentrate better. I may get to finally do *it* too. Finally I will be among people who know that there is not much difference between fingers and a bigger finger... and who won't go into fits of moral frenzy when it comes to sex,' he said.

Shrey always projected as if he didn't love her since it is cool not to be mushy. Just because he made out occasionally with other girls, didn't mean he wasn't in love with her. Yes, they had still not done *it*. He never tried convincing her. *He loved her.*

'Best of luck, man! But trust me, you will miss her.'

'No I won't. In fact, I will devote all my time to football and image processing. I have to read a lot too. I will try a little bit of photography too. It's not a tough thing to do if you ask me. A sunset, a crying child, a poor old woman... anything looks good if your camera is good. Take big prints in black and white and you are on your way... and with my modified camera and these focusers brought in direct from Sweden...' And it went on... nothing short of spectacular could ever happen to him, or so he thought.

'So, when are you leaving?' I asked.

'In a month, I guess. Damn! I have to get a paper signed from the principal. You are coming?' He got up frantically. I was sure he was late by at least a week.

'Naah! Vernita just messaged. She is coming here.'

'Bye then. Catch you later. That girl is nuts. And do tell her she can sleep with as many guys as she wants to. We don't give a damn.'

He walked off.

Although friends, Shrey and Vernita avoided each other's company. Shrey always had problems with Vernita's boyfriends whom she picked up from the strangest of places. Vernita never saw any point in whatever Shrey said and invariably pissed him off. Shrey cared, but Vernita was too blind to see that.

❧

'Why do you want to know?' I asked Vernita. The results of the interview were out and she wanted to see who all got through.

'Curiosity sake. Let's see who amongst us are doomed to a life of codes. Not everybody would have screwed up like you,' she said as we took the long walk towards the Training and Placement department. We crossed the OAT (Open Air Theatre), which stood witness to many Engifests, Troikas, INNOVAs and other fests, not to mention the innumerable romances that often sprung out of nothingness that had gripped this college.

Not that I gave two hoots about getting into a mass recruiter IT company with a sad gender ratio, but I would have loved to get selected. It helped to have a cushion placement and then go for better ones, especially when you don't have a great score.

'Hey Prasad! Did you get through?' Vernita shouted across to a loser.

'Yes, I did. I am sorry for you, Deb,' he whimpered back.

'Never mind,' I said as if I hardly cared. 'Prasad? He got through? He can barely talk.'

'It is not fucking about how you speak, Deb,' Vernita shot back.

'Okay, then tell me what he has that I don't?' I sounded like a jealous boyfriend.

'He looks like a geek. He looks serious for it and you didn't even shave. Fucking look at your hair. Terrible,' Vernita said.

'Oh, so now you finally get it. It's not about how you speak. It's about how dumb you look!'

'Whatever. I am glad I didn't sit for it,' she said.

'You would have got through anyway.'

'Yes, why not? I know everything. Computers? Haven't I been playing with it since the time I was born?' she mocked.

'Girls don't need that. And someone like you definitely doesn't. You are overqualified – too good looking to be rejected.'

You have great breasts and you look smashing in formals.

'Shut up, you chauvinist pig. I have the brains, you dickhead,' she said.

'Don't give me that crap. Okay, give me the name of one lab assistant who hasn't gone out of way to help you cheat in practical exams.'

'That's easy... I mean, sort of.'

'No wait, explain this. How have you been consistently outscoring the strongest and the most skilful of guys in the workshop? Now don't tell me those manicures give your hands super strength. Or you manage to do it with your brains? Just accept it. It helps to be a hot and pretty girl in an engineering college.'

She never stuck around the workshop for long. The pervy lab assistants were always too eager to help her out. What did they get out of it? Nobody knew. I would rather see her bend over and sweat it out. At least there would be something pleasantly hot other than the threatening molten metal alloys.

'Okay, shut up sucker. Look, Ayush is coming. Looks like he got through too.'

'Don't ask him. Can't take it anymore.'

'Fine. But I guess he is coming this way. No. He definitely is,' Vernita said.

'Hey Deb, heard about you, am sorry dude. Never mind. Anyway, I got through, Mohit too. Bye. Take care man and take it easy. Such things happen,' he said and walked off.

'Bloody hell! When was the last time he talked to us? Or did he ever talk to us before this? Sorry dude? As if I was dying for the job.'

'Shut up, Deb. You don't have to get paranoid about this.

Poor guy. He is happy that he got through. That's it,' she said.

'Whatever. Not another one. Don't tell me even he is coming towards us.'

'He didn't even give it, ass.'

I hoped he wasn't walking towards us, but as my wretched luck went, lightning could strike me twice that day. Never did I feel the option of killing somebody and rotting behind bars so tempting.

'Hi Chitiz. I heard everybody except me got through? They are so lucky. I wonder what they did in the interview. Maybe they just know everything. Or maybe they are just young Einsteins... and NO, we don't want to know who all got through. We just want to keep the suspense alive. Do you mind?' I said. He was lucky I still hadn't taken my hands out of my pocket.

'Excuse me. I can understand. Sorry to have bothered. Bye,' He walked off visibly perturbed after my uncalled for rudeness.

He can understand? What?

'Whoa! That was mean and totally unnecessary,' Vernita said as she hopped on the stairs leading to the T & P department.

'Whatever. But I can do without their sympathy. Especially when all they know is my fucking name.'

'There is the list,' Vernita pointed out.

'Ohh! How eager I am to have a look at it. I am not coming. You go and tell me about the assholes who got through.'

'As you say,' she said and left.

'Vernita… can we go now?' I shouted across to her.

'Wait,' she said, her facial expressions were changing each passing second. Seemed like more bad news was coming my way.

'So who are the lucky slackers who got through?'

'You've got to see this,' she said and grabbing my hand took me towards the list.

'I don't need to see this.'

'Yes, you do, Deb. Just read.'

'What? Ashish dumbhead, Ayush dickhead, Ankur loser.'

'Deb can you do it a little faster.' She punched me.

'Okay, okay. Ar… az… ba… be… ch… cu… di… what?'

'At the end of the list, Deb,' she said.

'Yogesh… Zohrab… Debashish… Debashish? How is this possible? Okay, wait, what the bloody…'

I was numbed. It was right there for the entire world to see.

Debashish Roy – *barred from all placement activities for the year 2007-08 on account of misbehaviour.*

⁀

The higher the ball falls from, the harder they bounce back. I was hit hard for sure. Being barred meant I would be jobless at the end of the academic session! I had almost fainted when I had first read it on the board.

This isn't happening.

Sitting at home and watch months go by, as my fellow students would get placed one by one was a horrendous enough feeling to contemplate being cut on railway tracks. I was screwed. I had never thought it would come to this. Getting debarred is something which always happens to others, not us.

I had been a complete ass. I had let my mom down, who used to be up all night to wake me up in whatever durations I asked her to. And dad too, who was in tears even after his brilliant son had once again underachieved by getting through an entrance he should have been through the first time around. I felt worse for them than for myself. They would have nothing to tell people around. I would not get placed that year. I would pass out from college without a job in hand.

No, Deb, there are some companies that hold off campus interviews before the session ends. And, NO, call centre is not an option.

Vernita called and broke the string of ridiculous options and way-outs.

Dumb Girls, Drunk Girls, Hot Girls

'She is depressed... something to do with Paritosh. You've got to do this for me,' Vernita said.

'I just had the *happiest* moment of my life. I just got barred, let's do this! Sorry Vernita, not coming. Anyway, it is very late and I would rather study for the exams.'

Sixth semester exams were less than a week away and I had decided to rock this one up. My fifth semester marks was the last good thing that had happened and I was dying to feel that way again. Anyway, I knew my career was going just one way – downhill. I needed those marks to get placed in off-campus interviews.

'Please. You will be placed off campus. That's not bad,' she pleaded.

'Don't give me that. My profile sucks. And my situation is definitely worse than hers.'

For a night out with Avantika, I would have sold my soul but that day was different. Not only was I aware of the fact that I was dumb and ugly, I was barred too... and she would know that. She wouldn't want to see a loser like me.

'Worse than hers, Deb? Smriti ends up writing your name on a suicide note and dies or you get debarred. What's worse?'

'Did Paritosh actually do that? Did he kill himself?'

'Not exactly. He just bashed up three of his classmates in the US with a baseball bat. One of them is dead. He was caught with drugs, bags full of it.'

'Where is he now?'

'Police custody, of course.'

'And?' I asked.

'And what?'

'Where does Avantika come into the picture? The suicide note thing?'

'She was the last person he met in India before he left for the States, after his family and his girlfriend... and a few friends.'

'Suicide note?'

'What suicide note?' she asked.

'You said her name was on a suicide note or something,' I said. Vernita had exaggerated again. I wondered in what words she would describe her own breasts. Hot air balloons?

'I never said that. I just gave an example. There is no suicide note, silly.'

'So what's the big deal then? Why is she depressed? She can just stay in her hostel and relax.'

'Don't you get it? She loved him. Now he is gone. Forever. She tried to get him clean off drugs, she couldn't. She thinks it's her fault.'

I learnt later that Paritosh was a drunkard and nearly flunked his ass out of school. He loved rock, as it was hip to do so, drove like crazy and spat blood and bile after crazy night outs. In short, a despicable creature. And more so for me. He even had half a tattoo on his right hand, half a man, half the pain. Avantika had the complete one.

'Is there nobody else? Shawar? He should be the one. Not me. I am dumb and ugly.'

'Shawar is the last person she would like to meet right now. I am picking you up in twenty minutes sharp. You have to do this. Just this night.'

More than anything, I dreaded meeting her again. I was not in a mood to deal with a work shirker heart and a rampaging tongue. It was already 11:30 p.m. and I had to convince mom that an important assignment was pending which could not be done sitting at home. Moms always know that you are lying, just that they don't have proof for it. Like movie tickets that you forget to throw off.

'Bye mom,' I said as I finally decided not to tuck in my shirt.

'Bye-bye. Did your result come out? The interview?' mom asked.

'Yes. I wasn't selected. Only 5 people got through,' I said. *At least 50 people did.*

'Never mind. Sit for others. These IT companies anyway are biased against Mechanical students,' she said. *I was perfect.* I would not ever put a foot wrong. Her son would do nothing wrong. How could I tell her that I would not be allowed to sit for others?

I left.

'Hi Vernita, hi Tanmay, hi Avantika!' I greeted everybody as I entered the car.

The best part about his car were the tinted windows that not only did a world of good to Vernita and him, who could do their thing in the college parking without raising any eyebrows, it also helped Shrey and me in our times of need.

'So where are we heading to?' I asked looking at Avantika, before she said anything and cast a spell on me.

She was looking no different that day, beautiful. Her eyes barely kept the flood of tears from running down the dried streaks of tears. She was in an extremely depressing, dull blue T-shirt and dark blue jeans teamed with sneakers. Her Orkut profile had her pictures in spaghettis and skirts with junk jewellery hanging from every part of hers but those days were long gone.

She was staring expressionlessly outside the window as if somebody had just sucked the soul out of her. A teardrop caressed her eye for a while until it could no longer stand her gaze and trickled down her cheek. The drop so clear, so radiant yet full of darkness and sadness. It hung from her cheekbone as if not wanting to leave it. Who would? *What would,* in this case. I caught the tear just as the ill-fated tear left her face. I held that tear in my hand.

'Now, you may suffer from dehydration.' Silly joke, I thought. She looked at me. Sadness never looked so heavenly. I wished she were sadder. *Can I slap you for looking great?*

'Hi, Deb.' She actually talked to me. It may have been out of sympathy. I was *dumb* and *ugly,* after all.

Somehow seeing her cry made me feel more comfortable. I had found a chink in her otherwise flawless armour. I had always proved myself to be a good agony aunt. Many of my relationships were rebounds. No girl in her senses would date me otherwise.

'Hey, you don't have to cry. Look at the better side. He can come out, sign a book deal and be rich... and famous. Oops, he already is.'

'Excuse me?' she said startled, her eyebrows making a small hill. She was taken aback and I expected that. I had seen that expression a million times. It was working. It is always easier to talk and kid about relationships than actually brood over it and not talk about it at all. For this very reason, people around me said that I was insensitive. But who was to tell them that it was for their own good. I was insensitive too. I had not been through a break up, so the whole sense or nonsense surrounding break ups eluded me.

'Excused. Why are you crying? And just think your

grandchildren would be so proud when they go about telling their friends, my grandma's ex-boyfriend is one of the looniest criminals in Arkansas. Now that would be cool.'

Don't kill it. Don't be over-smart. Chill. Focus.

'Hmmm…' she said.

'When did you break up?'

'It's been more than two years, February 2005.' She turned towards the window. We were whizzing past Punjabi Bagh. A string of flyovers on the ring road had made the drive red light free. These flyovers, metro, high capacity buses made Delhi much more commutable. No longer were the sexier parts of Delhi being alienated. Delhi government had an iron rod up its ass to do all that. The rod – the Commonwealth Games 2010.

'Two years? And you are still crazy about him? Look at Vernita; Tanmay is lucky that she is still with him after six months. I think you don't realize that you can get any guy.'

I couldn't believe I was speaking so much. I think it came out, as in the state that she was in; she wasn't as fatal as she was that day.

'I don't need anybody else.'

'You didn't need a cell phone before you started using it. Start using me and you will feel my need,' I said.

You couldn't be flirting with her. You are a poor, dumb and an ugly guy.

'I don't like people who flirt so much in their first meeting,' she said. Quite obviously, I was being unnecessarily over smart.

'Technically, this is our second meeting. And those who don't flirt and stay shut in their first meeting, you find them *dumb*. Don't you? As for the ugly part, I won't say anything because I am ugly,' I said as I winked at Vernita.

'I can't believe you told him that, bitch. And you're *not* ugly,' Avantika said as she pinched Vernita. I was the happiest man on earth. I had just made the most beautiful girl on earth smile in her saddest moment. She looked ravishing.

'I couldn't help it,' Vernita answered as she looked at me and ground her teeth.

'I didn't mean that. Seriously,' Avantika said apologetically and touched me on my forearm. I felt... something.

'Oh! Then what did you mean?' I asked as I leaned onto her and fainted. Almost. *Why did I have to look her straight in the eye?*

'I mean. You have to admit. You were acting so dumb that day. You were just average.' She had more authority in her voice than my English teachers after they spotted a *didn't-went*.

'So you could have said that... I am hurt. I couldn't sleep for days, you cruel hag,' I said.

'I said that. But she wouldn't take it. You know how she is,' she said, wiping off her tears.

Wasn't I great? I just made a girl whose most loved person is going to be dead in a few days, smile. Well not dead, but it sounded more dramatic that way.

'Yes, I know,' I said.

'Anyway, what are you accusing me of? Even you didn't find me attractive. Or rather, you found me dumb. What do you have to say to that, Mr. Roy?' she said.

Didn't that sound sexy? Mr. Roy... will you marry me, Mr. Roy? Will you take out the garbage? Will you... Focus. Focus Deb, focus.

'Oh that? That was because I knew you wouldn't have kind words for me, so why should I?'

Vernita had been a bitch. But what she had said was actually helping me blow the ice away. I was just plain lucky.

'Okay. So? What were the real words?' she asked.

'You were just about average. Nothing great.'

And we all burst out laughing at the pretty average joke, but any joke under those circumstances worked. I was no less. I felt like god.

'You guys go in, I am getting a call,' I said as we stepped on the escalator leading to *Hype*. It was Smriti.

I waited for Avantika to go past the huge bouncers and through the huge red doors before I picked up the call. She was off the circuit for a year but everyone seemed to know her – the bouncers nodded, the manager had something funny to tell her, no cover charges. Avantika often scared the shit out of me. She had been the kind who made school hell. The guys I never could be, and their girls whom I could never get, both of whom hated me. Avantika belonged to both of these.

Smriti never called when she was back home, in Meerut, during holidays. So it had to be important and as expected was greeted by a frantic sounding Smriti.

'What happened? I can't hear you properly.'

'Mom *is in the other room*. There is something very important I had to tell you. I told them about you. And *us*.'

'Told them what?' I shouted as moms do, out of habit, on trunks calls even on cell phones.

'*ABOUT YOU*! I told them about you!'

'And? What did you say?' I asked. The last thing you would want in a fling*ish* relationship were parents. I freaked out.

'I told them the truth. I love you. I told them we were serious and it is long term,' she said.

'Are you nuts? Why did you have to tell them? Are you fucking crazy? What did you say? What did they say? Man, shit, shit, shit, shit. Man... fucking shit man.'

'Am I crazy? You told me that you want it to be long term. So I told them. That is it.'

'What did they exactly say? What the fuck do they want right now? Why the fuck did you have to tell them? I had said you don't have to tell them anything right now!'

'I was feeling guilty, Deb.'

'What the fuck Smriti... you didn't tell them that you slept with me. Didn't you fucking feel guilty then? Shit man. What did they say?'

'They want to meet you... and your parents. It was tough, but I convinced them, Deb.' She said what sounded quite like a death sentence to me.

'Are you fucking crazy? Why?'

'...to talk about us. My dad is extremely angry with me... and with you. But I told them I loved you and he agreed to meet your parents,' she said meekly.

'What the fuck? About us? Meet my parents? My parents will burn me at the stake damn it. They won't tolerate another inter caste after the one Sonali almost brought home.' I thanked god I didn't tell my parents about the interview. That with this affair news would have made things stuffy at my place.

'What am I supposed to do, Deb? I can't do anything. I am doomed either ways.'

'I don't know. It's all your fault. Why did you have to fucking tell them? We could have done that later. I had told you so many times not to talk about us to anyone. What got into you?'

'Is it my fault?'

'Yes, it's your fault. It's because of you we are in this mess now. You are...'

'It's always my fault. Isn't it? I came after you, didn't I?' she broke down and I hated it. I couldn't bear to see her cry. I didn't love her, but seeing her cry pained me. Her crying also meant she would keep the phone down, not pick up my calls and bitch about how uncaring I was to others. Not acceptable.

'Okay, now don't cry. Your mom will wake up. We will see what we can do. Just tell me what exactly you told your dad. Exact words.'

'They didn't let me speak. They just wanted to meet your parents. I just said that we love each other and you have no problems with our getting married in the future.'

'Okay, go to sleep now. When are they coming to Delhi if they are?'

'Next week.'

Fuck.

'Okay, sleep now. Goodnight. Love you.'

'Love you too.'

I cut the line. I was glad she didn't ask where I was. Not that I would have told her the truth anyway. She hated Vernita and didn't trust me with her. Especially when she knew that I wasn't the nicest of guys around.

A million things started running through my mind. I was fucking 21 and some oldie was to come and meet my dad proposing a match. This was the worst that could have happened. Deep inside, I knew it would be lot worse. They would accuse me of ruining their daughters' life etc. etc. Ideally, I would have spent the night sweating it out and thinking about the worst worst-case scenarios, but Avantika was inside, and I was dying to see her again.

I decided I would deny all allegations of an affair. I made up my mind to tell them that it was a friendship and it was Smriti who went crazy after me. *I am innocent.*

'Hey! What's up?' I shouted as the pungent smell of alcohol and smoke wafted inside my nostrils adding to the filth inside it. *Hype* was a small cosy place, never too crowded and was open until early morning. It catered to the not so affluent but still chic crowd, so it happened to be a good hangout place.

'Whose call was it?' Vernita shouted back.

'Smriti.'

'Anything worth knowing?' Tanmay asked.

'Nopes, looks like it's going to be a long night,' I remarked as I looked around to see sagging, wobbly breasts and flabby thighs on the dance floor. It was a strange retro-trance night (something like that!) and the younger/dancing crowd had wisely stayed away.

'Yes, I guess so,' Vernita said. That was a consolation. Except me, the other three could set the floor on fire within seconds.

So getting an indication that they won't dance saved me from the embarrassment I invariably faced in nightclubs. Plus, I would get more time with Avantika that way.

'Drinks?' Vernita asked.

'No,' we all echoed.

Vernita was the only one who drank. Tanmay and Avantika were associated with *Spirit of Living,* which forbade them to drink. And I never felt like drinking. Ever. The taste just never appealed to me and my highly developed taste buds couldn't take the torture. I had come to despise people who drank. I was often called a wimp for not drinking. I somehow always thought it was the other way round. It was always easy to say yes... especially when it is being forced upon you by a bunch of bullies and their fucking bitches. My school days were torturous and I have never moved past the memories.

'You don't drink?' Avantika asked. I had heard she had had quite some unmentionable sexy and wild nights before she left all of that for *Spirit of Living.* The tattooed snake on her lower back testified that.

'No. What so surprising? Even Tanmay doesn't.'

'No. But he has his reasons, *Spirit of Living* and everything.'

'I have mine.'

'And they would be...?' she asked as she rested her chin on her knuckles and leant forward. I don't know whether that is what she intended to do, but I was seduced.

'I don't relish the taste. It's just so... yuck. Ugh.'

'It is not about the taste. It is about the feeling. It's about the high,' she said. Words from a veteran, I thought.

'I can do without that feeling or that high. Definitely not when I have to puke my guts out to get it.'

'People would call you simply boring.'

'I get my high from other things. Trust me.'

'Oh! Now that is interesting... and probably a lie.' She rocked back and adjusted a fringe, spiking my heart with her grace. I was glad she wasn't dancing that night.

'It is possible. You can never tell with him. He is very popular with my girlfriends,' Vernita added. Although it was a lie, I didn't mind her projecting me as she did. Vernita continued, 'But the not-drinking part, I still think you are just a wimp... and a loser. You guys will have anything?'

'Sweet lime,' Avantika said and continued. '...and Deb, I liked that. You need courage to refuse.'

I love you too. Can I hold your hand? I don't drink.

'You are a wimp too,' Vernita butted in.

'Shut up, Vernita. I guess you are just a boring person who drinks as she doesn't have anything worthwhile to do,' Avantika said.

'Hahaha! We will see that soon enough. Never mind. Deb?'

'Some more of your catfight and a cold coffee,' I added. I could tell she was missing Virender and Yogender. They would have got the whole bar to the table.

'Let me come with you,' Tanmay said as he put his arm around Vernita.

'Don't go, I will get them for you,' Avantika said as she started typing out something on her cell phone. Within the next few seconds, I saw the manager rushing towards the bar. The order was on our table in a flash. Avantika was a privileged customer there.

Just as it would happen to any normal person, I fell more in love with her every second that passed. She was beautiful and it would have been unfair to god not to appreciate his hard work. It's surprising he didn't keep Avantika for himself.

We danced a little that night. But to my elation, the music didn't encourage any complex movements that would have put my disabilities to the fore. All I tried to do was get a little close to her, follow her moves and catch glimpses of her face hidden beneath her swaying hair, as she kept craning her neck from one side to another with every beat. Thankfully, the swaying and shaking of head became tiring and we flopped down on the couches.

'Seems like they have just gone to sleep,' I said. Vernita and Tanmay actually had. Vernita was as usual drunk from the minute quantities of alcohol she consumed. Tanmay had passed out of boredom.

'Let's go for a walk. It's getting suffocating here,' Avantika said.

That was the single most beautiful thing she had said in the entire evening. That meant she preferred talking to me to sleeping. That was encouraging. Only for a while. As soon as we sat down on the stairs, it took her just a fraction of a second to doze off with her head on my shoulder.

That wasn't bad, I thought, as far as I got to touch her and watch her sleep so close to me. She wasn't crying anymore. *It was heaven*... barring the chill that my ass was subjected to. Unfortunately enough, she was sitting on the carpeted part of the stairs and I on the concrete part. *Small price to pay*, I thought.

I started feeling like the king who endured the scorpion bite for years not to break a sage's meditation. I could feel my ass freeze out of existence. It was not letting me sleep after I had spent hours staring at her. I finally decided to try sleeping one last time. Just as I put my hand around her and rested my head on hers, she did the most amazing thing. She snuggled up to me!

Now it was definitely *heaven*.

Out of Bounds

'*WHAT THE HELL DO YOU THINK YOU ARE DOING?*' Tanmay shouted.

'Huh,' I froze. Did he just *have to* interrupt?

As we had snuggled, I spotted Avantika in tears again. With every sob, she clutched my arm tighter. I looked at her again. But this time I couldn't help it. She opened her eyes looked at me and closed them again making a teardrop peep out. Something told me she wouldn't resist or resent. I kissed it away. It was surreal.

Seeing her cry pained me and for no reason whatsoever I held myself responsible for it. With those beautiful welled up eyes she fixed her gaze at me, almost hypnotizing me into kissing her again. I did it again... on her lips, enveloping them, one at a time. She didn't resist this time either. I felt her tears run down her cheeks and wet my hands that held her face.

'Let's go.' Tanmay held Avantika by her hand and led her away. 'TO THE PARKING LOT. NOW,' he motioned to Vernita and left.

Avantika looked back... and my heart sank. She had just betrothed me to her with that kiss. Those tears may have been for somebody else's love but they found me mine.

'*What the hell do you think you were doing*? How did you do it? Are you bloody crazy?' Vernita shouted and whispered at me at the same time not sure whether to be bewildered, shocked or angry. 'Four months and Shawar didn't even get to hold her hand. And you? You have a girlfriend, damn it? And you know what she has been through!'

If she was trying to make me feel guilty about it, she certainly wasn't succeeding. Not only had I achieved something of gigantic proportions, I had found love too. Not that I exactly knew what love is, but it was supposed to be great and this was better than great.

'It just happened. I didn't intend to do it. I am sorry. But it wasn't just me.'

'It was just you, fucker. She was sad and drunk. And what did you do? Use her?'

'Drunk? She wasn't drunk,' I retorted.

'Yes she was. I had mixed vodka in her lime, you bastard.'

'Oh, but I had…'

No wonder the lime tasted funny. I resisted the urge to tell her. Avantika and I had exchanged our drinks.

Was I going crazy? Or was the falling in love process complete? Is this what it feels like? I hardly knew her but I knew that she would never leave my mind.

Avantika finally taught me that kissing was beyond the pointless slobbering of tongues.

Tanmay dropped Vernita at her place and Avantika at her hostel. Everybody avoided eye contact. Avantika was quiet too. She was crying, softly, but not softly enough.

Nobody exchanged a word.

'Hey, Deb,' Tanmay said as I got down from the car. I was feeling good till then. After Avantika got down, he didn't give me the time to come to the front seat. So we hadn't exchanged a word.

'Yes.' I looked back as he came and stood right in front of me. I sensed a big scene. Maybe a punch in the face and a few kicks on the rib cage.

'Stay away from Vernita and Avantika. You have no idea who you are messing up with. Avantika has been through a lot and I can't see her being ruined again. Do you get it? Think what you are doing to Smriti. What if I tell her? Leave Avantika alone. For me, for Smriti, for Avantika. Do you get it?' Tanmay said, alternating between being dangerous and soft. He too was a brat once and that was evident, the lines seemed to have been delivered many times before, but the *Spirit of Living* had changed him too. That too was evident.

'Hmmm... Sorry, Tanmay. But don't tell anything to Smriti.'

'I won't. Keep in mind what I said.'

He walked away. Smriti would have been broken. I didn't want that to happen; at least not when I had no clue as to what was cooking between Avantika and me. Even if something was to happen between Avantika and I – very unlikely – I decided I would break up first and then take a few months before I started telling people around about Avantika. It would have spared Smriti the trauma.

'Why are you crying?' I asked Smriti. She was in Delhi, but fortunately enough her parents weren't. Neither had Tanmay opened his mouth.

'Deb, why shouldn't Mahima get a divorce? The bastard, how can he ask for...' Mahima was her big sister who had just got married in a very conventional fashion a year back.

'Is that why they didn't come?' I cut her in between. Mahima's husband may have been a bastard but that didn't stop me from thanking him a zillion times... and counting.

'Yes. They want me to decide about you.'

'Decide?' I knew things would be easy there on. Her parents had bigger issues to take care of.

'Yes, whether this is a long-term relationship. They want to give me the choice of choosing who I spend my life with unlike Mahima. Tell me, Deb. I need to tell them in a month. It's either going to be you or it will be up to them.'

'What?' I asked. I wasn't listening to her. Her parents weren't coming. So, I was more interested in checking out whether Avantika sent me a message or not. She hadn't. It had been two days and fourteen hours.

'Didn't you get me? They are asking me whether this is serious.'

'As in? Me and you getting married? Are you crazy? My mom will kill me.'

'You don't have to tell her now. By the time I finish my medical you will be 28. Nobody would care then. You always said we will figure it out later.'

She was right. But I was busy reliving the kiss, pouting my lips and imagining things. *Maybe she doesn't have my number.* But I had seen her online. All social networking sites screamed out my number. She couldn't have missed out. She told me that day that her exams were on; *maybe she doesn't want a distraction.*

'They would care, Smriti... and eight years... Anything can happen. How am I supposed to commit?'

Yay! I had a point there, finally.

'At least give me an assurance. At least we can try. If it doesn't work out, I will take the blame.'

'What if you tell them that you have broken up and then if things are good between us in the coming days we will inform them?'

'That can't be done, Deb. They want it right now. After what happened with Mahima...'

'But...'

I was interrupted by her sniffy sobs. Crying is acceptable once, twice or at the most thrice, after that it, more often than not, does more harm than good. *Tears don't make guys melt, they irritate them.*

'You don't love me, do you?' she said. That was it; I had to call up Avantika.

'Of course I love you. Let's talk about this later. Bye,' I disconnected the call.

This was the best conversation I had with Smriti in a while, mostly because I wasn't concentrating on whatever she was trying to put across.

'Hi, Avantika.' I finally managed to call her up. It took me a few hours to kiss her, three days to call her up. Great!

'Hi, Deb,' she said. I wondered if she even remembered what happened that night. I assumed she had gone into her past and forgotten this as one of her wild nights. Not a very savoury thought that was.

'Delete this from your log. Tanmay would kill me if he gets to know that I called you up.'

'Positive,' she said. Her curt replies and an uninterested tone didn't actually sound too good for me. But I hardly cared. I couldn't have let her get away so easily after her giving me a life-altering kiss.

'I am sorry about that day. Or maybe I am not. It seemed right, didn't it?' I said and bit my whole fingernails off.

'Yes, it seemed right. They still think I drank the lime. Why didn't you tell them?' Her matter-of-fact answers weren't helping. My nail less fingers had started to hurt.

'I didn't feel like telling them. After all, I wasn't under its effect I am sure. I didn't have to be drunk to kiss you.'

It was you, not the bloody drink.

'It wasn't the drink? You used me? I didn't expect this from you. You filthy man!' she shrieked. And just as I was about to slit my nail less fingered wrist, she burst out in a guffaw.

'Oh shit! You nearly had me there.' I said. I didn't quite know what her laughter meant. But it surely started to sound good.

'By the way, do you think it is going to work?' she said.

What? Was she talking about *us?* What did she see in me? I loved it! She was even more audacious than I was. I only just kissed her.

'What is going to work?' I asked, just to be sure.

'We... I mean *us*. Together.'

'Yes... I mean I can... we can... ...try,' I stuttered.

'I am sorry, Deb. I know about Smriti I am really sorry. It is just that I am a little disturbed, with this exam tension and... Paritosh...' her voice trailed off.

'I don't mind you being disturbed.' I tried to be funny.

'Do you mind if we talk later?'

'Why would I mind? Do call. Bye.'

And that was our first conversation. I didn't know what to make of it until she called up the very next day. Obviously, after five calls of mine, which she didn't pick.

The phone call lasted a full seven hours. I was told about everything from her first bicycle to her present cycles. She had lived her life in extremes. She had had her share of alcohol binges, getting stoned for days, boyfriends, flings and soured relationships. She hated her parents and that I felt was something mutual. Her parents' whole family's prestige seemed to have some strange connection with her getting married young. They never supported her dreams of being anything worthwhile and all they cared was to find a rich enough businessman for their daughter. And all the while, she just had one aim in life, be something someday and run away. That was the reason she slogged and topped her college exams.

She was taking CAT that year but her parents didn't know.

But surprisingly enough, she was a virgin (not that I cared). I would have labelled that as bullshit, but it was quite apparent that it had been the reason for her last break-up. Though as I had expected, she had lost count of the guys she had kissed. It was strange falling in love with her. I had been in relationships with girls who had *been there, done that* types and it always worked in my favour. But this time, every time she counted a guy she had kissed, she got me writhing in fits of frenzy that used to end with her trashing the guy as a drunken bastard.

'But why did you kiss him?' I asked agitatedly as I paced across the room, banging my fists in the air as doing it on the table it would have hurt. I was getting possessive although it was just our second conversation. I already felt cheated.

'Deb? I was stoned. Do you know what that means? I didn't know what was happening.'

'Didn't know what was happening? You could have pulled back. Why continue kissing him?'

'I didn't know why I did it. I guess you have to be high to experience that!' she chortled.

'You enjoyed it, didn't you?' I said. It was paining now. I wanted to see if I was any different from the other guys she had kissed.

'What do you want to hear?'

'Something that is not too hard for me to take.' My heart was sinking. I would have liked the answer in the negative than the choice.

'I didn't remember anything of it the next morning. I am a different person when I am sloshed. And I don't think he was good enough anyway.' She chuckled again.

'Good enough? Who has been good enough for you then?'

'*You!* You wanted me to say this, didn't you?' she chuckled yet again.

'Yes, why not? That is why you didn't call me up? Because

I was good? Blah,' I said, hoping she would beg to disagree.

'Deb, I had heard a lot about you. I thought it didn't matter to you. And remember I kissed you when I was sober. That is a first for me, if it means anything to you. And I didn't regret it unlike the other times.'

'It meant a lot to me. I am glad we met that day,' I said, still irritated. 'But why did you keep kissing me back?'

'I have no idea, Deb. Destiny I guess. Sri Guru would have wanted it. Maybe he wants us to be together.'

'Works perfectly fine for me. I love this Sri Guru of yours. He makes a lot of sense, I guess.'

'Does Smriti know anything about me?' she asked. I hated the topic.

'No, and I don't care. I am falling for you and her being there doesn't make a difference to me.'

'It does, Deb. She loves you. It wouldn't be right if you do this to her. At least tell her.'

'I won't. She won't understand. You tell me. Do you love me? Or do you think there is any possibility that you may do someday. I am willing to wait and that's all I really care about.'

'Someday? Yes. But Smriti loves you now. Go back to her,' she said. Her voice sounded as tragic as she looked that day.

'I would rather wait for that *someday*,' I said. We disconnected the call after a little while. I was in love. I was still not sure about her. It was a strange feeling.

That day onwards, we talked for hours at an end. The amazingly long phone calls became a routine. It was almost unbelievable for me to know she wanted to talk to me every day. Delhi University exams were going on, but she didn't make me feel so. She called me up as much as I called her up and I loved that feeling. That *someday* was around the corner or maybe we had already passed it. We used to be all worked up and things could would get steamed up during the conversations but she never admitted that she loved me. She was dumped for another girl by Paritosh and she didn't want to do the same to Smriti.

It had been quite a while since I talked so much on the phone. The phone bills shot up. Mom's temper followed the same trajectory. I would get brain tumour, is what she used to say.

All that time we had paid no heed to Tanmay's and Vernita's incessant warnings and frequent checks on us. Tanmay had categorically told me to stay away from his sister, come hell or high water. He never forgot to give me the look whenever he crossed me in college. We both admitted it was fun throwing them off track... *We haven't talked since that day.* This was what Vernita got whenever she asked me about Avantika.

For Smriti, it was getting tougher, my sixth semester exams got fucked up, I was supposedly slipping into extremely bad moods and tempers frequently. Smriti was advised to leave me alone. By me, of course.

But Avantika kept making me feel bad about what I was doing to Smriti. All my efforts in explaining that it was Smriti who wasn't doing much for the relationship fell on deaf ears. Though I admit, I didn't have much to explain.

But the problem was not she; the big stumble was Shawar, her boyfriend. Academic brilliance being the last of his attributes, Shawar was doing a B.A. pass course in Shivaji College, which barely kept him busy, giving him ample time to surround himself with equally rich, powerful, wasted guys. He slept through his days and partied throughout the nights, and found time to deeply immerse himself in ultra-nasty brawls and fights, some of them even making to local newspapers.

'Where are you?' Shawar asked, as she put him on loudspeaker.

Incidentally, she was with me on our first unofficial, un-fleeting date, our first night out, alone, exactly ten days after we had kissed.

The day her exams ended.

I had been lucky with night outs. Most of the girls I had dated were hostellers with bend'able' rules or came from homes where night outs at a friend's place were allowed, and their folks didn't know what their daughters were up to.

Anyway it took quite a bit of convincing for the night out which was to end at her place. It was hard to convince her that we will not be doing anything that would require taking our clothes off. She thought I was with her because... well, she had kissed me and I wanted something more to happen. But what she didn't know was that I hardly cared whether we kissed again or not. Her presence was all that mattered, her words were all that I needed and everything else was just superfluous.

'Where else? Hostel,' she said as her face contorted with irritation. It happened whenever *he* called.

'Don't fuck with me. I called up at the hostel. You aren't there.'

'Shawar, they can't transfer the call if you call up at 10 pm in the night,' she said as she asked me to go on. The movie was about to start.

'Then show up. I am standing outside your hostel. Come to your balcony. I am not going till you come out.'

Her face contorted until it reached an irresistible degree of cuteness. 'Shawar, I was kidding, I am at my guardians' place.'

'Never mind. I will be there in half an hour. Let's see whether you are there. I am leaving right now.'

'Shawar don't you dare do that. They won't let you in through the society gate and I don't want you within a mile radius of my place,' she shrieked.

'They won't let me in? *Me?* They won't let *Shawar* in? Are you crazy? You know who I am. Nobody can touch me,' he roared.

'This is the last time we are talking if you come inside the society gate and I mean it,' she shouted, feigning anger.

'This is so fucking great. I thought I should have been angry right now. But just tell me one thing. Why have you been talking to this guy, Debashish for hours?'

'I don't think I need to tell you that,' she said in the angriest tone possible and still managing to wink at me and bite her lips seductively. God knew what she wanted. She didn't want me to cheat on Smriti, she didn't want to make out with me, but she had no problems with flirting with me. I knew it was all in good humour but my hormones didn't know that, neither did my heart. As Sean Kingston sang, *damn all these beautiful girls!*

'Yes you do. When you don't pick up a single call from me for days, you so fucking definitely do. Will you fucking tell me where you are? JUST FUCKING TELL ME.' His anger was picking up.

'Shawar, you swear once more and I will never talk to you. Anyway, I am getting a call. Bye and don't you dare call me. I am going to sleep. Love you,' she switched the call to another call she had to answer.

'Hi Tanmay… yes… hostel… yes… sure… bye…' she kept the phone down.

'Why did you get so paranoid? I don't think he would have driven down to Greater Kailash just to see you wave from the window,' I said as she rejected another call from Shawar.

'First, he doesn't drive. He has a million friends who for some inexplicable reason tirelessly drive him around the city. Second, he had his friends drive him to Chandigarh once, just to do that.'

'How does he know about me?'

'You? He probably knows about your whole family tree by now. I have some qualified boyfriends. They know a lot of *right* people. You are a baby, Deb. You have a lot to learn,' she said, as she pulled me to the auditorium. She hated to miss the advertisements.

She had been the man that night. She knew the places, she

knew the people, and she knew the routes. The dinner at The Big Chill Café was on the house, the movie was free and so was the petrol. Even the soft serve cones at McDonalds were free. I loved it. She had been nocturnal for years now and knew a lot of *people*. A little more than a lot knew her. *Everyone.* It's hard to forget a face as beautiful as hers.

'Why don't you just tell him? That you guys are over and you have found me.'

'It wouldn't be too good for your health. He is an uneducated brash bastard. You never know what he might end up doing. He is nuts.'

I didn't quite like that feeling but I loved the way she trashed her ex-boyfriend. The *other* boyfriend. The one who had all her call details and was wanted to tear me apart.

'So you are officially two timing me?' I asked her.

'You can say that... and you are no different,' she said thrusting her finger against my cleavage. Yes, I had one.

'Damn! We missed the trailers,' I said.

'Who cares?' she said and winked at me.

I had fallen in love with that wink... too. Like I had with every mannerism of hers.

The movie was awful. Probably that's why half the audience ended up watching us instead. Avantika kept showing them her middle finger. Avantika was a great kisser, her tongue worked wonders, and so did my hands. The movie ended a little too soon. Or so we felt. Our decision that we wouldn't do anything *funny* fell flat.

'Where to?' I asked. It was pre-decided that we would go to her flat in Greater Kailash, so I just wanted to check if she had changed her mind.

'I don't think that needs an answer. Let's go.'

She hadn't.

The third and the last click on the door of her house set my pulse racing.

Trespassing

I was trying not to be nervous. More so, because she was not. Her transformation from a tragic beauty to a *dirty-past-devil-may-care* one had been quick, unexpected and thanked for, by me. We entered her place. The lights lit up the room.

And I froze, yet again.

'I knew they would be here! I know this fucking *BASTARD*. I knew they would be here.'

The very next second I was ducking Tanmay's savage blows. All I could see was Vernita shouting at Avantika across the room.

'*What* did you think, Avantika? *Why?* What the fuck were you thinking? What the hell are you doing with him?' Vernita rained a flurry of questions.

It wasn't rocket science to conjecture what had transpired. Shawar would have asked Tanmay to check on her after some *buddy* from the places where we went would have told Shawar about spotting Avantika with some guy!

'Didn't I ask you to stay away from him? This guy is a bastard, didn't I tell you that? He has dumped a thousand girls. He is going out with Smriti and still sleeping with you? Why Avantika? Why? What were you thinking? You want to get back to your shitty life? He will do just that, fuck you and leave you. He has done that a million times and won't even think twice before he does that to you. And you asshole...' Tanmay said. He came charging up and slapped me right out of the atmosphere. I ducked and he kept doing so until he got a few jabs right at my face. I cut a lip and started to bleed. He backed off seeing that. Going the gym helps, I thought.

'Yogender was right all along. He always said you were a selfish guy. You lied to me? Deb? You are such a bastard. I can't believe... I warned not to go near her a million times, didn't I?' Vernita said.

Vernita was visibly hurt. But I still feel she overreacted... and slapped me softer than people pat kids. And I could have done without her moral lecture. She wasn't a nun herself.

All that high-emotion, high-energy drama seemed a little childish for me, as it was a small price to pay to be with Avantika. Any price was a price too little to be with Avantika. Only that Avantika was crying now. I didn't quite like that. Moreover, Avantika was big enough to decide whom she sleeps with, though I knew this wasn't a point I could have raised.

'Avantika, I didn't expect this from you. Tanmay hasn't slept for the last few days. He loves you more than he loves anyone and this is what you do to him? Lie to him all the time. Do you think we are fools? For the last five days both your phones were busy. Didn't we know what's going on? Deb, didn't I ask you to leave her alone? Didn't you fucking think what would happen if we get to know about this? Fuck you Deb, I can't believe you dagged me in the back,' Vernita shouted at me. Every time my phone was busy, she never forgot to ask whom was I talking to. I always used to take some arbitrary name and hoped she would believe it. She showed that she did. She didn't.

'Stabbed,' I corrected Vernita. It wasn't the smartest thing to do but everybody except Avantika did have a smile on their faces for a fleeting second before Tanmay resumed.

'Vernita, give me your phone. Let's call Smriti up. Right

now.' He walked up to Vernita and started dialling the number.

'You are not doing that. I will tell her tomorrow,' I said. I could have dumped her anytime, but I didn't want to do that this way. Never.

'Why do you think I care, asshole? You didn't care about Vernita. You didn't care about Avantika. Why do you think I would care about your girlfriend?' Tanmay shouted. He spat while he did so.

'Hi Smriti... Tanmay here... Talk to Vernita, she has something to tell you,' Tanmay had called Smriti up and put the phone on loudspeaker.

'Hi Smriti. We came to Tanmay's flat and Deb is here. With Avantika.'

'*What?*' she said from the other side.

'Yes. He cheated on you. He fucking lied to us. Talk to your boyfriend,' she gave the phone to me. I disconnected the line.

'I hope you listen to what I said this time. This guy will *destroy* you. I don't want you to be hurt again. It's either him or me. Don't ever talk to me if you ever see him again. You have the night to decide. It's either him or me,' Tanmay said and Vernita continued.

'Deb, it's over. You are after all a bastard of a guy. You fucking couldn't even respect my boyfriend's sister,' Vernita said. She was crying too.

They went into Tanmay's dad's bedroom and bolted it. Smriti kept calling me. Finally, I picked up the call.

'Why? Deb? Why?' Smriti said as she broke down. *Not again.* 'What do I do now? Why did you do it? Weren't you happy? Why Deb? Why?'

'I don't know Smriti. It just happened. I am sorry. You know things weren't right between us. I wanted to love you, but then you were not making it any easier for me. It was not working out and you know that. Things were not the way they were before.'

At this Avantika came and sat near me and switched on the loud speaker.

'You don't love me anymore? Please say you do. I will forgive you. Please come back. I am begging you. I will love you. I will never let you down, I promise. Please don't leave me Deb.' her sobs gave way to full scale wailing.

'It will be tough, Smriti. I loved you. But I don't know... We will remain friends. I promise. Our relationship was not working. If we don't break up now, I don't think we can even remain friends,' I said. I felt the guilt seep in. But it wouldn't go further in; my body had developed enough anti-bodies to fight against those situations. The friendship part never happened, and I hardly ever cared.

'Don't give me that crap, Deb. Avantika? Why didn't you tell me? Please come back. I need you. You can't leave me like this. I can't believe all this is happening to me. Please come back. You said we will work things out.'

'I can't, Smriti. Please understand. I know I have wronged you, but there is nothing that I can do now.'

'Wronged? You bloody slept with her! Why? Deb, I am ready to wait. Give me a time. When would you feel like continuing it? Give me a time. I will wait, damn it. We will start afresh. Please don't go. Please don't go.'

This went on for hours. She cursed, she cried, she wailed, she begged and she shouted. I contemplated going back to her but leaving Avantika would have been too costly a deal. We broke up. She was in tears when we kept the phone down. It wasn't as if I was untouched by her crying. We were together for more than six months and I cared about her. It may not have been the handsomest of breakups but maybe it came at the right time. She would now have an answer to her parents' questions. She wasn't bad, I thought. But Avantika was great, sexy, good-looking, smart... and I loved her. You don't let go of the person you love easily, do you?

Avantika and I spent the night balled up in an embrace, looking into each other's eyes.

'So, what have you thought?' Avantika said.

'About what?'

'Smriti or me?'

'I have decided about Smriti. It's anyway over with her.'

'And me? You think you can be with me? Do you even know whether I love you or not... and Tanmay?'

'Yes. It hardly matters to me. As long as you're with me. If you don't love me, that another matter but I am ready to wait,' I said.

'I think you should go back. It happened with me once. I can't do this to another girl. It's painful. Believe me. I don't want to be responsible.'

'It's not *you* who did this. *I* did this. And this had to happen someday. It's good it happened sooner than later.'

'But... won't you miss *it?*' she asked. 'You know why Paritosh left me. What if...?'

'Are you crazy? I will never leave you. And I would want nothing more than you being around me.'

'I was expecting something more,' she said.

'Love you.' For the first time I wasn't getting anything for saying those words. I wasn't unhooking or unzipping. I was longing for her to reciprocate.

'Love you too. Thanks for everything, Sri Guru,' she said and looked heavenwards and softly cried the night away. All calls from Shawar were dutifully rejected throughout the night. Some 65 of them.

I grinned the night away. I was in love! It had (supposedly) happened to me before, but it meant so much more this time.

It was the 20th May... the day, that changed it all.

'Take care, Shrey.' We hugged. I didn't want him to go. Vernita wouldn't be talking to me ever again and I would have no one to kill time with.

'Do get me something from France.'

'I will try. Actually, I am on a strict budget. But I will try and steal the university hard disks for you.'

'Bye,' he said as he disappeared behind the clearance gates. He won't be back before the seventh semester. Long time. Two damned months.

After every relationship of mine ended, I kicked myself for getting into one. I felt bad for the girl and made up my mind to never repeat such a thing. But then within a few days or months things were back to square one. The girl I dumped would be smiling and I would be robbed of the guilt.

Smriti was dumped. Though I couldn't say I loved her, but it wasn't very easy for me. For no fault of hers, I had given her a torrid time. Not only I had broken up with her, it was a terrible break up. I had cheated on her. She wasn't actually going through a great phase and ditching her wasn't very sensitive of me. I cursed myself for it but I couldn't help it. I didn't intend to cheat on her.

In fact, all this time I wanted *her* to break up with me. I wanted the break up to be a mutual decision... and I hated to see her cry.

Over the next few days, I couldn't keep the wails of Smriti out of my mind, often pulling back from brink of shedding a few tears myself. She was the only one who had thought of me as a good boyfriend even after what I had done to her. I missed her. I missed her bugging calls. I missed her irritating messages. I missed being with her. I missed her imperfectness.

But I was with Avantika now. I loved her. I loved her

perfect 'ness' more. *And I was sure this time.*

I was in a relationship. I was committed – not in my words, but in my actions too. But the most glaring fact of all was that I *accepted* this gleefully. This automatically meant I was unavailable, but it hardly mattered. I was neither single nor in any mood to be so. I still loved tinted car windows, empty movie halls and the like, but now the phone calls meant more than anything else. The short sweet messages now meant more. Holding hands meant more than a lot of things I had craved for in my previous relationships.

Though it would have been a little strange for the people who saw us together. I am sure about what they had to say – *'Shit man, that girl is actually with that guy.' 'Damn man, shitty choice.'*

I was way too ugly to be with her.

'Hi, Avantika. Where are you?'

'I am on my way. Where will you pick me up? I am about to reach Kashmere Gate,' she said.

Even though I had to reach the place where she already was, we still met midway and travelled the same distance again. It gave us more time together and I hated every moment not spent with her.

I was very dependent on Avantika. With no Shrey and Vernita, there was no one else I could talk to. Not that I even wanted to. Yogi and Viru had gone back their hometowns and I found no sense spending on STD calls to discuss why girls from Punjab have better breasts.

Where people were scrambling for an internship that would see them through to a great job, I spent my days with Avantika trying to not to think about the fact that I would not get any. I was faking my internship. Mom and dad occasionally asked me where all would I apply for a job when the seventh semester starts. I could do nothing but avoid their eyes, brimming with expectations and enthusiasm.

Avantika saw me through all my mood swings, there were many. Sad, for I had lost one of my friends, agitated, one was away in France, jealous, for people were gearing up for their job interviews, angry, for I was letting my parents down, worthless, for I was letting myself down.

'Hi Avantika, no see! It's been long.' We hugged as we met. Tanmay wasn't talking to her anymore. But she said he would be okay and the bigger problem was his ego and not I.

'True. It's been eighteen hours I suppose since we met. Very long. We should meet more often!' She smiled.

'Where to?' I asked.

'North campus, where else? Oh, wait! Take the Civil Lines route. There is a deserted place there. It's called *Bhoot Bangla(ghost house)*. We used to go there often. It's sealed now. It will be fun.'

'As you say, baby.' I always hated to use terms of endearment, but things had changed now. And this was one of them.

'So where is it? There?'

Driving had become insanely tough now. She used to look at me while I drove and it was hard not to look back at her.

We reached where she wanted us to. It did look like a haunted place. It was a modestly big clock tower surrounded by overgrown trees from an adjacent park. I remembered spotting it once from the metro. Big thing jutting out from vegetated area meant reminds me of only one thing. Ugh.

We climbed the fence and reached the main tower. It was locked. I was not a National Geographic lover and never did I have the tendency to spread my wings and swirl around a mountain edge and try to fly. But the place was beautiful. And so was she.

'So this is it?' I asked.

'Yup.'

'I see.'

'What?' she asked.

'I see that I see nothing.'

That was enough indication for our frenzied hormones. We lunged towards each other and within seconds, we were all over each other, searching for things inside each other's T-shirts. She hadn't quite left her wild streak at the *Spirit of Living* conventions. We were much in love but who says you can't in lust too?

'Hey there?' a big voice boomed behind us.

'Oh! Fuck!' I whispered as we separated and pulled down our shirts.

He was a huge guy. Or a small guy with a huge paunch. He was the most dreaded creature under those circumstances - dishevelled sparse hair, untrimmed moustache, red-stained and decayed teeth, and a pumpkin sized face – the Delhi Police!

The only thing worse than being caught pants down by your parents is to be caught by the cops.

Not that it was within their right to do anything about it, but they always played the *we-will-tell-your-parents* ploy well. Traffic policemen were getting richer by the day thanks to the exorbitant fines so the others type of cops didn't quite relish being left behind. It became expensive to get caught.

'Sir, we are sorry.' I almost broke down and bent down to catch hold of his feet. I pulled back just in time. Overacting wasn't cool. As I was getting up Avantika put her hand in my back pocket.

'Sorry? What the fuck do you think you are doing here? What If somebody puts a knife through you here? Who will save you then? There is nobody within a mile from here.' he shouted.

'Sorry, sir.'

'Give your names and your addresses,' he said as he came

closer and sprayed the betel he was chewing on me. Although he was still a meter away from me but that was the closest his paunch allowed him to come. 'I will have to inform your parents about this.'

Ah! C'mon! At least say something new!

'Sorry, sir. We will never do it again,' Avantika said apologetically. *We will never get caught again.* She was a natural, finding time to blow kisses and winking at me in between. Not to mention sticking her hand in and squeezing my butt again.

'No, nothing will do. You will have to come to the police station with me. Give me your names. Right now,' he said and whipped out his notepad. He was taking it too far. He went through the full motion of writing down our names and addresses, not even bothering to look up our Identity Cards once. It was all a sham.

'Sir we are sorry but can't we just settle it here?' she said in a *cut the crap, get to the point* fashion, bent backwards and placed her hands on her waist. His big moustached face lit up. I was sure we were the first ones to get caught today.

'No, that won't do. Give me your names. Right now. You can't be let off easily,' he said, trying to make it sound like a big offence.

'Sir... we told you we are sorry. Let's forget it sir. I am sure *something* can be done,' she said.

'I know how you kids behave. Your parents should be told about this. Let your parents come here and then we will decide.'

'Please don't do that sir. Let us settle things between us, why drag parents into this? Sorry sir,' she said. She was the *man* again. I would have sobbed my way out of that, with the same result. The act was over; it was time for some money to exchange hands.

'Okay, if you promise that you will never do such a thing ever again, then I will leave you.'

Oh. You fucking saint!

'We promise, sir,' we echoed. We were being preached at by someone who had unlawfully caught us and would unlawfully accept a bribe. *Sweet.*

'Where is your car?' he asked.

'There.' I was thankful the game was cut short by Avantika, it was getting boring... and the stench of his uniform was getting unbearable.

'Let's go,' he said and asked me to follow. Avantika followed us. 'How long have you two been doing this?' he asked, as he climbed into the car, which seemed too small for his two hundred pound frame.

'I...'

'Anyway, how much do you have? Take out your wallet.' He was getting impatient with the preaching stuff.

'Sir, not much. Plus, we are students sir and we don't have much. It's the end of the month-,' I said as I brought out my wallet.

'Show that to me.' He snatched it from me. As expected, there were just a hundred bucks in there. *Good job done, Avantika.*

'Sir, I need to go back home. I need fifty bucks for that,' I said.

Avantika had not squeezed my butt. She had squeezed out the wallet from my back pocket and all the money in it!

His face shrunk to the size of a Coffee Bite. The ethics of bribes guided them not to take money from a female accomplice. I was sure he wouldn't ask for money from her.

'I will leave you this time. But watch out. Next time I will inform your parents. You are lucky that I didn't do that this time.' He took the fifty bucks and left, disappointed and empty-handed.

'Not a bad deal, eh?' I said.

'Nope. You owe me a treat. I just saved you a thousand bucks.'

Avantika was intelligent and experienced…it showed. I hoped her experience was a traffic violation incident and not kissing an ex-boyfriend of hers in public.

We kissed again. And the world stopped to matter.

The two months were breezy. We met every single day, every single night during those two months. We crashed farmhouse parties, weddings, even stayed locked up in her college classroom for a night, as it was her fantasy to make out on the professor's table. I loved the way our night outs ended, especially when they ended at her place. Most of the times it used to be a bubble bath, after which we used to wrap ourselves in a single white towel, her head on my chest. We used to kiss and I used to feel the wetness of her hair on my face and it surely felt like heaven.

Night outs were now much more than groping. Much more. They were not a pretext to make out. They were a necessity – the only way we could have spent more time.

We dodged Shawar

and his friends a million times during those days. A lot of them hung around the places we did. Avantika obviously couldn't tell Shawar about me. Tanmay had not spoken anything but Shawar had by this time guessed that it was not sisterly love that I had for Avantika. The last time she talked about a break up, Shawar spent three days drinking and asking about me and cursing me. So, dumping him for another guy meant two of us going down. Shawar and I.

He will hunt you down and kill you, not beat you up, but kill you for real. Trust me, he can do that, Avantika once told me.

Flowering and Deflowering

'Hi baby, what time is it?' Avantika asked in low husky groggy tone.

'7:50 a.m. We still have ten minutes.' I had changed my number again, to the one that had reduced call rates up to eight in the morning. Invariably, at least one of us used to wake up minutes before 8 am to have those few minutes of dirt-cheap ecstasy. It is amazing how money and love changes one's biological clock.

'What's up Deb?'

'Nothing, the *doodhwala* did not come today. So coming back from the grocery store,' I lied.

'Why didn't you call me up when you woke up?' she asked. With others it was always an accusing cross-question, with her, it was just a question. The other details of place, time, nature of work and most nagging of all questions – *how was the work more important* and *why couldn't I have taken out a single minute to call* were secondary in nature.

'Nothing, was in a bit of a rush,' I had reached her place. 'Will call you in a while.'

'Okay, bye. Miss you.' We kept down the phone. It had been a long time. I wanted to feel it again. It mattered to me. I drove around and parked the car. I called her again.

'Hi Deb.'

'Hi! What's up?' I asked as an ambulance passed by me and it blared its siren in full blast.

'Hey! Fuck? What is that siren behind you? I can hear the same here. Are you here, Deb? Outside my hostel? You are here, right?'

'Yup, now what will you take to come out?'

'I will be there in ten minutes. I got to change out of my night suit.'

'Shut up and get out. Nobody is around, and I love you in your night suit.'

'But…'

'You have two minutes. Quick!' I kept the phone down. I waited for her.

She came, we hugged, more of an embrace. Her unruffled hair, her dull pink night suit, comb in hand, I loved it all. Or the fact that she was so pretty that whatever she wore or did with her hair, it ended up looking good on her.

'Such a surprise, Deb! Thanks for coming. I missed you.'

'The pleasure is all mine. Can we sit in the car?' I asked her, in anticipation, I waited.

'Yes, sure.' Bang. She closed the car door. A little harder and it would have fallen off. But then, you always have poor quality mechanical engineers to blame it on.

'Your car smells great! New freshener? Showing off? ' she laughed out.

'No,' I said as I adjusted the rear view mirror. 'Look,' I pointed out to the mirror.

'OH MY GOD! Deb!' she shrieked covering her mouth with both her hands trying to keep within it. There it was, hundreds of yellow and red petals strewn across the back seat and covered every inch of it, with a huge card in pink screaming in bold red letters. *Love you Avantika.*

Her wet eyes told me that I had done a good job. She read the card, which had some very sweet things written on it, and was immediately in tears. She lunged and hugged me.

'Love you, Deb, love you so much.'

'Love you too, Avantika.'

We spent the rest of the day driving around in the car. She didn't want to leave the setting. And she was still in her night suit. The good part done, I later had to do an even better job of cleaning the car before I handed over the car to dad. It helped that Avantika stuffed a lot of them in to her night suit pockets, fists and armpits before leaving. I so loved her. Our love was flowering.

It had cost me hardly a hundred bucks for the roses, but I couldn't have expressed my love in a better way. Six months and the biggest wholesale flower market in Delhi in front of her college and I hadn't bought a flower for Smriti.

And there I was, waking up at six, haggling (for my own good though), stripping the petals off the roses (three bleeding fingers, not so good), driving for another hour or so without braking to keep the petals in their places. I was so in love. I had to be. Or I had to be crazy to do all that. I was being cheesy but I didn't mind it.

I loved those two months. I hated it when her college reopened on the 15th of July.

And in the background somewhere during the end of the second month, Shrey came back from Paris. I had missed him... whenever I needed his car or tell someone how awesome Avantika was.

'Hey! Welcome back,' I said as I hugged him. I looked around for some gifts that he may have got for us but I couldn't see anything.

'Before anything, give me the filthiest Hindi abuses you have ever heard of. It's been a while I have heard any of that.

Missed them a lot man.'

'I am sorry. But with my impaired vocabulary, I don't think I can be of any help. Why don't you call up Vernita instead?' I said.

He hadn't changed. I dreaded him coming back smarter than he was but fortunately but he was just the same.

'Yes, I can do that. But tell me. Is there something wrong between the Vernita and you? I heard something.'

'You can say that,' I said, not wanting to go into all the details.

'Whatever. Are Yogender and Virender coming over?'

'They should be here any moment. Rohit is coming with them too. Oh, guess they are already here.' They barged in through the door. I hated their enthusiasm.

'Dude! So tell us. How many girls did you sleep with? Do all women have anti-gravity boobs there? Was your professor as sexy as she sounded? Did you make a girlfriend?' Virender asked pinning him.

'That's more questions than he would have been asked in his research in France.' Yogender quipped.

'Ha!' Shrey smirked.

Damn! Looked like he had loads of fun.

'So, how was it?' I asked.

'It was fun. I just hope I don't end up with a couple of white kids claiming to be my sons if I ever visit that place again. The worst out there would make the best here seem like baby elephants. Even the older ones. They are just so young,' Shrey said and licked his fingers.

'Did you sleep with older ones?' Virender asked as he swigged his Fosters' down.

'No.' Shrey shrugged.

'Never mind, tell me more.'

'My professor, she wore hot pants on holidays. She is 50, beat that.'

'Did you sleep with her?' Virender asked. I resisted gouging his widened eye out.

'No,' Shrey said. Maybe it wasn't fun after all. I was relieved. I didn't order another *parantha*.

'*Why* not? Why the hell not?' Virender was getting restless.

'Why the hell not? I respected her dude. She is the first person in the world to have successfully digitalized the entire electrochemical broaching process. Even at National Physical Laboratories...'

'Fuck that man. Is that your reason?' Yogender asked.

'Not acceptable, man,' I added.

I loved that he had not. My superiority was still unchallenged. I was still dating the hottest girl ever. Yeah, we are men – we are shallow and silly. But that didn't stop me from getting envious of other people's escapades.

'That and the fact that her sister wouldn't have liked it,' Shrey smirked.

'What... what do you mean?' I gasped. There came the challenge.

'Obviously he means that he slept with her. Didn't you?' Virender answered quite intelligently. I needed something to eat. Or beer. French girls would have done best, but...

'Yes. I did,' Shrey said, his chin pointing up. He had just had the most amazing two sex-filled months any one could ever have. *I am dating a goddamned goddess*, I told myself to calm down.

'What was it like? Man, did you make a video? Don't tell me all you got us are these stupid Eiffel Tower pictures,' Virender added.

The video, apart from the obvious viewing pleasure would have also meant free membership of the greatest Indian porn site – www.debonairblog.com. Like every hosteller, DCE hostellers too had just four avenues for time pass – porn, movies, sex talk and alcohol. A few of them had a fifth – a girlfriend.

'Obviously, no videos.' He held his head so high he might have touched the ceiling any moment. I hoped the fan would come in between. I was glad there was no proof of his sexual conquests. It would have been disturbing.

'Tell me. Is it as easy to hook up as they show in F.R.I.E.N.D.S and other sitcoms?' Virender asked.

'Pretty much. You just have to look out for the drunken girls, approach them with an English-to-French dictionary and boom... you are not a virgin anymore,' Shrey said.

'Is it that easy?' Virender asked. A few cars could have passed through his gaping mouth. He had probably started fantasizing about having a drunken French girl on his knees. *I had.*

'So how many did you sleep with?' I asked hoping the number wouldn't be mind boggling.

'Six. Beat that.'

I could not.

'Six? Man, you are lucky,' Yogender shrieked. He was yet to see a topless girl off-screen.

'But what about Vandana?' Rohit said who had been quiet all this time, wringing his face to signify different degrees of disgust.

'What about her? She is good,' Shrey said.

'No, I mean, have you told her?'

'No, are you nuts? Obviously not.'

'No?' Rohit asked, and his face contorted beyond recognition. He was still going around with a school time sweetheart and probably had accepted every other girl as his sister. Since he was from the IT department, he never realised what scarcity of girls around us felt like.

'But I think you really should. It's not right what you did to her. Anyway, you guys carry on. I better leave now. Bye.' He got up and left.

'Deb, I heard you have started going around with Avantika. How is it going?' Shrey asked.

'Did you sleep with her?' Virender added. 'I have heard she is hot as hell.'

'It's going fine. Hot is an understatement. And for the last part, I will never confirm.' I winked at them. I had not. But I really wanted to tell them how we made out in a graveyard parking and the freaky looking guard freaked the shit out of us.

'They may be hotter. They may have figures one would die for. They may be even better at blowjobs, I still long to do it with an Indian girl. You are a lucky dog. I would love to swap places with you,' Shrey said.

Yeah, right.

'But why is that?' I asked. No matter what he did in France, I would have given up the time I had spent with Avantika for the time he had spent in France.

'I don't know. There is a sense of achievement when you run around after someone and finally get her,' Shrey said.

'Or the frustration when you run after someone and then you don't,' Virender said and looked at me.

'I understand your pain. If it were up to you, you would turn all girls into little sluts. Even your friends... say Vernita.'

'Is she not a slut?' Yogender asked. His body not taking in the expensive liquor too kindly for it soured its relationship with cheap Old Monk rum he used to have.

'Shut up. Of course she is not,' Shrey said. There was silence for a little while.

'How is Vandana? Did she miss you? Of course, you didn't miss her,' Virender asked Shrey.

'I hope she did. I did,' he said wistfully. I told him, he would.

Shawar was becoming a menace now. Avantika told me that he

was tracking me but she said there was nothing to worry as long as both of us were careful. Night outs became a little tricky when Shawar started calling Avantika's roommates every day to check on her.

If that he wasn't enough, he even called at my landline once to ask where I was. My parents obviously told what they knew. For them, I was in the hostel, studying. But mom never forgot to ask why a drunken sounding guy was interested in knowing my whereabouts. I lied, whether she believed it or not, I would never know.

A few rebukes from Avantika stopped him from calling, but then he started calling me up. He could be called just barely polite in the first call. After that, he had just one question to ask – *What is going on between you and Avantika?* Often laced with the filthiest Hindi expletives.

He was a year or two younger but he made me pee in my pants. I was clearly indicated by Avantika to call her up if and whenever I were to spot more than a few guys hanging around big cars and puffing on cigarettes, beer bottles in hand.

They could be them. Be careful, Deb.

Avantika – The Witch, Shawar – Her Bitch

'Jealous?' Avantika asked.

'Certainly not! A paid foreign internship… replete with sex. Why should I be jealous? Naah!' I said sarcastically. I had told her about Shrey's wonderful time in Paris.

'I cannot say that I am particularly sad for you. Though I can make it up to you in ways you have only imagined,' she said. Most of the times this used to be an empty promise, but the sheer sexiness with which they were delivered made me go bonkers with passion.

'Oh, yeah? No, I would love to see how you do that. Three chocolate syrup fantasies are already pending if you remember, sexy!'

'Oh yes I do, baby! All of them together… you would like that, won't you?' she said in a low husky voice.

'Yes, I will, but shut up right now. I am in no position to talk dirty right now.' I was dead tired. Mom and dad weren't asleep yet. So I couldn't have shagged away to glory, however sexy she might have sounded. She loved to arouse me at times and in places I used to be absolutely helpless.

'Not even if I say I bend down on you…'

'Will you fucking *stop*? I've got to study,' I shouted non-angrily. This had to work; she could fuck me over the phone, but not my career.

'You have to study? Ha! DCEites study? Don't give me that crap.'

'Why? I do study. I know I am intelligent enough not to study. But then...'

'Yeah yeah... whatever! But seriously, go and study. CAT is on your head, ass.'

'As if you are studying your head off!' I shot back.

'I won't get through anyway. But you can. Do study.' That always gave me a kick. Deep inside, there was still a nerd in me who still wanted to score the highest marks and get patted by teachers.

'Okay. Will think about that. What are you doing tomorrow? I mean can we go to your place?' I said. The dirty talk showed its effect.

'Ohooo! Baby now wants to make out? What happened to the studious Deb? I am sorry, but I am a little busy tomorrow.'

'Don't fuck with me. Tell me.' I was already feeling a twitch and felt she was playing around.

'I am serious. I am going to my rehabilitation centre. Something to do with SOL.'

'What exactly?'

'You will not understand. Go and study.'

'What? See, there is no use of me studying. Even if I get through there is no way I can clear the interviews.'

'And why do you say that?' she asked irritably.

'Why? There is nothing in my profile, Avantika! Four years of college and I had practically done nothing!'

Except stacking up shameful girlfriend history.

'You have been part of those societies and stuff, won't that help?'

'Obviously not. Everyone can see through it. Even the guy from that software firm did.'

'Then do something. Pick up something. Anything. Say you love cooking. And that you can cook anything under the sun and mug up recipes. What say?'

'Crap, they will ask me to go and be a cook. And cooking? I would need something that can act as pretext to bad academic score. Cooking doesn't quite fit in.'

'Writing? Say blogging? That would be cool. You anyway will say that you weren't ever interested in engineering, so you spent a lot of time writing on your blog,' she said. I wasn't very interested. I couldn't see how it could have enhanced my fucked up profile.

'What exactly is a blog? What exactly do I do?' I asked, completing a mere formality.

'Nothing, just a free website, a log of whatever happens to you or around you. You can write about anything under the sun. A photographer friend of mine has a photo blog. He uploads all his pictures over there. So people go out there, read stuff, see stuff and comment on how they like it. In short it is networking, but through written stuff or photographs or videos. Even Amitabh and Aamir Khan have blogs.'

'Whatever. I will think about it. But we can go on a night out tomorrow?'

'I will be too tired tomorrow, Deb. Later, I promise, baby,' she said.

'Okay, but I won't take no for an answer the next time around. I swear.'

'Sure, tell me one thing. How's D.E Shaw as a company?' she asked.

'D.E Shaw? I would give an arm to work for them. They literally bathe you in money. It's a huge package!'

'But isn't it software? I thought you weren't interested in software, especially after that day.'

'That's because I don't like working. I will flush toilets if you pay me that much.'

'Shut up Deb, it doesn't work that way, it's about interest. Like I am desperate to have a career in finance, there must be something in your mind?' she said forcefully. All she wanted was to have something that would pay her well enough to move away from her family. Lately her uncles' marriage related jabs at her were getting unbearable for her.

'Nothing. If I give you a choice, McKinsey & Company or Dena Bank, consultants and finance, where would you go?' I knew I had her. For fresh graduates it's all about the cash. It's simple, fire the HR guys, pump the money into benefits and watch your company grow. But nobody listens.

'I don't know. Tanmay just called, Vernita is through D.E Shaw,' she said.

'What? What?' I spluttered. The same flapping of tongue struck again.

'Yes. She is through.'

'I cannot believe this. That bitch-' I went supersonic.

'Don't swear.'

'Why shouldn't I? Why shouldn't I? That slut has a lesser percentage than me, doesn't know a thing about software. Why do you think she got through?' I was still beyond the audible range; I was expecting hyenas outside my place.

'It's not her fault if the interviewers liked her.'

'Don't give me that. Do you know what that means? She fucked her way through college and pocketed the highest package. Why is every average being around me suddenly transforming into a genius? People are going to France and fucking their brains out, someone's ending up as the youngest millionaire, and I am fucking stuck here talking to you. *Great.*'

'What do you mean?' Avantika said.

'Oh, I am sorry baby. I didn't mean to say that.'

'Better. Now tell me. Who is more important? Baby or the job at D.E Shaw?'

'Silly question. You... of course.' Though it would have been better if I had the job along to go with it. We always did the *who-is-more-important* thing every time one of us was depressed.

It started out as a joke but soon it became quite a soothing factor for me given the number of times I had to be soothed.

'Keep studying, Deb. There will be scores of off-campus interviews,' she said.

'We will see.'

'You will never get the pants ironed if you don't take them off,' she said.

'Chill Avantika! I don't need to work. You will do that. I will be home taking care of our kids,' I said.

'Is it Deb? Ohh! We are getting married. I am so obliged you told me that.'

'Obviously we are! You know I am not into short term relationships. When have I ever been in a short term relationship?' I said, jokingly.

'Yes, I know. You have had just ten long-term relationships until now. Haven't you? Bloody ass!' she said.

'No, baby, but seriously, this time it is long term.'

'Long-term till the time you get bored of me,' she said dejectedly.

'I will never get bored of you. You are the only girl I have ever loved. I just lust*ed* the rest of them.'

'Oh yeah? And you don't lust me? I am not good enough for you? Or were they better?' she let out a wholehearted laugh.

'You are the best. You are a porn star strapped in Avantika's body! Okay? You turned down tomorrows' plan, not me!'

'Ohh! That is why you are upset with me? I knew it all along! You filthy ass.' She laughed out again.

'Shut up. I love you, my sweet porn star. By the way, I have decided the names of our kids too. We will have around seven of them, five girls and two boys and hopefully no hermaphrodites—' I was interrupted.

'You can keep all that nonsense to yourself and study. Don't make a long face when others beat you in the placements scene. I am serious, Deb. Do study.'

'Okay. I will.' We kept down the phone after a while.

I didn't like people beating me but even then, I wasn't doing anything to change that. Toying to change it also meant poking at the beehive - failure. Failing when you don't put in an effort always hurts less.

Even if you win the rat race you still end up being a rat... okay maybe, let's say a rich fat rat.

Avantika always made sure I never lost *hope*.

But that day had to be one of the worst days of my life. After Vernita and I had drifted apart, I somehow always looked at her, full of contempt. If given a choice to kill six people on earth I would pump all six into her. She too left no stone unturned to see me being kicked out of classes and practical exams. Also, her constant bitching about me to our classmates and common friends didn't do any good to our soured relationship either. I was giving it back in equal measure. We were becoming obsessed with making life hell for the other. She was trying harder though.

Shawar was not making my life easier either. He called me up numerous times from different numbers but I never picked up his calls. Avantika asked me to get myself a private number, the one where you can bar your incoming calls, but it was too much of an effort.

'The hair is *fine...* and you are looking perfectly okay.' I reassured Avantika for the millionth time as she brushed her hair again. McKinsey and Company was on campus. Obviously, she was quite nervous. This was her shot to run away from a potential uneducated businessman husband and she would give it her all.

The placement season had started at SRCC too. And the line-up of companies was better than what was scheduled for

DCE that year and that shocked me. It didn't even have a placement cell a few years back! I was pretty disappointed at their progress, as my college wasn't making any. College life treated Avantika well. Especially after she got rid of her drug habit. It did not have a hostel, though she lived in one. A very expensive one... with some rich brat girls. Everything was taken care of! That was quite in contrast with DCE hostels where students used a bed sheet until it turned grey.

Also, living in a hostel in Delhi University had its own charms. You never ran out of places to hang out. Tom Uncle Maggie Joint was where Avantika and I spent most of our day dates. We loved going there. It was open air, cheap and had a great view – Miranda House, the famed girls' college. Avantika spent her time branding the girls I liked as wannabes.

'Will I make it?' she asked nervously.

'You will make it. You are my baby.'

'That's not qualification enough, I guess,' she said.

'Don't ask me, then. I am the barred one.' I couldn't help being sarcastic. I had lost it many times whenever the talk hovered around placements. Even Yogender and Virender had managed decent jobs. They didn't offer great salaries, but any company was good enough for them, given the huge number of papers they had failed, their rotting intestines and smoke battered lungs.

Avantika would soon join their league and that wouldn't be comforting either. Shrey would be with me, only that he didn't care. It was a long time before I could start applying for off campus placements and I wasn't too hopeful about that either.

'Oh. Never mind. You will get a better job than all of us,' Avantika said as she checked out her pointy-black-witch shoes. She stood as tall as I was. She would look great in those... just those. I often wondered if it was just me who thought dirty all the time.

'Isn't it? That's easy for you to say. You will be employed in a matter of minutes.'

'Oh shut up. You are a blogger now. No one knows, your blog may get famous and all, you might end up richer than all of us.'

Avantika had made me blog on her mail account and invited me to write on it. She pestered me to keep writing and uploading stuff on it.

'Yes, how can I forget that? The blog, which I stopped writing after the first article. The same one you trashed!'

'I didn't trash it. I just said I felt that what you wrote was dragging in parts... most parts,' she laughed out.

'Drag? I wrote about my school life, damn it. I am a drag for you?'

'Do I get to say yes?' she asked biting her nail and yet winking at me.

'Whatever you say, I got about 45 comments on that post!'

'Whatever, Deb! All your stupid comments are filling my mail box up.'

The blog had her mail ID on it. All the comments reached her ID, not mine, but I never had the drive or interest to change it.

'Avantika.' The placement coordinator shouted her name and called her in.

'Best of luck.'

'Thank you,' she said and rushed in, brushing her hair again.

I prayed for her to do well. I knew she would get it and felt a little sad about it. Somewhere deep inside I knew I wouldn't end up too badly either, just that I felt left out then. I pushed out those negative thoughts and concentrated on more important things in life. I looked around to see everyone dressed to entice, in short black skirts, stockings and stilettos.

I loved coming to SRCC. Avantika and I had spent a lot of time in its libraries, front lawns, Irfans' and the co-operative store. I had more attendance at her college than mine. More people knew me there. I missed my own college fest but never missed hers – Crossroads. Avantika got me passes to every fest in Delhi University, a lot of them, out of bounds for Delhi College of Engineering guys after a few drunken brawls. *Many* drunken brawls.

Her interview ended in fifteen minutes.

'Hey, how did it go?' I hugged her as she came out of the room.

'It went fine. What did you do all this time?' she asked. It went great. Had it not, she would have cried her way out. She was unbelievably child-like when it came to anything about career. Even coaching classes.

'Nothing, just some bird watching. It's not as if you are the only good looking girl in SRCC.' I winked at her.

She wasn't. She was still definitely amongst the top few. But the average quality of girls was astounding. Out of every ten, seven would surely pass any damn test of trendiness or sexiness. Most of them were stinking rich and dolled up every day before coming to college.

'That's not very exciting to hear,' she said, making a fake sad face.

'You tell me. What did they ask you?'

'The usual. They got stuck to *Spirit of Living*. The guy himself is a part of it, so it was pretty easy! Plus, I think they liked me. Does that make me a slut?' she winked at me.

'Obviously not. But that doesn't make Vernita a *non*-slut,' I said and pointed out to a girl. 'Look at her, you know her? She drives an Accord, short skirt, great goggles, what else can anybody possibly want?' I had been tracking those legs for quite some time now.

'That's our senior. She works at Deloitte. Had a super-rich boyfriend, took her to Goa and stuff, so out of your league.'

'What do you mean? You had a super-rich boyfriend and I ended up dating you.'

'She wants her boyfriends to be super rich. Not a miser like you. Get the difference?' she said tapping on my head.

'I am not a miser. You never let me spend. Not my fault that you know everybody around.'

'I know, but as if you could have afforded the places we hang around in,' she said. It did hurt but I knew she didn't mean it. I was a poor kid by her standards. Some of her friends never dated someone who didn't have a car of his own.

'Then I guess you should go to yours senior's ex-boyfriend. He will take you to Goa and dump you. Won't you be so happy?' I said irritably.

'Aww... my baby... I am sorry. I love you and you know that. There is nothing that could change that, Deb. I am addicted to you,' she said while pulling my cheeks and thus putting things back in order.

'You have some really hot girls in your college.'

'Jealous?'

'A little. But then I didn't expect anything in the girls department in DCE.'

'Let's just say all the engineers are terrible looking,' she winked at me.

'Ohh... that's not totally correct. There is a reason for it. The richer people take commerce. The poorer ones take up engineering. That explains the good looking-bad looking phenomenon. Get it?'

'No, I don't. I don't get that poorer ones take up engineering crap,' she said, stationing both her fists on her waist, visibly pissed off.

'It's quite simple. The richer ones tend to take up commerce. They have a lessened sense of responsibility. Career isn't the be-all and end-all of everything for them. So they take up something that allows them to have more fun.'

'Lessened responsibility? People around here have an equally bright career as you have, dumbass.'

'But they weren't so five years back, when you actually took up commerce. It's just been two years since the placement thing started in your college.'

'You do have a point there. But I still don't agree with rich is equal to good-looking *funda*.'

'That's easy, if you are rich, you have access to all the better clothes, better places, so you learn more and you implement more. Most people here may not be inherently beautiful. But they dress smart, bathe in expensive creams. And look what you are seeing: Ugly ducklings to beautiful swans.'

The richer the girls get, the sexier they are. The sexier they are the better guys they get, who invariably are more bed-able. Better guys who are better in bed lead to superior craving. Once they are doing it, they are more assertive about their needs, which stems from a confidence that only money and power provide. More assertive is what is labelled as lusty. Rich is sexy, but what matters is, *rich is lusty* too. You never say, poor horny housewives, it's always rich horny housewives!

'Okay, I lose, but that doesn't mean you are right...' she said easing up.

'The list is out.' The placement coordinator shouted out.

'Please, please, please, please go and see. I can't,' she clung to my arm and squeezed the place to pulp where I would have had biceps and triceps if I were two stones lighter.

'As you say.' I loved the jostling and pushing around. I was the only guy in the crowd shoving around in a sea of great smelling massive breasts.

I have to stop thinking dirty!

She was selected! Predictably.

'Am I in?' she said as she tried to look for a slight smile on my smug face.

'YES, you are!' I shouted. We hugged. They had selected just three out of the eighty students they interviewed. The one I sat in took fifty out of hundred and I didn't figure in their list. *Opposites* attract! She was immensely intelligent while I was totally stupid.

'Thanks Sri Guru,' she whispered.

'What? *I* was the one who was praying for you and your *Sri Guru* gets the credit. I don't know how you can believe in hideously bearded, stupid god men.'

'Hey, dare you say anything about Sri Guru. If you don't like him, keep that to yourself. He is family for me. It's because of him that I am what I am right now. I have been in some shit. You won't understand.'

'Okay, am sorry.' I wasn't. 'Anyway, the basic point is, I need a treat.'

'Anytime, Deb.'

I was very happy for her. But it did hurt a little. I felt like a complete loser. I had spent a year at home trying to get through an engineering entrance, spent four years in engineering and there she was, a commerce graduate, *just* a commerce graduate, who will end up having a better career than I will. I hated to be envious.

'Hi Shawar,' Avantika said as we were leaving college and looking for a rickshaw to Kamla Nagar, which was a ten minutes' walk from her college.

'Hi Avantika. I heard you got through. Who are you with right now? Debashish? Stay there. I want to meet you and him.'

She looked at me almost pitifully as I wet my pants. We both knew what *meeting-me* meant. The last time he *met* a guy, he made him end up with six stitches and a couple of broken ribs. I was a big guy but nowhere near a fighter. Not even the least bit. I pretty much stayed out of fights after one of them left me with a chipped tooth. That was around a decade and a half ago.

'Shawar, he has to rush. I am sorry he can't stay.'

'Why not? Give the fucking phone to him.' He didn't sound

friendly to say the least.

'He is drunk,' Avantika whispered in my ear.

'Hey dude. Where do you have to go? Busy...eh?' Shawar said to me.

'Yes, kind of. Have this exam tomorrow. Got to study for it.'

'Ohh, do you? Both of you think I am a fool, don't you?' he bellowed.

'No seriously, I do have to leave. I can't meet you right now.'

'Just wanted you to know that I called up Vernita and she told me everything about you two. And you don't have an exam. That means you have a choice. Either you meet me right now or I will see you at your place. It wouldn't seem too appropriate if I beat you up in front of your parents. The *choice* is yours.'

He banged the phone. I wish I could *choose* to be invisible.

'Fucking shit, I am so dead. Will he actually beat me up?' I was petrified.

'Yes, he will. But stay here. I can at least try to save you. And I agree. Vernita *is* a slut, after all.'

'What do you think he will do? Is he big?'

'Naah, he is half your size.' She punched me.

'Is that supposed to be a joke? I haven't fought since the time I started wearing pants, you witch.'

'No seriously, he is half your size, but he won't be coming alone. He would come with five guys at least, big ones. '

'Thanks for the consolation. Can't we do something? Go to some place. Police? Some *thulla*? What say?'

'The last guy who tried to do something ended up in bed for four months. Calm down. It's just a street fight.'

'Calm down? You're not getting your ass kicked, I am! Yes, sure. Street fights? That's pretty okay too. Don't you know that's what I do for a living?' I started walking around in circles wondering how fast I could run... *could I possibly tire him out...?*

It was too late for that, the Chicken McGrills and the chicken buckets had taken their toll. Damn McDonalds and KFC! I thought I would die of obesity, not of a fucking smashed head.

'You want to call the cops. Go ahead. Just a few problems. What will you tell your parents? And yes, he owns the Shababs' chain of restaurants. That incidentally makes him rich and powerful beyond your imagination. He can bribe the whole police department, for god's sake. Just calm down. Let me handle him when he comes here.'

'Fuck, fuck, fuck, fuck. Fuck man, I will so fucking kill Vernita.'

'Deb? Can't you get some guy to side with you? They won't have to fight, just to keep Shawar's guys from fighting,' she said.

I couldn't get any. I didn't have any friends. I either had girlfriends or ex-girlfriends. All the guys from school were tired of being ditched for my relationships and... I couldn't involve Shrey in it.

'No... '

'What about Virender? Yogender?'

'I don't think so. They will take an hour to reach... and I can't drag them in to this, they are hardly friends.'

'Shit!' she said covering her mouth.

'I am officially dead. Is that what you are trying to say?'

'Not exactly. He loves me. That can save you... If something can.'

'You know what? I hate your guts so much right now. How can you be so bloody chilled out? Your boyfriend's going to be stripped and beaten up and you are just standing there, looking sexy. I hate you.'

'I love you, baby. Here they come, I guess,' she said pointing to the red light. Two massive cars screeched to a halt near us. I knew their makes quite well, else I wouldn't have recognized them with their hideous modifications and gross stickers that screamed *'drink beer, fuck fear'*. I couldn't do any. But the cars were massive, which only meant more guys.

A door opened. And a dark complexioned midget popped out.

Shawar was barely five foot three, two inches shorter than Avantika. He had strange curly hair and blood shot eyes. It was quite a funny sight watching him take big strides like villains from Z-grade movies. He was in a black shirt, sleeves rolled up, and desperately tried to look menacing. The dog he almost tripped over looked more threatening.

He walked up to me and stopped barely inches away. He was so short that he could have had a whiff at my armpits without bending. I wish he had. My greatest weapon, that is, if he didn't allow me to place my butt on his face. I had a faint feeling that he won't. His teeth had decayed, as Avantika told me. Too much Meth does that to you. His skin has red sores all over it. The drugs leave you with an itching sensation. Avantika had survived all that, and it shudders me to this day as to what would have happened to her if it were not for SOL.

'Let's go,' he grabbed at my hand. It wasn't funny anymore.

'No… no… I can't come…' I struggled for words as I fixed my eyes on the bald patches between his curly hair. He would be bald in a few years. Smoking sheds. It also makes you impotent. I was about to be thrashed by a half-man.

'What makes you think you are in any position to decide?'

'He is not going anywhere Shawar,' Avantika said as she freed me from his puny hands.

'Avantika, I am not talking to you,' he said as he grabbed my hand again.

'C… c… can't we j… u… s… t… just talk here?' I stammered. I was glad there was nobody around to see the terrified woman in me. There was usually a crowd around in my school days.

'We fucking can't. There are certain things we need to settle. You bloody fucked my happiness. I will now do the same to you. You are not getting away with this.'

'What did I do?' I squeaked.

'What did you do? You bloody took my girl away from me, that's what you did asshole. Get it. I will fuck your whole life. Can you do something about it? Go. Try it.'

'Shawar, mind your language!' Avantika shouted.

'Avantika, I love you. I am not doing anything to you. But stay out; it's between the two of us.' He looked at her, his shoulders dropped and seemed to melt and sublimate. He reminded me of myself when I first met Avantika. I prayed to god to turn me into a girl then. You can't be beaten up. You can have unlimited sex... and you wield more power than ten big guys.

'He is my friend. There is nothing between the two of you. Whatever happens will happen here right now. In front of me.'

'Yes, in front of her.' I said.

I repeated. They looked at me. I knew I had said something outrageously cowardly, but I didn't care if it saved my ass. I was surprised I didn't hide behind Avantika and stick a thumb up my mouth.

'He is a friend? Vernita bloody told me everything. She hates him. And you? What are you looking at fucker? Vernita told me where you are and asked me to bash you up. This is what his friends think about him. And you left me for this asshole? Why?'

'Vernita is not a friend,' I said. I was hurt. I hated her too. But I didn't want her to be hurt. Deep down she was still a friend. Or maybe I did. But what Shawar said shook me up. I was angry and I thought about taking him on. Only a little bit though. Maybe in a video game.

'Shut up, you ass hole. Come with me.' He started dragging me towards the car.

'SHAWAR!' Avantika shouted. 'What do you think? It's not his fault. Leave him.' The mere frequency of her voice shook him enough to let go of me. I thanked her. She continued, 'I love him. And you can do nothing about it. You do anything to him and everything will be over between us. I never loved you. I loved Paritosh. I dated you because I wanted to hurt him. Who the fuck do you think you are? You think you can be my boyfriend? My foot! I could have bloody stoned myself to death and you would have hardly cared. Shawar, was there a single time when you showed a little bit care? Once, when you asked me not to drink? Or smoke? Fuck you, Shawar. I love him. You do anything to him, I will fucking *destroy* you. You know I can. Love is not stalking Shawar. Love is what Deb has for me. I was wrong with Paritosh. I was wrong with you. I have finally got it right. Touch him and you are not getting away with it. I will so fucking *ruin* you. I so will. You have a choice.'

Now that was something. She said she used to be a rude bitch before she joined *Spirit of Living*, though I never believed that. Now I did. She could have blown a few buildings apart with that outburst. Shawar was just a rich powerful guy. Now, a *crying* rich powerful guy.

'Deb, can you leave us alone for a second?' Avantika asked me.

'Sure,' I winked at her, but she didn't respond as I would have liked her to.

I loved to see him cry, although I hadn't done anything to do that, but I won. Shawar sat down on the pavement and continued weeping for quite some time. Avantika was sitting right beside him. They talked for an hour or so and Shawar left in those hideous cars, not once looking at me. I had emerged victorious.

'Thank you Avantika.' I hugged her. 'You beat the shit out of him. That was great!'

'You found it funny? I had to hurt the poor guy,' she said and looked away.

'I am sorry,' I said.

'Don't be. I loved that too,' she winked and hugged me again.

'Oh, love you.'

'You know what? He expected you to get some guys with you. He was somewhat disappointed. And yes, there were cops too, in the car. Just in case. Who knew my new boyfriend would be such a wimp?'

'A sexy wimp?' I asked trying to gain at least somewhere.

'Yes, a *very* sexy wimp. Thanks Sri Guru,' she whispered and I suppressed an urge to ridicule her. I always wondered if these god men had to shave off their beard, would they evoke the same saintly sentiments.

Shawar had wasted a lot of time. It meant Avantika had to go back to her hostel sooner.

'I think we will have to settle for Tom Uncle, then,' I said.

'I was thinking about a night out,' Avantika said and winked at me.

CATting and Cutting

'Now that was a close shave,' Shrey said, as he put the form in the envelope.

'Yup, nearly had my face boxed in,' I said as I darkened the bubbles in the form. Despite being a technophile, for some reason, he too was taking CAT (Common Aptitude Test), the management test that decides the fate of many. Around 2.32 lakh, students to be precise.

'How do you rate our chances?' Shrey asked me.

'Can't say. It all depends on that day. Of course, if we do get through it, from then on, it will all depend on the IQ.'

'Yup, that's true. But you have been studying for it. You will obviously do much better than I do.' He hadn't joined a coaching institute and quite apparently couldn't see me score more than him in the mock exams that both of us took.

'Fuck that. CAT isn't about preparations. Maths and Data Interpretation are purely IQ and there is nothing much you can do about English if it isn't above average by now. They can't teach you how to read, damn it.'

'Whatever. What happened to Shawar? Any further news?' Shrey asked to take focus off that topic. We had had numerous arguments on the topic. I had joined it purely because my dad thought it was necessary to do so... and coaching institutes generally had some good-looking girls too.

'I heard he was planning to ask his long-time friend Purvi out; the one he goes on night outs with.'

'Do you think he has slept with her?' Virender butted in as he wrapped up the form too.

'I think so. I mean it's highly likely. They are on a night out every second day and they get sloshed all the time. It's possible that they have done it. Anyway, Purvi had had scores of boyfriends, so it's inevitable.'

'Nay, if he was doing it with her, why would he think of taking the next step? Who wants a relationship, when you are getting to do it?' Shrey debated.

'It's not as if it would be totally guilt free sex. She would do it for a while and then ask for a relationship! That's how it works.'

'Deb. I don't think that is right. How many friends do you have who are girls?' Virender said.

'What do you mean? I have had quite a few. But they all ended up as girlfriends,' I chuckled.

'See, that's the reason why you say things like these,' Virender said.

'Ohh! Mr. Virender, how many do you have?'

'None.' The only girls he ever talked to were the ones on the metro counters. The only one he had an affair with was on customer care. It lasted fifteen minutes.

'See, that's why you say this,' I said.

'But he does have a point there,' Shrey said. 'A very weak one, though. Most of these long flings do actually end up as girlfriends.'

'I told you.'

In a world of engineers where there are no major hetero-groups, we never treated any girl we met as a friend. Everyone was a prospect. *Every* girl was an *opportunity*. Vernita had been one too.

As for Shawar, his male ego had taken a huge blow too. Everyone in his circle knew that Avantika had dumped him for another guy. He had to do something to redeem himself.

Everything was okay as long as he kept his hands off me, which he did.

The last two months before CAT went exactly as I had not planned. Shrey and I had planned to study together but our study sessions, more often than not, ended up as movie/TV series watching sessions. The lesser time you have, the more you have the urge to splurge time on nonsensical things. Occasionally, we switched our phones and PCs off, ready to bring the world down to our feet, but that never lasted beyond an hour. Avantika, meanwhile, slogged her ass off and the results showed. She even threatened to match our scores occasionally. A job had already ensured freedom from her parents, but clearing CAT would mean doing it in spectacular fashion. Her parents didn't know she was preparing for CAT.

'Hey Avantika! All set for tomorrow?'

'All set? I am so nervous.'

'Nervous? Chill! Just go out there and try to attempt the easier questions and you will be through.'

'Easy for you to say that. You have been the one topping all the mock exams. Not me.'

'All that doesn't matter tomorrow. It's what you do in those two hours.' I had been doing really well in the mock ups to the main exam and people had really started to expect a lot from me. Though I showed I was irritated by their constant *you-will-get-through-thing*, but I liked it.

'Anyway, I just hope Sri Guru helps us.'

'Helps you. I would better rely on myself.'

'Whatever. I am going to sleep now. My centre is way off. Have to leave early. Bye. Good night. Love you,' she said.

'Love you too. Bye. You will do great.'

The exam was horrible. And once I started screwing up the paper, I started picturing all my fellow classmates (a few of them from school too) laughing down at me as if saying '*you couldn't do this, you are such a fool.*' And laughing the hardest amongst them was Vernita. I screwed the exam big time.

Avantika didn't pick up the phone for the rest of the day. I assumed she had screwed it up too. Shamefully enough, I was happy about that. I spent the day writing about my CAT story on my blog. My make-out escapades were a huge hit among visitors to my blog. It is a pervert world, I tell you. I knew many people would start turning up at secluded, make out feasible places that I mentioned. People had started expecting frequent updates to my blog.

That was better, because I didn't want to call up Shrey, as whenever I did, used to start his speculations about the cut offs and his chances. And he did better than me, so I tried to stay away from him. There was no way I could have got through any of the IIMs.

But bad news travels fast and people didn't fail to bring it to my notice that Vernita had indeed done pretty well in the exam. So consequently, I started trashing the exam itself and began to harbour dreams of making it to Stanford a few years down the line. But all of this was just an escapist route and didn't keep me from making my mind up for taking CAT the next year.

I spent the entire December trying not to bump into my classmates who all had calculated their score and fancied their chances. *Bloody assholes.* I took a few other exams and screwed them up too. I was getting good at it.

The only good thing I did during December was going out partying every night with Avantika. We did all that for free and in those two months I saw it all. I ate out and partied out like never before. My dancing skills now extended beyond stomping of cockroaches! It felt good when people started treating me as one of the regulars.

Although gorging and partying out for free meant you couldn't go to the same place too often. *It is uncivilized*, Avantika once said. I never agreed. After the crash diet I had gone on after school ended, this was the first time I loved eating. I loved the attention I was showered with. Having a regular seat at top-end restaurants... What else can one ask for?

Somewhere in all that gulping and shaking, the eighth semester started. It was the last one of my college life, the time when attendance ceased to matter and subjects failed to make their presence felt even during exams. And you spend more time deciding what you can do in the few months to end your college life with a bang.

'Hey Deb! I have good news for you,' Avantika said.

'What?'

'Eighth semester, baby! I thought you would be now eligible for some off campus interviews and I forwarded your resume to Lehman Bros. You have got a call.'

'No shit!' This had been the second most exciting news to me. First was that nobody who was close to me got any calls from any of the good management institutes. In fact, I had done better than most people around.

'Yes, shit! Before I forget, they are paying exactly thirty percent more than the company you shag on, D.E. Shaw pays. Like that? I told you Sri Guru is great. Isn't he?'

'Excuse me. *You* are great. Not *Sri Guru*. Anyway, when is the interview?'

'It's tomorrow. Don't you screw this one up.'

'I won't. Will you be coming? And message me the place.'

'Will do that. And no, I won't be coming. Sri Guru is coming to town and I am going for his convention. He won't be coming to India before March. I know you wouldn't listen, but you should attend this once. Anyway, I will mail you your curriculum vitae. I had made some changes to suit their need. Do check.'

It was one of the many times that she had dropped a plan for Sri Guru and Spirit of Living. I hated it when she did that, but then she made it very clear that it was because of them that she was living. We had had many arguments on this, which I invariably lost, convincingly. Just because she was so cute.

'Perfect. I *so* love you! They are an investment bank, if I am not wrong?'

'You aren't. And best of luck. Do well.'

'I will try.'

'Hmmm… it would be fun, then. You will be a rich guy and you fly down to Bangalore anytime you want to! What say?'

'That is so true. By the way, have you tried getting your posting shifted to Delhi?'

'No, I haven't, Deb. I see no point in that. There is no tangible growth in the Delhi office. And we anyway can meet whenever we want to. We have great paymasters, or we will have, won't we?'

'Ohh… that means baby is not important? Only your growth is?' I said in a baby voice. I hated to think that she was leaving Delhi in a few months. I hated to be an impediment in her career plans but then, it was hard to let her go. This was the first time I showed my disapproval, that too very indirectly.

'Aww… baby is very important, but then…' she said. I wished I had been a little serious in my displeasure of her going away.

'It is okay, Avantika, I understand.'

'Okay, Deb, I will try. I surely will. First say, you will never let me go, only then will I try.'

'Of course, I will never let you go. You are my baby, how can I let you go? You are mine, all mine. Muaaah.'

'I won't go. You are so sweet, Deb. Love you,' she said. 'I will talk to the main office tomorrow. Or after my exams are done. I love you more than you do.' *Yay! Was it so easy?*

'Thank you. Love you. I will call you in a while. Dinner is served.' I was ecstatic. Good times were here again.

The next day, I went for my interview. As it was an investment bank that paid quite a packet, the turnout was huge. Most of the guys seemed excessively smart for me… and knowledgeable. But whatever it maybe, I was the best-dressed one. My fat thighs were skilfully hidden behind the slick Mark & Spencer's suit that Avantika got me on a huge discount.

Somebody once told me that investment bankers are so busy that they don't get time to get home and *do it*. And so, they end up sleeping with their colleagues. It was always good for an investment bank if the applicants are fuck-able. I wished to gain there at least. Avantika had done a good job on my curriculum vitae. There were projects on terms I hadn't heard about before. But she had given me a half an hour class about it and said that was enough.

'Are you there?' Avantika asked. She had called me up for the twentieth time that day. The previous ones were to check whether I had gotten up, bathed, brushed etcetera. She really wanted me to get through. And with the resume that lied with every syllable and consonant, it shouldn't have been tough for anybody. I hadn't bathed.

'It's been an hour. The list was out just a few moments ago. I am the fourth to get in.'

'You are the fourth? Just one before Vernita? Cool.'

'Vernita?' W*hat?*

'Yes, she is giving it too. Tanmay just told me that she is fifth on the list.'

'How the fuck did she come to know?'

'I told Tanmay about the off campus. He had seen your resume on the computer. He may even have flicked through it,' she said. For the first time I felt like slapping her somewhere other than her ass. She was close to blowing my chance at a great job.

'What the...? Why didn't you hide it? Are *you* all like this? First there was Smriti, who couldn't hide a bloody relationship and now it's you? You all are the *same*, aren't you? I didn't even tell Shrey about it... and you? I cannot believe you did this. Couldn't you just have lied to him about this?'

'Deb, I didn't want to lie to him. I did that before and I regret that. I was not going to do that again.' I have never understood why people make a big deal about lying. It doesn't even figure in the seven deadly sins!

'Have you completely lost it? It was a different matter. It was about a goddamn relationship. This is about my life, *my career*, which you just royally fucked.'

'Excuse me, Deb, *goddamn relationship*? I got you this interview, damn it. I am sorry I did that.'

'Hey, hey, hey! You didn't do me a great favour doing that. Tanmay did that for Vernita too, didn't he? Anybody would have. But they wouldn't have told the world to fuck up his or her chances. You did that. Thank you.'

'Deb, I am sorry.' She broke down. 'I'm really sorry. But did you ever think why *I* didn't apply for it? It was something I always wanted to do. Finance.'

Click. She disconnected the call. I looked around to see everybody staring me down.

Then on, I spotted Vernita everywhere in the hall almost like you start to spot a word you just looked up in the dictionary everywhere around you. I couldn't talk to anybody around me as I had just established myself as a swearing shouting ass. In short, a typical Delhi *dude*.

'Debashish Roy,' the HR person called out. 'You are in.'

History repeated. I fucked up the interview once again; thanks to the brilliant distraction Avantika had just created. I knew the answers, but just couldn't say them. Or that's what I would like to think now. I stammered, blabbered and stuttered. And I was kicked out. Vernita was through. Avantika was to blame.

'Deb? Can you come to my place? Right now.'

'Shrey, I am not exactly in a mood...' It had to be one of the two reasons he called out to me. It was either a new movie he had got hold of or he had come out with some robotic bullshit of his. He usually had to lie for the latter.

'You have to. We have broken up,' he said sounding as if he was asked to stop going to NPL.

I had to go.

'What happened?' I asked.

His eyes were wet. He had been crying before I reached. I had seen quite a few girls do that in front of me before they fell in love or lust with me. 'She found someone else at work,' he said. Vandana had been working at an analytic firm that had a world-renowned vibrant work environment. A *vibrant work environment* generally means a healthy gender ratio and a great sex life.

'Who?' I asked. I was somewhat bewildered. I never thought Shrey would go to the extent of crying for her. That's something girls are best and prolific at. For us, what better than a girl offering a break up on a silver platter?

'It's some guy. She said they came close during the two months I was away.'

'But did she give you a reason?'

'She says she can't rely on me. He incidentally has a great career in front of him. She has even met his parents. It's over.'

'Are these guys getting married or something?' I said. I had always been a gossipmonger. So was Avantika. And she would kill me if I didn't give her all the details. I knew he would be all right in a while. Once he would find a new girl. But I also knew this one would take a little longer than usual.

'Not right now. But a few years down the line,' he said.

'How old is this guy?' I continued with my research. 'And how the hell does he have a better future than you?'

'I don't know. He has just done English honours or something and claims to earn a lot. He's just twenty four,' he said as he located that guy on a popular friendship site.

'Damn! He looks thirty. Or probably even more... and is awesomely bad looking. How can anybody possibly like him?' I wasn't trying to soothe him. The guy really looked like a monster. With big fat lips jutting out, a square face. He'd put up some stupid snaps before the Petronas Towers with some Thai people. He either was a very smooth talker or was a monster in bed too. The latter seemed unlikely for a person who wore bellbottoms in the name of boot cut jeans. Even they weren't particularly in vogue then.

The *nobody-is-a-stud-except-us* thing struck again. We found something wrong about a perfectly normal guy, again. Apart from his previously established grotesque looks.

'That can be true. Anyway, what do you plan to do now?' I asked him. We had proved that Shrey was phenomenally better than the guy and Vandana had got a raw deal.

'Nothing. I will wait for her to come back and dump her once she does. Meanwhile, I am talking to your Smriti. She is not as boring as you claimed to be. She really has to say some nasty things about you. She even recounted how horny you used to get and grope...'

Smriti? I thought she wanted somebody to get married to! With Shrey, all she would get would be painful love bites. I didn't know how to react. Not because it was Shrey. My friend. *How can he do this?* Of course, I didn't love her. But I was feeling a little strange about the whole thing. It seemed like Smriti's way of getting back at me.

'Cut it out. I can do without the explicit details. Anyway, best of luck with her. Hope it works out.'

'I hope too, man. I thought Vandana would write the patent application for the aggregate assembling robotic arm I had designed...'

'Don't start all over again. I am too tired of technocrap.' I was feeling way too sleepy. It had been a long day, and a very frustrating one.

'Sorry, Deb. How is your blog going? Any fresh readers?'

'Pretty bad. Had a fight with Avantika regarding that a few days back.'

'Why?' he asked as he started checking out the hot girls in

Suhel's list of friends. He tilted and let a small fart out. I was glad I could hear it. The soundless ones are the smelliest.

'Nothing. She didn't like certain parts where I had written some good things about Surabhi. Remember the Hotel Management girl? She had great legs, man! So whatever, she asked me to take it off and I didn't. Obviously. People loved it! She got pissed off and swore not to read it ever again.' I sniffed for any effluence. There wasn't any.

'So are you still writing it?'

'As long as you give me such interesting stuff to write about.' I was already asleep, only my lips weren't.

'That sounds good,' he said.

'Avantika said I was wasting my time on it. Anyway, I am crashing. Super tired.' I slept off at his place.

Shrey loved her. It seemed even more so, after they broke up. Shrey hadn't been perfectly loyal to Vandana but she knew nothing about it. And after the way Shrey treated her, she wouldn't even believe it if somebody told her. For the first time, by his own admission, something bad had happened to him.

Post breakup, Shrey never lost an opportunity to hit on whosoever he thought deserved him. But he never forgot to slow down his bike whenever we passed Hindu College, *Vandana's* college, on our trips to Kamla Nagar. He used to stare at it until it went out of sight. And then he spent the next few seconds with his head tilted upwards to keep the tears in check. It was only after parking the bike at a suitable distance from where I used to get down, that he used to take his helmet off. Then he used to take a moment in the washroom and come out eyes reddened with Delhi dust... *amongst other things*.

It was only after Shrey was dumped that I realized why the friends of the girl who are ditched are the most agitated lot. It had never happened around me and I had never seen a friend in pain for no fault of his or her. If I were to lay my hands on Suhel, I would have fucking cut his guts out and hung him with it.

Of Dad, Drunk Drivers and SRCC Internals

'Hi Deb! Why aren't you picking up your phone?' Avantika asked, frantic.

'I didn't feel like.'

'Are you still angry?' she asked.

'Naah, kidding. Was at Shrey's place. Had slept off. Though, I am still a little low.'

'Why is that?'

'Why is that? I still do not have a job, Avantika! And it sucks real bad. People have two, and I don't even have one. No wait; I do have one at a software firm.'

'Software firm? I didn't know you sat for any off campus?'

'No, I didn't.'

'So you mean... what?'

'I lied. What am I supposed to do? Everybody knows the placement season is over. I had to get dad something to tell the mysterious relatives who God knows why appear in these sorts of times.'

'But—'

'And yes. Dad still isn't happy about it. He says everybody can get that job. Ha! The sad part – he is right, just that *I* can't.'

College was ending and every conversation I got into with

dad, started with the topic of placements. People around my dad with kids in inferior colleges had jobs. So lying that companies weren't recruiting wasn't an option. I gave them different reasons, each time they asked me.

I am not interested in technical. And non-technical companies aren't recruiting these days.

I am concentrating on taking CAT again. Jobs come and go, education stays.

'But what are you going to do now?' Avantika asked, worried.

'Wait for off campus, what else? Just like you said. Never mind, you had to tell me something yesterday. What was that?'

'Shawar is jailed. He ran over a few people. Purvi is critically injured. God knows why he attempted to drive. I am so scared for him.'

I sinfully loved these incidents. Being an awfully slow driver, I always hid behind the pretext of road safety. And these incidents just made my point stronger.

'Am I to take this as a bad news or what? Because I am happy he's off my ass. But the cover charges...'

'Are you crazy? You are so insensitive. He was a friend, Deb. I am feeling bad. I met him today. He is in a terrible condition, bleeding from everywhere. I could barely look at him. He is battered, multiple fractures in the right leg, few teeth missing and a broken wrist. They might have to amputate his leg, if the bleeding doesn't stop. He is on an artificial ventilator for now. I am so scared for him.'

'He will be okay.'

'I just hope so. I don't know why are these things happening around me? First, it was Paritosh. Now it's him.'

'It's just with your ex-boyfriends. Oh yes, that reminds me. Shrey was dumped. He didn't even have sex with her. That's not the point. But he is sad. I don't know why! I never expected this from him. I wonder... what it would be like if you dump me.'

'I won't,' she said.

'Avantika, will he get out? The cover charges will hurt otherwise,' I said. I had come to love Shawar. His contacts gave us free passes to almost every gig in town!

We knew he would eventually get out. Shrey and I had hacked into his mail account and seen her sister's marriage photographs. All big politicians were there. I then sent a few mails to his professors that got him suspended for a week. Avantika wasn't too happy about it.

'Shut up, Deb. I will catch you later. I have to study. Law tomorrow and I am so fucked up right now. I can't get Shawar's image out of my mind. It scares me a lot.' Avantika's internal examinations were on and generally, she left no stone unturned to maximize her score. She hardly slept on the nights before her exams.

'I am going to sleep. Catch you tomorrow,' I said as I hugged the bolster tight, the one Avantika had gifted me. I had a hard time explaining my mom why my *guy* friends gifted me a *bolster*.

'No catching me tomorrow. Be at north campus, sharp eight thirty. Be there or I will think you don't love me. I am serious,' she chuckled. I heard a few girls laugh behind her.

'But why?'

'I will tell you tomorrow. Bye for now.'

'Don't act kiddish, tell me now. Right now or I won't come.'

'You will come. Bye, bye, bye. I am switching off my phone and studying. Be there. Please, please, please.' Click.

I had a faint idea of why they were calling me there.

I went back to contemplate whether I should wait for some time or should I go and talk to dad at once. I was waiting to get through some management college but since that didn't happen, I was in deep shit. There were no off-campus interviews in sight and as per some seniors, there weren't going to be many. Not talking now could have meant disastrous. However, the company I was supposedly *selected* in had joining dates in

August, leaving me with loads of time to find a job. Offer letters were still due, so dad wouldn't know.

Avantika had promised me to get a job in a broking firm at a decent salary if I ended up with none until September. That promise was what kept me sane. But there was no final word on it.

I just had to talk to dad and tell him what had transpired.

<hr />

I turned up at SRCC sharp at 8: 30 to see three girls wrapped in dull shawls. Their heads were totally wrapped around in scarves. They walked towards me with a bundle sheets of hand written notes tucked in their armpits.

'Hi, Deb,' Avantika said, 'this is Yamini and this is Radhika,' she said and pointed to her friends. They were both *averagely* sexy.

'Hi. So why…?' I asked as they handed over the papers to me. They had practised more on their hands rather than notebooks last night.

'See, extremely simple. These are the papers we have got Xeroxed. The questions are going to be asked from these sections only. All you need to do is dictate these to us on the phone. All four of us will be on conference. We have written the keywords to the answers to every question. Yamini will tell you the keywords and once you find the keywords, start dictating. Be slow, but not painfully so. Get it?' Avantika laid out the entire plan. It was indeed quite simple. They had tucked in earphones behind layers of hair and scarves, so they couldn't be caught. It was good enough… and it had been tried and tested in a Bollywood movie too.

'You're sure the questions are going to be asked from this only? And what if somebody drops off conference. Will you be able to call me back?'

'That is our problem. You just keep on dictating,' Radhika said as if she was paying me to do so.

'Deb, Radhika has talked to Murari Sir. He has confirmed the sections,' Avantika added.

This was the best about SRCC or Delhi University in general. If you are hot, if you are sexy and your professor is a guy/man/oldie, you can have the paper in your hand. It wasn't the first time that I had heard from Avantika that she knew the questions. But these stunts were also reserved for internals, where there were lesser things at stake.

'Okay, I will do that,' I said.

'Great then. We will leave now. Call me up and let us set the conference.' Avantika said.

'Alright,' I said.

They left and we set up the conference call as soon as they entered the examination hall. The exam started and Yamini started reading out the keywords.

'Memorandum of association... Conditions... Companies Act... Annual general meetings,' Yamini whooshed into the microphone. 'Quick.'

'According to section 173, a company and every officer who makes default is holding AGM is liable to a fine which may extend to Rs. Five hundred... blah... blah...blah...then there is something like a three *Ws*.'

'What?' Avantika shouted in whispers. I heard somebody shouting the words *stop talking* in the background.

'It is like three *Ws* and followed by...t...e...d. Make it look like three *W*. Write what I tell you to. Make three *W* looking things and t... e... d... then, blah...blah... blah...'

This went on for an hour or so before they finally decided to stop for the day.

'Thanks, Deb,' Yamini said, came forward and hugged me.

'Yeah, thanks Deb. You saved the day for us,' said Radhika as she hugged me too, a little too hard, a little too long. Both of them were now looked better without the unnecessary accessories of scarves and shawls. It hid their revealing, stringy tops that they wore, anyway.

'Pleasure is all mine,' I said.

'Can we go now, Deb?' Avantika said.

'Yes, sure. Are you guys coming along? Lunch at Noodle House?' I asked Yamini and Radhika.

'Ohh! You guys going to Kamla Nagar? Great, I have to get the books for the next exam. I can come along. Radhika, are you coming?' Yamini asked Radhika and she nodded in affirmation.

'Actually, we are going to Connaught Place. You guys carry on. We'll catch you later,' Avantika said and ground her teeth at me.

'Okay, never mind. Bye then. Bye Deb. Catch you later. And now that you know what to do, I may need your services more often. Avantika is new to this, I do this every time,' she laughed and hugged me again.

Avantika and I walked away from them and started walking towards the metro station.

'Deb, who is it?' Avantika asked as soon as my cell beeped.

'It is Yamini. A *Thank you* picture message. Cute, eh?' I said as she snatched the phone from me.

'Bloody bitch. And why have you stored her number, Deb?' she asked, not quite impressed.

'I just stored it, in case I had to call her if she happened to drop out of the conference call. At least she thanked me! You forgot that,' I said. I could see that Avantika didn't like the on-going argument. I did. It was nice to see her get possessive about me.

'Shut up. So, I can delete it now,' she said and didn't wait for my answer.

'Why are you getting so worked up? I would not even look at her twice.'

'Cut the crap, Deb. I saw you staring at that bitch's cleavage.'

'Firstly, I wasn't. And secondly, even if I was, I am not going to start going out with her. And what is the big deal? You yourself point out so many cleavages to me!'

'Deb, I know her. She is a *slut*. She sticks on to guys. And you hugged her, damn it. Not once, but twice?' she went red in the face and slightly wet in her eyes.

'Aww... Avantika, I love you. *She* hugged me, *I* didn't do it,' I said as I put my hand across her neck and pulled her close. It was quite an embarrassing thing to do on the streets of Delhi University.

'Bloody bitch... and you are not replying to that message,' she said, as she broke free from my hold.

'I won't, baby. But you have to admit, there is something about me.' I winked at her.

'There is nothing about you; she even flirted with Shawar once. She is a slut and that is about it.'

'Whatever. But she was hot, you have to admit.'

'Fuck off. Hot, my foot! Just because I don't put my breasts on display when I come to college doesn't mean those fucking girls can beat me in it,' she stomped down her point. I had never seen her so full of spite. But I had to agree, I had seen her yesteryear snaps on Facebook and she looked like ramp walk material.

'I know that baby, you are the best,' I said and blew a kiss at her.

'I better be.'

We walked for a while before she asked in a very meek voice, 'Deb, do you want me to wear all that?'

'If I had it my way, I would not let you wear anything,' I chuckled.

'Asshole,' she said and held my hand as we started to walk towards the metro. 'By the way, what are you wearing on your farewell?' Avantika asked me.

'It is two months away. A lot of time.'

⁓

Finally, I got my words in order. I was ready to talk to my dad, and I did. All the preparation done the day before to tell dad the truth about everything went waste. All I could say was, 'Dad, I really want to work in BHEL.'

I knew I could get a job at BHEL. But I couldn't admit that I had failed in getting placed and it was my last resort. April had ended and so had my college exams. I just had to do it.

'Why?' he said, putting the vegetables in my bag. It was a Wednesday. Every week on Wednesday, dad, mom and I used to go for an outing. It used to be to the weekly vegetable market, where I acted as a porter. I underwent the whole ordeal week after week, year after year with my head bowed down, lest anybody spots me. Even if somebody did, both of us would be so embarrassed that we wouldn't exchange anything beyond the upward twitching of eyebrows.

The clangour of the market used to be impossible to bear with aunties and vendors matching pitch to pitch. That's what middle class families do. They do not dress up as light bulbs and scheme and talk to oneself to bring the whole clan down. *Damn those soap operas.*

'I want to work in the Mechanical industry before I go for an MBA later,' I said, pushing a beggar child aside. They sell irritation, not sympathy.

'Why? What happened to your software dreams?' I knew the sarcasm would start flowing. 'Or those KPOs, analytical firms and investment banks? No longer interested in working for them? Your non-technical jobs?'

'Kids don't know what they want to do. This is the problem with the whole generation,' Mom said. Her voice was already squeaky with all that bargaining with the vendors, which wouldn't amount to more than a few rupees saved. Maybe it just satisfied their ego. Probably gave them a topic to talk about in their next kitty party.

'I know, mom. I want to work in BHEL and then go to ISB or something. I have it planned out.' I hadn't. I was just looking for some security before I started going for the off campus interviews. I was just as clueless and aimless as the moths buzzing around those halogen bulbs those vendors used. Just that, those moths didn't need an aim with all those veggies in front of them.

'Please talk to Mr. Malhotra and try to get him in,' mom said.

'I will do that. Which department do you want to work in?' Dad asked. I could sense he had just won a moral war against the present generation. His rotting company still had young takers.

'Piping,' I said. It was the only department I knew, besides the one dad worked in. My dad's department was not an option. His perfectionist attitude made me feel nervous as shit.

I got my first job. The *interview* was shorter than expected. Thank God for the rogue vegetable vendors who then had to be accused rightfully or wrongfully of faulty weights/pesticides/exorbitant prices.

At the end of the day, I too ended as them, the rich bastards. I had a job I had not earned. I was nothing without the job dad got me. Dad probably knew I had failed in getting a placement beyond a silly IT one. What he would not know was that I failed to get *any*. But whatever it was, I knew he will never pick that topic up. I was a hero for him and he would never make me feel otherwise, no matter how many times I faltered. He loved his work. It was a government job, and he never slipped. But now, everybody would have something to level against him.

You know, Mr. Roy? Yes, the one from the planning department, he got his son in. Heard he is from DCE. Must have failed or something. People like him are spoiling this office by getting everybody they know inside it.

An office he had upheld over anything else. For 32 years. Dad would feel all that, but I would never get to know. He loved me. I loved him too.

'I got the job. Aren't you so proud of me? Now we can go shopping for the farewell.'

'So you did finally talk to your dad about it,' Avantika said, clearly unimpressed.

'Yes I did. I told him I really wanted to work in BHEL. And that's it. I get the job. Ha! I didn't screw this one up.'

'That's not *talking* to your dad. That's *lying* to your dad. You will be in a big trouble one of these days.'

'I won't. Guess what? Mom, dad and Sonali are shifting to Hyderabad for a couple of years.'

'So?' she asked nonchalantly.

'So? *So?* Are you asking *so*? I will get a chance to live alone. The whole flat to myself. You can come over anytime you want to! If I were you, I would already be heading to a lingerie store,' I mocked.

'Shut up, Deb! For now, let us head to some place else. A suit store! Farewell just a month away.'

Avantika wasn't in the best of moods that day. What happened to Shawar still haunted her. She took me to his hospital room, guarded by police officers on both sides. My heart sank as soon as I set my eyes on him. The image would never leave my mind. His condition was pitiable. He was extensively bandaged and every bit was soaked with blood. He had still not regained consciousness and was on the ventilator. I could notice it. He had lost his right leg. I held on to Avantika, who almost fainted. I felt sorry for him. It was a terrible sight. We did not exchange a word for the rest of the day.

The Farewell Night Molestation

'That's so cool. You have so much to write about in your blog. The Shawar incident and then the cheating one,' Virender said as he adjusted his tie. It didn't do him any good. He just ended up looking like a low budget movie star with his skin-hugging suit.

It was mid-March, and more importantly, our farewell night. There were four of us cramped in the miniscule JCB 208 hostel room, and tried to look our best for the day.

'I am not writing any more controversial stuff. Radhika got to know what all shit I wrote about her. She cannot do anything about it. But Shawar will kill me this time if I write anything about him. And Avantika will do the same if I write anything about Yamini. But Yamini was awfully sexy, man!' I had started liking blogging. But I was dropping a lot of shit on a lot of people and not everyone liked it.

'C'mon, how will he get to know?' Yogender said. He was looking good. As he couldn't look as bad as Virender did. But in isolation, the *sherwani* on his scrawny frame was looking more like a huge rugged invisible cloak. But he looked good in the snaps we took and at the end of the day, that is what matters. Ten years down the line, that is the only thing that would be there to remember of this day. Or even the next day, when the pictures go up on Facebook.

'For your extremely kind information, my blog has some fifty dedicated readers. And I know, there is one who knows Shawar through someone. Though it is slightly far-fetched, but why take the risk?'

'Who reads your blog?' Shrey asked.

'Gitanjali, one of my most regular readers,' I said.

'Who is Gitanjali now? Deb, tell me just one thing, where do all these girls keep coming from in your life? It is almost unrealistic!' Yogender asked.

'You just have to keep your eyes open. Even the worst looking girl around you is important. She may just have a hot friend,' I said.

'Is she hot, then?' Shrey asked.

'Naah, not quite. But she is well read. So her opinion counts.'

Gitanjali was intelligent but didn't look that great. But then, I had started comparing everyone to Avantika so it wasn't really fair. She was studying at Jesus & Mary College. So getting close to her had other advantages. Although I didn't think about all that, Shrey wanted me to have a presence in JMC so he could have a shot. He had just one *dream* – one girlfriend each in both JMC and Lady Sri Ram College before college ended. These two colleges had the best Delhi could offer in terms of breasts with brains. His dream remained unrealized.

'Leave all that, *yaar*. Can I meet Yamini sometime? Accidental meeting types?' Shrey asked me.

'No chance. Avantika wouldn't let me miles within Yamini's reach. You can talk to Avantika, though.'

The farewell was great on the eyes. It left me wondering that if these girls could actually look so good, why didn't they do it every day? Everybody seemed to have come armed with pad ups or stuffed socks in their bras. Finally, after four years of college life, I saw more woman boobs than man boobs in my college. Many of those breasts, I never knew existed.

The evening wasn't anything spectacular. After the dancing

and the nickname session got over, people pounced on the food. It always tastes better when there is no bill following it. Meanwhile, Yogender and Virender, drunk as shit, found it difficult to stand straight. However, they danced with the college dogs with unmatched finesse and grace.

'Hey Messenger! Where are you going?' a voice called out from behind as I walked away from the main stage. *Messenger* was the name given to me by our juniors in the nicknames part. Apparently because I was always caught texting somebody or the other. *Very* creative indeed.

'Huh...? Nowhere. All this noise just got to me. Going for a walk for a while,' I said. I had no intentions to stuff myself that night. Especially not after the major trouble I had fitting into the suit I had bought myself barely a month back... and my tastes were more refined now and free food wasn't a rarity! *Thanks*, Avantika.

'Can I join you? If you don't mind?' Vernita asked. She bent down to strap open her stilettos and handed them over to me. I hadn't yet said yes. Vernita looked ravishing in her peacock blue glittery *saree* wrapped tightly around her, accentuating her fabulous ass and baring her midriff all the way. An equally glittery blouse, held in place only by threads, *and* an equally glittery gold bag completed the picture.

'Of course, you can.'

'See, Deb. Now that this is the last day in college, I thought let's end it on a good note. We may not end up being good friends after we move out of college. But at least be friends for this last day,' she said.

'Sure.'

I shot discreet glances at her massive cleavage. I hadn't had the opportunity to do that in a long time. It had been months since we had talked to each other. And we had been hurting each other in some way or the other. She had sold me out to Shawar. And I hadn't been all that innocent either. But I was happy that we did finally talk, even if it was for one last day.

'Now tell me, you were the sucker who told Sethi sir that I missed the practical for a date, right? Don't lie. I knew it was you bastard,' she said, laughing. 'You nearly got me a back paper that day.'

'Ok! *Did I?* And what did you do? With the Shawar incident you nearly had me dead there.'

'Don't tell me. Could he do that?' she giggled.

'A lot more than that! But he is behind the bars for good.'

'Tanmay told me that he would be out in days.'

'Even I thought so. But he had hit an MLA's car on the way. The MLA's son was injured too, so it may be a little tough. Shawar lost a leg too.'

'Okay, Isn't it good?' she said.

'What? Shawar?' I asked.

'The *walk*, you asshole.'

'Yup.' It was. It was a beautiful night. No stars or anything, but still the long road from the hostel to the campus, which had in it, four years of great memories, made it beautiful. Not that we couldn't come back and experience it. But it wouldn't be the same. We would no longer be a part of the road, or the buildings and the college. It just wouldn't be the same.

I wasn't in love with my college. My four years had been eventful, but the college had nothing to do with it. Not when I wasn't even a hosteller. I hadn't made many friends as most of them were not my type. I was anyway too busy pursuing and going out with girls, most of whom I found intolerable. When I used to see huge groups of guy buddies, I used to feel a little jealous. But then, I was not comfortable in large boisterous groups after a few unpleasant experiences in school.

But I would still miss college. It was still the place I first made out, first had sex and first finished in the last ten in class rankings. That was the place where I made my transition from a fat nerd whipping boy to a semi-fat semi-stud. It was much better than the torturous time in school, where I was a bloated bag of people's jibes. At least I had the girls' department working right. No fucking one could have made fun of me anymore; I had beaten each one of them at the girlfriend count. I wasn't the nerd any more. They were. I was getting laid, they weren't. I had gotten back at them. Only partly.

'Vernita, I am sorry, I lied. But I really didn't think you guys would make such a big issue out of it... and it seems pretty stupid now that Avantika and I are happy with each other.'

'Deb, let's not debate that. It was a big issue. For Tanmay, it was. You were bloody fucking his sister when you already had a girlfriend. For me, I was upset that you lied to me. You could have at least tried to make me understand,' Vernita said.

'I am sorry for that. But I just didn't know what I was doing. We couldn't have met had we told you. I am sorry, anyway. But I missed you and hated you. You didn't even bother to contact me—' I was interrupted by a screeching Vernita.

'I didn't bother? *I*? Even today *I* bothered, not *you*. All this time, I have been bothering, Deb. I know everything that you do, everywhere you go. I had to listen to all the NPL bullshit of Shrey just to know how you are doing. And you? Was it so easy to walk off with her? Just one night and you killed our friendship? Three years, damn it! How could you do it? Did it ever occur to you what I was going through? I love you, Deb. I always have.' She broke down. For the first time in four years, I had seen her crying. That could be the first time after the time she was born. *It was unreal.*

'WH... what?' I asked, as we sat down on the pavement.

'Deb, don't read too much into it. I had this huge crush on you in the first year.' She sniffed the last of her nasal fluids in. 'And don't look at me that way. I am not crying anymore, sucker.'

'Sorry. Go on,' I said. I felt like the handsomest person in the world. I knew I wasn't, but there had to be a reason for all the luck I had had, with the hottest I had seen. And I chose this one. *I must be handsome.* Made perfect sense.

'I mean, I had boyfriends. But they weren't as funny and smart as you were.' *Funny* and *smart*, I noted those down.

'But why didn't you ever tell me that?' I asked. I was sure I would have said yes, at least my hormones would have made me do so.

'Why didn't I ask you? Can you remember a single day you hadn't trashed me for something or the other? I was always this loud brash girl for you. You never saw me as girlfriend material. I didn't want to be one of those girlfriends that you had during those days. It was hard. You would have probably laughed at me then and walked off to sleep with somebody else.' I wouldn't have laughed at her, not *before* making out with her, at least.

'Excuse me, I was never that lucky. I have just made out with four girls in my entire life. But I still say you could have tried.'

'Poor you... Just four?' She took out a small mirror and started setting her smudged *kajal* right.

'So do you still...' I asked.

'Obviously not! That was just an emotional outbreak. I love Tanmay quite a lot now.'

'Do you? I thought you just had to go on with him till the time Avantika and I broke up,' I said.

'Why so?'

'*This guy will just fuck you and leave you.* Remember this? That would have been a little hypocritical then.'

'Yes, maybe. But I love this guy. I met his parents at the *Spirit of Living* thing. They kind of like me. Saw Avantika too, wasn't looking very happy. Are things all right?'

'Pretty much.'

Avantika? Sad? She always is, whenever she is with her parents.

'She is beautiful. You are a lucky ass. You are not planning to dump her. Are you?'

'Not in the next hundred years, I suppose.'

'She is lucky too, then,' she said.

'I guess we should leave now. If you don't want Tanmay to see us. Just tell me one thing - what is it that girls find interesting in me?' I said as I got up. I didn't want to see Tanmay either. There wasn't a single moment in the entire night that I spotted him without girls wanting to get clicked with him. *Fuck that, I am not photogenic. That is it.*

'Need an ego massage?' Vernita answered as she got up too and ironed out the pleats of her *saree*.

'Wouldn't mind that.'

'I told you. You are funny and smart. You haven't changed and so haven't I. So if you want me to tell you that you are good looking, forget that. I won't lie, sucker.'

'Whatever. Let's go,' I said. There went my *I-am-good-looking* dream.

'Yup. Wait. There is something I always wanted to do,' she said and turned towards me.

She, all of a sudden, grabbed hold of my tie and pulled me close. She forced her lips on to mine and kissed me deep, holding me close against her. My pulse touched a hundred. She bit, licked and rolled all over my tongue and bit the hell out of my lips. I could feel her lipstick change its resting place... After she transferred all her wetness and left my lips bruised from her savage kissing, she grabbed hold of my hair. She pulled my head back and dug her teeth on my neck. Then she started to suck on it. I put my hand on her exposed waist and clawed in to keep from making a sound. Just as I started cursing myself on missing out on four years of fabulous sex, she pulled back and walked away. I stood there and tried to string my words to say something.

'So... any last words?' I shouted as she walked quite a few yards away.

She looked back and adjusted the tuft of hair falling on her eyes and shouted, 'Now I know why Avantika is crazy about you. And the other girls. I hope now you feel that I was girlfriend material after all.' She smiled and walked away.

Did that mean I was a great kisser? Obviously yes! But that didn't answer the question – why did girls like me? As more often than not, kiss chronologically comes *after* the liking.

Silly answer, I thought.

Great kiss, though!

I got the hottest girl on the farewell to kiss me. *Nobody is a stud except me, not even Tanmay.*

Avantika was sad and I was yet to know why. It had been two months since Vernita said that and I had forgotten all about it. I didn't ask her why. But I suspected it was because her application to change her posting to Delhi had been rejected. And so, she had to leave the city in June. We didn't have much time left together. We spent those two months trying to spend every possible minute with each other, spending hours at coffee shops till the waiters asked us to fuck off.

We held hands till they became sweaty, we kissed each other till it became it embarrassing, we said we loved each other till we got tired. We never got tired. We started to plan ways we could meet each other, compare the merits of Google talk and Skype, among other things.

With every passing day, I saw Avantika get sadder. Sometimes, she just cried all night and didn't receive any of my calls. All that made me equally sad. Though even in Bangalore, she would be a call and a flight away from me. But not meeting her thrice in a week was depressing enough a thought. We knew whatever we might say; we wouldn't be able to meet more than once or twice in two months. I looked for jobs in

Bangalore, but it wasn't anywhere. I would have flushed toilets but all I got were IT jobs.

I had already started missing her and every time I said anything like that to Avantika, she sobbed like a little child.

She was a little child, my baby, my sweet little baby. *Tattooed* little baby!

All that crying and not sleeping for nights at an end gave her bags beneath her eyes. It took me to the time when we first met. She was sad then. She was beautiful then. She was beautiful now. She will always be beautiful to me.

She may be ninety, her breasts may sag, her teeth may fall, her gums may bleed, she may miss a few limbs... but she will always be my baby. I will still kiss those hollow cheeks, I will still hold her wrinkled hands and still say that I love her. Because I will love her forever.

She was the only one I ever loved and it took me eight years after I hit puberty to find her. I was going to keep her until the next eighty.

The Spirit of Losing

'Deb, I need to tell you something,' Avantika said. She didn't sound great. I knew that tone. That came up whenever she thought ours was a purely physical relationship. First muff dive, I heard that. First blowjob, I heard that. The times I begged for sex, I heard that. But she wasn't at fault. We were so bed breakingly good. Anyone could have thought that.

'What?' I asked.

'We need to break up.'

'WHAT?' I was speechless. I felt like somebody had driven a ram though my chest. I started feeling dizzy. For a moment, I thought she was joking. It was almost as if everything we had done suddenly flashed in front of me. Just like life does when one is about to die.

'Deb, just listen. Please, do this for me... and don't ask for explanations. I don't have any. You have given me the most wonderful relationship of my life. And I love you and will keep doing that. But...'

'But...? What? Why? What? *What?*' I was in tears. It took a split second for that to happen. I must have looked worse than Shrey in those moments. But I didn't care. I loved her. I hadn't even cheated on her ever, as I count the encounter with Vernita as molestation. Avantika was all I had, I had never thought beyond her in all those days I was with her. My days started with her and ended with her. She filled everything in between.

'Sri Guru told me...'

'Sri Guru? Your Sri Guru? Did he ask you to? I can't believe this, Avantika! Are you fucking out of your mind? You are breaking up with me because your stupid Sri Guru asked you to? Shit, I can't believe I am in this. How can you just walk away like that? Are you serious?'

'Deb! Deb, you can say anything to me, but please not a thing against Sri Guru. He didn't ask me to break up.'

'Then what? Did he just ask you to marry some ugly long bearded disciple of his? Huh? How can you be so irrational?' It still sounded like an extended joke and she would crack up any moment. She didn't.

'No, Deb. Will you please listen? I have been somewhat disturbed with what happened to Paritosh and Shawar. So I talked to Sri Guru about it and...'

'Great! And he loaded it with astrological bullshit about you and that you are responsible for it. Hasn't he? Tell me Avantika? You never loved me, did you? Why? All you fucking care is about your Sri Guru.' I shouted at her. I heard mom and dad stop talking in the other room. They were then trying to listen in. I knew mum would come into my room and ask for something she didn't need.

'Deb, will you listen for, God sake? Don't call me unless I call you. I am hanging up. I can't be the reason for your pain. I can't see you suffer because of me. Check your inbox and you will know. Bye, Deb. I love you. I always will. It may hurt you for a while, but it is for your own good.'

'Avantika, listen. You cannot leave me just like that. Please, can you at least tell me why you are fucking doing this to me?'

'Deb, it is no use. Go check your mail. It is not easy for me to do this. Bye.'

She hung up. Her crying didn't give me the least bit of

consolation. I checked my mail after I handed over the paper puncher Mom asked for. After I read the message, I was sure about two things.

First, I would definitely kill all the God men before anybody, if I ever get the chance. Especially since Vernita was off the list, after that lipstick smudger of a kiss. And second that this was the silliest break up ever. Avantika still had a wild streak in her intact.

The message read:

Sri Guru: 'It's you who is responsible for all the trials and tribulations that people around you go through. You determine the happiness or the sorrow that they experience. You have to make their lives worthwhile. It's you who define their lives. What fate they have is your giving. It's you, only you who can make or break their lives. Child, if you think that somebody is suffering around you, it is only you who can set it right. You are the one responsible. It is because of you that they suffer. It is because of you that they don't.'

Deb, I am not strong. After what happened to Shawar and Paritosh, I am scared. I won't be able to carry on if something ever happens to you. You were barred, you screwed CAT… maybe it was all because of me. I am not sure, Deb. I'm scared, after seeing Shawar in the condition he is right now. I don't know Deb. I cannot take it. I would rather be away from you and see you safe and happy.

Sorry Deb. I love you. Avantika.

Now what was that supposed to mean? If Paritosh and Shawar did something freaky, it did not mean *Avantika* was at fault! If she couldn't get Paritosh off drugs, how was she responsible? If Shawar was a drunkard, it is not because of Avantika. And even if it was, it did not mean I will end up in the same manner.

I couldn't believe she could be so dumb! I knew she loved and respected Sri Guru more than anybody else, but this was downright stupid. And he did not ask Avantika to leave me!

But there was nothing I could have done. Avantika could be extremely stubborn and I knew that.

She called up a few times but never said more than a hello and broke down after that. She was in pain, but she had her reasons to end this relationship. I had none. I wanted this relationship. It was the only thing I had. It was the only relationship I had given my all in. That relationship was the only thing that kept me going those days. It defined my days.

I tried to talk her back into the relationship, but nothing helped. From the next day, she started rejecting my calls. I stayed the night up and went to north campus that day. I spent hours below her hostel, sending her messages, begging her to at least meet me once. She refused. Just a message saying that she can't come. Just a single fucking message. For all the times, for all the dreams, for all she had promised, *just a message.*

Maybe she wanted me to hate her, but I was falling even more in love with her. Frustrated and tired, I called up roommate Isha. Isha had helped us innumerable times on previous occasions and was the only one who knew what Avantika meant to me. I kept holding on the phone for the entire night while Isha engaged Avantika in conversation. That was the closest I could have gotten to Avantika. At least I could hear her voice. At least I now knew it wasn't just me who had been crying his heart out. At least I could hear her take my name. I kept doing that for eight nights and nine days, until the time she shifted out of her hostel and went back to her flat. She had to start packing to leave for Bangalore.

It had been days since I had slept, eaten, breathed or smiled to my heart's content. It was only Avantika that I craved for. One touch, one hug was all I wanted. I wanted to tell her only once what she meant to me. I wanted to tell her how much I loved her and how badly I wanted her. The worst had happened, she had left me and I couldn't think of anything worse.

Mom, dad and Sonali were leaving Delhi and they thought

it was because of them that I was in that condition. Mom contemplated staying back, but I pestered her to go. I understood what life is without your most loved one without you. Life ceases to mean anything.

Things changed for the worse when they left for Hyderabad. I no longer had to check the flood of tears. They flowed.

I kept calling her, she kept rejecting my calls. I started calling her up from different numbers. But the moment she would say hello, I would burst out crying and begged her to come back. She kept saying she owes her life to Sri Guru and she can't go against his wishes. She had apparently taken close to two months to take this fucking decision. Maybe she was just waiting for our exams to get finish.

She used to bang the phone down without saying anything after the first few times I called her.

'Move on Deb, you have to. For me. For you. Bye. Best of Luck.'
This is what her message said, days before she had to leave for Bangalore. That was the last time I called her. I stopped giving her blank calls after she asked me to forget her and make her life easier.

It all went downhill from there. I had asked Shrey to leave me alone and he had done exactly that. He left for Germany in a few days for a technological start up with up some guys he knew from IIT. Viru and Yogi had joined work. Anyway, their being with me would not have made a difference. Their relationship with me was restricted to treats, which they never forgot to ask for. I had to give them one for getting through BHEL too.

Quite obviously, they gave none in return. I couldn't have talked to them. They weren't friends I could call my own. There were a few people that I called up, whom I knew loved me once, but it made no difference. I didn't want to meet them either. The tendency of thinking that meeting others would mean cutting on the time with Avantika still hadn't left me. Avantika had sucked me out of all my energy, love and optimism.

Talking to anybody didn't help. I ended up in the same damned state. I didn't need a distraction. I didn't need a diversion. I didn't need company. I needed Avantika.

It all came back to me. Every iota of pain that I gave to others came back to haunt me. Every break up came back to haunt me. Every friendship that I had not respected was back to haunt me. I never felt responsible for the shit my friends found themselves in. I had no one now.

Everywhere I went, I couldn't help but see her all around me. *May be she is stalking me. Maybe she is behind that pillar to see how I am doing.*

The emptiness of my place had started to bite me. Mom, dad had left me the car and I spent days driving around her flat. I hoped to catch a glimpse of her. Nothing happened. I drove back and forth from North Campus to Greater Kailash, where we first met, more than a dozen times each day and hoped to bump into her. Nothing happened.

I spent hours at the Delhi University metro station and hoped that she would walk by, spot me and then come running into my arms. Nothing happened. I called up her friends to help me track her. They too had no idea as to where Avantika was. Vernita refused to talk to Tanmay about it, though she told me that Avantika was living with her uncle those days.

My world had crashed right in front of my eyes.

Avantika was my world. I never needed anyone else. She was a friend when I needed one, she was a punching bag when I wanted one, and she was a lover, always. I never had someone who actually had the capacity to control my moods. I was an extrovert loner. I wanted people around, but I didn't need them around.

But since the time I met Avantika, things had changed. Everyone around me had ceased to matter. The world around me ceased to matter; I didn't even want people around. Now there was none. I had never thought I would need anybody else. But now that she had left, there was nobody around. I was a kid in the big city with no one else. I had no friends for I never made good ones. And Avantika, my best friend, had left me for no reason whatsoever. No human company and days away from a social life – the job at BHEL.

Had I been a drinker, I would have wasted myself dangerously. But since I wasn't, I ate with a vengeance. I bloated up from all sides. I ordered everything home. I couldn't have gone out... every place reminded me of her, and the time we had spent there. Moreover, I didn't like the feeling of sitting alone and eating. Back home at least I had the television for company.

I spent many of those days writing the defunct blog, but ended up writing her name repeatedly. I was glad nobody read it because all there was on it was Avantika, about how much I missed her. I missed the time she cribbed about my comments filling up her mailbox.

I kept tracking her on social networking sites to see if there was anybody else in her life. But there was absolutely nothing in her Orkut scrapbook except some random friend requests from *cool guys*. There was nothing on Facebook either. She had not been online for about a month now, since the time we broke up. As a last resort, I enrolled for the *Spirit of Living* course, hoping I might just bump into Avantika, even though I knew she would be leaving for Bangalore anytime, to join work. Probably *forever*. I knew it wasn't forever, but I had started loving the pain. It felt better when I thought that all the doors had closed in on me. It was better than the times when I felt there was a glimmer of hope. It's better to die in an atmosphere without oxygen than struggle in one with traces of it.

Not surprisingly, I did not bump into Avantika during the course. When I joined the course, which they claimed to be a spiritual uplifting process, I thought I would trash everything that goes around there and move out. But once I was in, I couldn't do any of that. It may not have been spiritually uplifting for me but I did see people with the most rotten of moods going out with a smile on their faces. Stressed out couples, out of job executives, broken hearts like me, everybody there smiled and tried to get rid of their problems.

All it did was get a few miserable people like us together, made us pour our heart out, sing, dance and play. And behold we were in wonderland. They were in wonderland. But I did start accepting my break up. I forgave *Spirit of Living*. Not because I had started accepting the crappy philosophy (which wasn't crappy anymore) but because I started seeing with my own eyes how much people revered Sri Guru. He was a father figure to millions. I had seen people's faces light up just at the mention of his name. He was a God to many. I hate to say this, but I started respecting him, even loving him. But I did not forget that my break up was not my own doing. *For once.*

The weeklong course helped and I hate to say that because had it not been for the *Spirit of Living*, I would still be with Avantika!

I called up Smriti, half out of guilt, half to get over Avantika, but just ended up crying. Smriti tolerated me for a while and then asked me not to call her ever again.

Everything went on like that for more than a month. I had driven everyone around me away. Now, it was I who was driven away, from friends. I had nobody to talk to, nobody to laugh with, nobody to cry with, nobody to celebrate with… I wanted nobody, I wanted *her*. I wanted the time she had promised me. Now it was all gone. I had been dumped, unceremoniously, painfully, unreasonably… and a lousy job beckoned me.

Me, Myself and Amit

'Are you sure you are going to be fine?' Shrey asked. He'd called from Germany. So he was spending quite a lot on me. I liked that. 'I know it's been kind of hard for you. Avantika and then your family moving out. But it isn't that bad, there are a million girls out there. Go for them you will be just fine.'

'I hope so, man. Hang up now. It must be costing you a lot,' I said. I didn't want to be sympathized with all the time. I hated it after a while. It made me feel like a loser, which I probably was.

'Are you crazy? I hacked into their telephone exchange and so actually I am calling from their... let me see... oh fuck, it's their parliament's line...fuck... bye. You take care...'

'You haven't changed.'

'And you don't need to change. *The girls are waiting.*' He hung up.

I was the only one going to a government office amongst us. It wouldn't pay me a lot after all kinds of funds and taxation, about ten thousand less than my peers and half of what Avantika would be earning. To make things worse, BHEL hadn't heard the word *appraisal*. Vernita's office had already started a fortnight ago. Shrey was working with some IITians in a start-up of some kind. They were trying to make some hybrid car in

Germany. Tanmay had joined his uncle's business; he wanted time to prepare for CAT.

Virender and Yogender had joined their job in the research and development department of a tractor making company in Punjab. Back to their homeland. It suited them. *Everybody is happy*, I thought.

Vernita had everything she wanted. Virender and Yogender had each other, their homeland and loads of liquor, I was sure. Shrey had his techie crap quite well for him. It was just I who didn't get what he wanted.

Avantika's words rang in my head - *you will never get the pants ironed if you don't take them off.*

Even that was bullshit. I didn't care whether I was going for a government office or a plush investment bank. The only thing that mattered was she. Or maybe if I had her, those things could have started to matter. For now, they didn't.

I looked at the huge office at Bhikaji Cama place. It was some fifteen stories tall but looked at least thirty. It was a huge building made out in brown stone, in ascending and descending staircase fashion. *So this is the place*, I told myself. I had lost the drive to sit for any other interviews so that was pretty much it. It was the twentieth of June, the first earning day of my life.

The guard asked for my ID. I fished it out and flashed it as I moved through the automated doors. I had been there before, but always looked at it as a place where losers or old people worked.

I wasn't a loser. I still hadn't come to accept that. I had just lost her. The world was there for the taking. I just had to figure out how. And whether I wanted it more than I wanted Avantika.

I looked up the huge board that had all the details about the building.

'Piping. 6th floor.'

I tried to memorize. The building was about five decades old. But it was surprisingly well maintained, for a government office. The lift was a little tricky for me, though.. Different lifts stopped at different floors, so it took me quite some time to get used to it.

'Is this the piping department?' I asked a bespectacled man who I was sure had spent all his life there.

He took full two minutes to chew upon what I had asked and answered, 'This is the eighth floor. Piping is the sixth floor. New joinee? Tricky lift, eh?'

'Yes. Thank you.'

'You will have to work really hard here. Our principles of integrity and hard work are well known around the globe,' he said and became suddenly strangely demonic. 'And get a haircut. Such long hair is unacceptable.'

'Okay, sir,' I said left before he could comment on how my falling jeans would further rot the company.

As I jumped alternate stairs to reach the sixth floor I thought whether I would end up like him. I would not, *this is just temporary,* I told myself.

It was. I did intend to leave the job in a few years and go for an international MBA. Or the one at ISB. Or maybe go to Middle East, they needed a lot of Mechanical engineers there.

I may even meet Avantika's parents. Not that they would have liked it. They were Punjabis and they wanted the same for their daughter. But then, I could have be an oil magnate and impress them out of their wits. Or become the President of United States. My daydreaming had no bounds.

Just as my mind started to drift off to Avantika, another old voice called out. 'Deb?'

'Yes?'

'I am Deepak Malhotra. DGM, Piping. Your dad talked to me. Welcome to BHEL. I hope you like it here.'

Mr. Malhotra was one of the better-dressed people in BHEL. Most people there in the office wore the same shirt for a month before putting it out to laundry.

'Thank you, sir.'

'Amit is waiting for you in cubicle number 5. You are a management trainee under him. He will show you around. Any problem, see me or Mr. Goyal. Cubicle 5 is the third one from left along that aisle. Go ahead. Nice meeting you, young man... nice jeans,' he chuckled.

He reminded me of my father, who kept asking me how often it dropped down. *Whenever Avantika wanted it to.*

I decided to love him. He didn't have a paunch, was tall and had a perfectly trimmed peppered moustache. He was a man of consequence and that showed.

I walked down the aisle. It dispelled quite a few doubts. It wasn't as dilapidated as I thought it would be. They were definitely not using MS DOS.

The computers were all upgraded. The desks were swanky and clean, with no spit stains on them. Nice little cubicles with two cabins on the floor. One for the DGM and another one for the HOD.

That's another matter that the computers missed people. There was a bunch of people in some corner discussing the new receptionist in the office. Another bunch discussed the cricket match the previous day, while they sipped tea and occasionally run their hands over their bulging stomachs.

But overall, the office was impressive. I liked it. *I had to.* I reached cubicle 5.

'Hello sir,' I said.

'Hello!' he said as he swirled around his chair to set his eyes on me. I saw his desktop screen. It was Monica Belluci in a gold bikini, signed Amit beneath. He wore a shirt tucked deep inside his hideously faded jeans and wore glasses whose frame was heavier than him. He had not yet grown out of his fifth grade hairstyle that his parents had decided for him. A crew cut. Unlike other desks, his was a tutorial on how to keep a desk organized. For someone like me, who had more books sleeping with me on the bed than stacked on an unused study table, this was new.

I decided to like him too. Not that I had a choice.

'So you must be Deb?' he asked. He gave the pencil in his hand quite some rotations.

'Yes sir,' I said.

'I am Amit. Call me Amit. I am no sir. I joined just last year. So it is cool.'

'Fine, Amit.'

'How many trainees have joined? Any girls? Any hot ones?'

'No, Amit. Not that I know of,' I said. I was little surprised. Not that he looked old, but I didn't expect this question so early. Not from somebody who looked like the king of Nerdsville. He desperately tried to sound urbane, but his small town upbringing was dripping from every consonant and syllable. Strange small town accent.

'Not that you know of? If somebody would know that, it's you. Want to see around?'

'I would love to.'

The ice between us broke the very second we met. It lit my dull life, suddenly. My longest conversation in over a month.

He stood up. He wasn't more than five feet five and barely had anything in him. He was skin stretched over bones. I could have flicked him into orbit.

'Okay, let's go. Let's start from the least glamorous to the most glamorous department. First on our list is planning department.'

'The least glamorous?'

'Yes all the oldies work there. The excruciatingly slow department. It's like a very slow dentist,' he said and started to hop off. His imitation Gaffar Market shoes were in sharp contrast to my All Star Converse ones. He still had a lot of things to learn from Delhi. Breaking up on a mail was one. I wondered where Avantika learnt that.

'My father worked there,' I said. Not that it mattered to

me; it was just that he worked hard enough for a government employee.

'Oh! Debashish Roy? Now I get it. It just slipped out of my mind. You want me to apologize for what I just said. I won't, because you don't want me to. But yes, your father. He worked really hard. Why do you think he got the transfer?'

'Okay.' Dad never ceased to make me proud. Although working in a PSU after IIT(D) isn't what people expect. If only he worked in an MNC... I missed my Lexus.

'No, it's not okay. Count and tell. How many people are at their desks? Quick you have ten seconds,' he said and started looking at his watch.

'Everybody, I guess.'

'That took 18 seconds. 18 seconds and still a wrong answer. The answer is nobody. You are not at your desk if you are not working. Okay, another question. On how many screens do you see the screensaver on?'

'Everybody.'

'That's 3 seconds. And that's the right answer. That also means nobody has touched their computer screens for at least the last 10minutes. And it's just 10:30. Extended Monday morning blues huh?'

'Yes, maybe.'

'You don't speak much, do you?'

It's useless trying to blow spit bubbles in the direction opposite to a gale, I thought. He looked like a nerd but definitely didn't talk like one. I mean, he wasn't a stud but he sounded like a hyperactive hyper vocal genius.

Piping, Cost Engineering, Rotatory Equipment, Civil Department etc. etc. He was desperately trying to explain what each department did, but my brain diligently rejected such useless information.

I felt I knew more about BHEL than people get to know in their lives. This office was in sharp contrast with what I had imagined and heard of offices in DCE. Small town guys and girls flocked this place. From where they belonged, there was still a certain amount of prestige associated with government jobs. So consequently, whatever girls were there in the office, stuck to their group, the guys stuck to theirs. There was minimal interaction. Shrey was wrong; not everybody sleeps with everybody in all offices.

'This is the last department. Chemical processes. And that is my dream girl.'

'Who? What? That?' I exclaimed.

'Why? Isn't she good?' he asked with the innocence of a two year old who had just sketched his first drawing.

I looked at her. She was about ten shades darker than I was and I was, by no means, fair. She stood at five feet and wore an awkward pink suit. She could have passed by me a zillion times and I wouldn't have noticed. She had a sweet face but after Avantika and Vernita, I had set myself high standards.

'I know. You wouldn't like her. You must be going around with sexy mini-skirted girls. But she is a nice girl.'

'I am not going around with anybody,' I said. I didn't need to say that but I wanted to check whether it still pained. It so fucking did.

'Why? You broke up? I tell you this is the problem with Delhi girls. They are all like this. That's why I like her. She comes from my homeland, Bihar. Will you meet her?' Delhi girls? I wondered if it had anything to do with it. Maybe she actually had dumped me for somebody else.

'No... it's...'

'It's okay. Don't be shy.' He pulled my hand and pulled me all the way through the aisle. I was standing right in front of her. *Yes! I am so shy.*

'Hi Astha,' Amit said.

And for a moment, I felt I was back in the time when I first met Avantika. His cheeks had turned the loveliest shade of pink and his milky white complexion didn't help his cause either.

'Hi Amit. You here?' she said. She pulled her head out from beneath feet long sheets that had lines, semicircles, three fourth circles crisscrossing all over it. She fumbled with the sheets thrice before she managed to fold them into neat bundles. *Damn, all these guys are so organized, I wonder how they do it.*

'Err... umm... meet my new MT, Deb,' he stammered. For the first time that day, I saw him stumbling for words. I checked for stuffed toilet paper. None, nowhere.

'Hello,' she said.

'Good morning, ma'am,' I said

'Call me Astha.' She was sweet sounding too, a voice that matched her kind, docile face.

'Perfect,' I said.

'Amit, I have some work right now. Lunch break?'

'No problem. Bye,' he said, still blushing.

'Welcome to BHEL,' she said and wiggled her hand. Her inner palm was darker than the back of mine.

'Thanks. Bye.' We walked off.

As soon as we were out of her audible and visible range, he started to tug at my shirt and ask, 'Isn't she cute? Isn't she cute?' She was, without any doubt, the first girl Amit had talked to. There was no way Amit was past twenty. He could have hopped around in a school uniform and would have escaped notice.

'Hey, chill. Yes, she is cute. Are you guys going out?'

'I don't know. I once said I like her. But nothing then on.'

'What? Why? You said you like her, then why didn't you ask her out?'

'No. What do I say? What if she says no? How do I say that? Where do I take her?' he continued to tug and his eyes didn't leave me.

'The same way you said you like her.'

'You mean I should mail that?' he asked, his gaze never left me. His tone got more paranoid with every passing second.

'You mailed that? *You mailed that?* Did you actually just mail that? And you have never talked about it, you motor mouth?' *Not again! No mails again!*

'Why? What is wrong in that? She sent me her Piping Stress sheets and I mailed her back saying I liked it. I even said I loved them.'

'You liked her *designs*? You didn't say you like *her*?'

'NO! Obviously not. Are you crazy? I cannot say that. But I said I liked her work. I even said I loved them. Isn't that enough?'

'*No, it is not!* How do you plan to lay her? Or marry her? Sex? Or will you do it with her designs?' DCE legacy strikes. Sex is all we can think and talk about.

'Deb? What are you talking about? There is still a lot of time for that... and I will learn when the time comes.' He was visibly scandalized. So was I, the *dumbness* of Amit had caught me off guard.

'There isn't a lot of time, dude. You are what? Twenty three. She must be...'

'I am twenty five, she is twenty four.'

'Oh great! She is twenty four? When do you plan to say something? When she gets married off? By Bihar standards, she is already over age.'

'Don't say that,' he said and hung his head as if it was his fault. But he was a twenty five year old virgin. In circles in which Avantika and I moved around, people did that number in a year.

We had switched places. He was not in charge then. I was. He was the trainee. I was comfortable.

'Anyway, we will figure something out,' I said.

'Yes, now tell me did you like anything?' he asked.

The process department had twice the number of girls all the other departments had, combined. No one was smart enough, though. After Avantika, my tastes had changed too. I was spoilt. I was hers.

The girls are waiting.

Amit Moves In, Turned Down

'Deb, watch out. Open the first file in the second directory,' Amit shouted at me in whispers as he walked closely behind a big bulky drowsy eyed old man. I still hadn't learnt doing anything in the first two months at BHEL except getting coffee for Amit from time to time. I pretty much did whatever he asked me to.

In BHEL, there were no parties, there were no gorgeous girls, and there were no office trips. It was an engineering firm, and as expected, it had a sad crowd, mostly guys, sad ones – the *ghissus*. Gender ratio is what I missed. I passed out from an engineering college to reach another. Same discussions. Same jokes. Same porn preferences.

Some classes used to happen thrice a week under some of the senior employees. They introduced us to fundamental concepts of piping and other things that – to my surprise – no one listened to. There were some eight of trainees in the piping department. Each one of them was dutifully told by their mentors that all classes were sham. You learn everything on the job, this is what the buzz was around the classes. I did not think it was necessary to talk to anyone else other than Amit. Sometimes Astha.

I did go around the office looking for some good-looking people to talk to, but I found none. None close to what Avantika was. I did initiate conversations with a few (which used to raise quite some eyebrows given the kind of people I was surrounded with) but used to lose interest after I exchanged the first hello. Avantika had left me in deep, *deep* trouble.

Just as I had opened the file, the oldie reached my cubicle and started to stare at my computer screen. He didn't say anything just stared at the strange combination of pipes that lay in front of me. He bent over and moved his face within microns of the monitor; his armpits stank of sour yogurt.

I had a look at those pipes and at once, I realized it wasn't my cup of tea. I started sharpening my pencil again.

'So, working hard?' he bawled in my ear.

'Huh? Yes sir.' I stood and breathed.

'Sharpening pencils won't do. Do something. I know how you got here. But don't think it's easy working here. You have to work to survive. You have to be smart, just working hard won't do,' he said as he leaned on to me.

Surviving hadn't been too tough. All it meant was getting coffee and writing semi-mushy mails to Astha on Amit's behalf, which were wrenched out of all their mush once Amit edited them. Training period anywhere in the world is a honeymoon period. And just in case it's a government office, you can be gone a year and nobody would notice. Unless, of course, your father used to work in the same office.

He continued, 'Get it? How is your dad? In Hyderabad? Whatever. Get back to work and I want to have your first isometric sheet done by Monday. I haven't got even one yet.'

I saw him for the first time and he already acted smart with me. I just kept myself from sticking that pencil up his hair-infested nose, which had more of hair than his barren head.

'Okay sir.'

He went off.

'Gosh! Now *that* was a narrow escape. He nearly had you in,' Amit said.

'Excuse me? Who the hell *is* he? I didn't think anybody

around me can be of any damn consequence?'

'No. Not anybody. He can be. He is just back from a tour. Mr. Goyal is the one who was passed over for your dad's promotion. So he wouldn't take kindly to you. He is the HOD.'

'*So?* What can he do? He can't possibly kick me out,' I said. I was an employee of the Government of India. I had to be dead or mentally unstable to lose the job. *Mentally unstable* I was, but he would never know about Avantika.

'He can,' he said.' Till the time you are a trainee. This one year, he can. He will take your viva one year from now. He can easily kick you out then. So better be careful.' *This is just a temporary arrangement*, I reminded myself.

'Nothing will happen, especially when you are here.' I swirled around in my new chair. Amit and I were the first ones to get them as I had pestered the hell out of the store in-charge.

'Deb! You are taking things too lightly. Did you read the manual I gave you yesterday? Obviously, you did not. What the hell do you think you are doing? You haven't even bothered to go to the site once. I tell you, you are going to be in big trouble. And how do you think you will do the pipe section he asked you to complete?'

'How am I? What are *you* here for, genius? You are going to do it, not me.' I broke my record of eight complete three-hundred-and-sixty degree revolutions, I pushed even harder. I wasn't taking things lightly. These chairs were better.

'And what do I get this time?'

'A gift. A beautiful romantic gift. You want that? Or should I just start the pipe section? Maybe I am taking things too lightly. Maybe I should start working.' I started to fiddle with the files.

'Okay... okay, okay. Don't touch those files; you will mess up the order. I need that. I will do it for you. What are you making for her? Is it expensive? That's not a problem; I will pay you for that. But please make something good. When are we giving that?'

'It will be good. Don't you worry,' I said. This was the usual. During the first two months, I wasn't required to do anything other than type out certain things or fill out excel tables. It was all the mentally numbing work that seniors didn't want to do anymore.

All the MTs were required to do that. Except me. Amit did everything for me for the return of my services in the Astha project. And that was fair in a way too. Amit was too smart to be working in a government office. What used to take me hours to do was just a minute's work for him. He tried really hard to teach me certain things but I was too stubborn about letting nothing affect my ignorance. We were living out a symbiotic relationship. It was the *only* relationship I had at that point.

'So, are you shifting in today?' I asked him. I badly needed a roommate. Even now, the moment I stepped out of the office, I was clouded by thoughts of Avantika. The intensity was much less now, though. *Maybe*. It had been three months since I had last contacted her but she was still very much around me all the time... I missed her. The laughs, the seductions, the touches, the winks. I missed it all. Still no movement on her Facebook account.

Nobody was a better choice than Amit for a roommate. He too had nothing much in his life. Everybody in the office who didn't matter hated him. He was excessively smart for them to handle. For those who mattered, he was a gem. All the seniors loved him. I think they saw a little bit of themselves in him when they had joined, not for the lure of a lazy sinecure job, but the passion to do something. What did they make out of it? Nothing.

Most importantly, I had come to love him. He was a cute lost kid in love, who knew nothing about it. I was the kid in office, who wanted to know nothing about it. A few months had passed and Avantika vacated a tiny part of my brain, which was promptly hammered in with CAT by Amit. He knew I would fuck up my career if I were to stay there for more than year. I knew that too, but... It was still three months to CAT and Amit was the only one who had the patience to remind me of that every day, every time.

'Yes, I am moving in today. The truck would arrive at 8:30. Wouldn't it be so cool? Then I will call up Astha whenever I want to and you can tell me what all to say. Thanks, Deb. But I will pay you the rent. You will have to accept that.'

'Fuck off, Amit. Either you get the house without the rent or you don't get it.'

'Okay, as you say. But—' I stopped him. I refused, although the temptation to add to the meagre salary was great but I had started to love him. Moreover, he was doing me a favour by staying with me.

'Deb... Deb! Will we call her tonight? I mean, can we?'

'Sure, Amit. Can you now please complete the sheet?' I had been trying to make him call her since the time I had joined office but he had some or the other inexplicable reason not to call her.

But that night we finally did. Amit left the office early that day to oversee the shifting.

And I spent the rest of the day sharpening pencils. I couldn't break my record.

'What the fuck?' I exclaimed. 'Did you do all that? You know what? You have to be gay to do all this.'

He had cleaned up the entire flat. It wasn't my place anymore. The place had been a mess since the time mom left. And not only did he clean up the room, he had also replaced all the flowers in the vases or put some where there weren't any. But I should have expected that. He was the only one in the entire office who used a dustbin for pencil shavings. There was even a paper Mache lamp that he had put in the drawing room. It so suited the setting, it seemed to have grown out of it. Avantika loved paper Mache lamps.

'You like it?' he asked.

'I like it? I love it. See, this is the reason I won't take any rent from you. I don't need a housemaid anymore.'

'Do you have a housemaid? This place didn't look as if it had been cleaned in ages...'

'No, I do not.'

'Never mind, now that I am here. Everything will be just fine,' he said rubbing his hands together.

I hoped so. We spent the next few hours unpacking his stuff and placing it in his new cupboard. My house started as a modest two-bedroom apartment, but then as we grew in size, so did the flat. We extended our house wherever and however it possibly could. It ended as a huge three bedroom flat with a humungous balcony, though we never felt it was big enough. I shifted into the master bedroom and Amit shifted into mine.

I was relieved of the unpacking duty when he finally said that I wasn't arranging things, I was stuffing them. I lay back then and watched him arrange his clothes, the idols and the photo frames in neat patterns. I wondered how people like him think. What makes them think that a perfectly, or almost perfectly arranged closet can be arranged in a better manner? Where does that thought originate? What drives them to do it? What difference does a neat closet make in their lives? If I do it, will it bring Avantika back? Just as I was slipping into arbitrary thoughts of Avantika, Amit brought me back to my senses.

'So, do we call her up now? I have been waiting to do this for a year now. Please. Please. I promise to be your pipe sheet slave all my life. Please do this.'

'As if it's me who has stopped you from doing so. Go ahead. Call her.' I tossed the phone to him. *Are you crazy? A year? It took me three days to call Avantika up! And we had kissed before that!*

Astha and Amit never talked to each other. They had the strangest relationship possible. They liked each other. Everyone knew that. But they were downright terrified at the mere thought of talking to each other. Even during their lunch meeting, they used to transform into dumb, smiling statues after the first few seconds of customary hellos. All my attempts to start a conversation fell on deaf ears.

The only one who used to talk was Astha's best friend, Neeti. I knew that Neeti had a crush on me. To make things worse, she made a thousand nails on a blackboard sound like pure symphony. She talked or *shrilled* and *shrieked* a lot more than required. I had decided I would hold her responsible if Amit and Astha never became a couple.

'Are you sure I should call her up? Is this the right time? What if she is not awake? Maybe we shouldn't. Or can I just send a message and ask her? What do I do?' Amit repeated these things as he paced around the room.

'Okay, I will call her up. And then you can talk. Is that fine?' I said as I stretched for the first time on my bed. For the last two months, I had been sleeping on the couch because I turned out to be too lazy to clear the newspapers and Dominos' boxes strewn across the bed.

'Yes, you can do that. But then don't tell her I am here.'

'Great. How do I ask her to talk to you? Telepathy?'

'Okay, do whatever you want to. Do it quick.' He was still shaking up the foundations of my flat.

'Hi Astha!'

'Hi Deb.'

'What are you doing? I hope you are not busy.'

'No, Neeti and I just finished the dishes.' Amit had already drifted into his daydreams. This was the longest sentence he had heard from her.

'Okay. Actually, Amit and I were kind of getting bored. So we thought we would bore somebody else too.'

'No, it's okay. You tell me. How are you finding the work?' Amit had shit his pants for all I could say. I could tell he was feeling insecure. He always did that when he saw other guys talking to her.

'It's good. I was just wondering, I mean, if you aren't doing anything, whether we could meet up. Amit really has something important to tell you.'

'Am… it? Oh… it's very late. I won't get an auto back home. I… am… Sorry.'

'Don't think about that. I will drop you home. I don't think that will be problem.'

'Um… Err… Neeti isn't well too. Can we do this some other time? If he doesn't mind?' Amit stopped pacing and sat down beside me, pretending to read the newspaper, big tears edging his eyes.

'Never mind. It's okay. It wasn't anything important. We will meet up whenever it is convenient for you.'

'I am very sorry, I couldn't come,' she said. Amit rolled over the bed covering his face with the newspaper.

'It's fine. Never mind! Ohh! The match is on. Can I catch you later?'

'Okay, bye. And I am sorry. I am very sorry,' she said.

'It's alright, bye.' Click. I disconnected the call and turned to Amit, 'Hey dude! Are you crying?'

'No, I am not,' he squeaked and sniffed.

'Yes, you are. It's okay. She said, we would do it some other time. She couldn't help it. Neeti was ill.'

'Shut up. She was lying. First, she said she couldn't come because she wouldn't get an auto. Then suddenly Neeti fell ill. I tell you, she doesn't like me! What if she already has a boyfriend? Or maybe her parents have already seen a guy for her? Maybe she likes Kumar from the equipment department? Damn Deb. What do I do? Why did she do this to me? What did I do wrong?' Amit had again slipped into one of his hyper paranoid motor mouthing sessions. *Why did Avantika turn me down?*

'Hey. First, you haven't done anything wrong. You haven't done anything. And she definitely doesn't have a boyfriend. Or a suitor. Whatever.'

'Then why did she turn me down?' he asked and wiped off discharges from various places. I wondered whether he would allow the yellow stain to become a crust before he wipes with his shirt again. He didn't.

'She didn't turn you down. She just said we will do it some other time.'

'But why?'

'Maybe it was just too sudden. Maybe she wanted some time to get ready and stuff. You know that, don't you? These girls... they need a lot of time to decide what they have to wear on their first date. That needs a lot of planning. Maybe she didn't want to disappoint you by looking bad on her first date.'

'But she never looks bad. I like her the way she is.' Amit sometimes behaved so cutely that I felt like kissing him. He reminded me of myself, pre-college, pre-make outs, and pre-night outs. *I like you the way you are. Please come back...*

'Maybe, but she doesn't know that. Have you told her that? No, you haven't. So how do you expect her to know? You don't speak much. Do you?'

'No,' he said. *I had said.*

'I knew that. Maybe she even wants to look better.'

'Better?' he exclaimed. He again reminded me of myself. When I used to look at Avantika without even an iota of lust in my eyes, before I first saw her naked. But he was much dumber than I was.

'Yes, better,' I said.

'Deb, you always get the girls you want. That is why you don't understand me. I love her, but there is nothing I can do. I cannot talk to her like you do. I cannot be as cool as you are. I am scared Deb. Will I ever get her?' he asked, as he sobbed softly.

'That is not true, Amit. And you know that. I loved Avantika, but...' I trailed off.

'I am sorry, Deb. I forgot. I am very sorry. Let us not talk about this.'

We kept quiet for a while. Before he started again. 'But tell me, have you ever felt like I am feeling right now?' he asked.

'As in?' I asked. He intended to change the topic as he saw life being sucked out of me, but he couldn't do it as well as I would have liked him to.

'I mean, have you had a crush? Like running after somebody and trying to catch her attention? Being helpless in expressing your love? I have never liked somebody the way I like her,' he asked.

'For better or worse, I was quite like you in school. I had this ten-year long crush on a girl, Manisha, but I could not get her. I could never tell her. Not in the way I wanted to. You at least exchange hellos. I didn't have the courage to do even that. All I did was to stare at her for days hoping something would happen. Quite obviously nothing did. Before Avantika came, I always dated girls that resembled her. Small, fair, cute. I thought a lot about her, till Avantika came around and change everything,' I said.

Ten years? Fuck you, Deb! You were a loser! That is what Avantika said. Manisha sort of knew about my crush and so did my entire batch. But in those times I defined the word – undate-able. That would not have changed even if I happened to be the last guy living. But after school, I lost weight, lost conscience, gained oodles of confidence in the year I had dropped before getting to DCE and dated with vengeance. I became directionless personified. Many girls, Manisha look-alikes, were dumped in the process.

'Are you trying to scare me? What will happen to me? I cannot wait ten years. She will get married. What should I do, Deb?' He went paranoid again.

'Chill, Amit. You have me. I didn't.'

'Do you think I will get her?'

'Yes, you will.' I was glad I didn't get her. I would have never known how beautiful life could be. Not to forget, how sexy and wild too.

Great Challenges, Symbiotic Lives

'Get up. Get up. Get up, Deb! DEB!' It took me quite some time before I realized that it wasn't a dream that Amit was trying to wake me up. He actually was trying to do that.

'Ahh... it's just 8, Amit. Go to sleep,' I yawned.

'The punching time is 8:40. We've got to leave right now,' he said.

'We will be going by car, you ass. Won't take more than 20 minutes. Let me sleep. Anyway the guard will do the punching thing.'

'What guard?'

'What do you mean what guard? He is the one who punches my card. So I can go a... a... as late as I want to. Or miss it if I want to.' I turned around to see Amit, as he stood there, dressed and his briefcase in his hand. 'Oh shit! You are ready. It will still take me an hour to find my underwear.'

'Please hurry. I will let the guard punch my card tomorrow too, but please get up now. Just today. Tomorrow, I promise we will sleep together. And go a... a... as late as you want to, but hurry up. Have you done your sheets? Obviously, you haven't. Have you made the gift? No, you haven't. What the hell do you think you are doing? If you don't want your ass to be kicked out, get up and get ready.'

At last, I felt like hauling my ass up to office. Getting kicked out of a government owned firm? Now *that* would have been a failure.

We reached the office about five minutes late. The guard was quite surprised to see me so damn early. I handed over Amit's ID to him and instructed him to do the same. It took me quite some time to convince Amit to do the possible career-damaging move. It is only the punching of your I-card that counts. The accounts department had no idea whether you had been to office or not, if you card is punched every day. I owed the guards at least half my salary.

Just as we settled down at our computers, the sound boomed again. It was the sound I had come to hate the most. It was Mr. Goyal again.

'So, Deb? Are you ready with your sheets?' he asked with the same demonic smile running across his face. I could break that face without a speck of guilt in me.

'Yes sir, I am almost done with it,' I said. I didn't even know which sheet he was shouting about. But I didn't want him to win.

'Ohh? That's good to hear. Finding it too easy, gentleman? Quite like your dad. He never used to respect the Piping department. He too found it easy. So, it's easy?' I knew he was throwing me a challenge and it would be foolish to accept it. But then, this was my father's battle. I didn't want to let him down, even though he probably wouldn't even know about it.

'It is not that tough, that's all I can say.'

'Okay, then I want the full isometrics of the BINA refinery project ready by tomorrow. Sharp 9. Best of luck,' he said and rolled away. I could now break open his jaw, burst open his tummy and hang him by his sack till it burst open too.

I knew I had won the psychological battle, but he won the verbal one. There was no way the whole piping floor combined could have completed the work. Let alone, Amit. For me, I had to take at least a hundred births just to think about doing it. I was told all this by Amit. I did not know what Goyal had asked me to do. It was only after I repeated what Goyal said word by word to a flabbergasted Amit, that I came to know what I had put my hands into.

'*Are you mad?* How are you supposed to do it? Okay, how am *I* supposed to do it? That's designing at least twenty five pipes. *In a day.* Even if I do at the pace of one an hour, it will still take a whole day. Oh great, we are already an hour short. Why are you looking at me like that? I am not going to do it. Not for anything that you give me. It's twenty five pipes. The whole department takes a month to do that. No, not this time.'

I knew he would do it. His non-stop blabbering meant he was thinking how to go about it.

'Okay, fine. I was thinking of asking them out tonight but since you won't do it for anything in the world, let's drop that plan.'

'Were you? Seriously? What if she refuses again? Please do something. You promised you will.' Our symbiotic relation kicked in again.

'I will do it. But just in case... '

'Okay, I will do it. But I won't be able to do all of it. It's a lot to do. But I will try. I promise, I will try.'

'Why do you think I care? That bastard knows this can't be done. Just do five or six and that would be enough for me to kick his ass.'

'Fine, but when will you ask them about tonight? I mean, do that early, you know, girls take time for planning their first date and all,' he said, trying to mimic me.

'Ohh! Is it? Why don't you go and do it yourself, then?' I said.

'Why don't *you* go and do these sheets yourself, then?' he challenged.

'Okay, you win. I am off.' I left for the eighth floor where Astha worked.

The only thing that made my days was the unsaid love between these two. They were these grown kids who had never loved or lusted before. I loved being around them. In a way, I felt close to Avantika. I too loved her, a lot. Just that it didn't work out. But I wanted this to work out. I knew it wouldn't be easy to convince Astha and Neeti to agree for a date... let alone one extending beyond sunset. But the refusal the day before was kind of smoother than what I had expected from a small town girl. She hadn't been very clever while turning it down, but I had expected it to be worse.

Amit had been trying to convince me for a day date, but I knew that would make no sense. It wouldn't make any difference. Both of them would have found something interesting around them to stare at, rather than actually talk.

I entered the eighth floor. It had been quite some time since I actually moved out of my small world of office, Amit and my place. So, for a moment, I did find the girls there bordering on attractive. *The girls are waiting.*

I tried to shrug off thoughts of Shrey. He had been having quite some fun with his equally desperate IIT buddies. He never did forget to mail me about that. I never replied.

Astha wasn't there. However, I spotted Neeti at the coffee dispenser.

'Hi Neeti.'

'Hi Deb? Sorry we couldn't come yesterday. I wasn't well. Hope you didn't mind. Plus it was so late in the night... Can't we do it in the morning time? Weekends. Fun, no? But I am *so* sorry.'

'It's okay. Do you have any idea as to where Astha is?' I replied after trying to make sense out of what she just shrieked.

'Oh, Astha! Look. Think of the devil and she is here. Hi Astha, Deb is looking for you.'

'Hi Deb. I am really sorry...' Astha said as she put a few strands of hair behind her ear. She almost dropped the fifty odd rolls of sheets precariously held beneath both her armpits.

'It's okay. You don't have to apologize.' It had almost become a kind of reflex action for them. I had cancelled a million plans with my friends and could never recall a single time when I have apologized. Maybe *that* was the difference.

'Anyway, now that I see Neeti is pretty much okay and I know Amit and I would have nothing to do tonight as well, I am asking you out again. And this time you don't have an option. I will pick you up at nine. Right?'

'Perfect. I would be only too happy to come,' Neeti screamed as if she just saw her positive pregnancy report.

'And you, Astha?'

'Yes, sure Deb. Nine it is.' She couldn't possibly blush with the complexion of hers but had she been any fairer, she would have looked like a ripe tomato. A pink tomato.

I bumped into Amit just as I moved out of the process department. Apparently, he had been there all this while, trying to gauge something from our expressions. 'So, Deb? Did she say yes?' he asked.

I didn't answer and stared at him with a dull stolid expression. I loved to do that.

'Deb? Please don't do that. Tell me. Say something.'

'You should better get down to work. You have a hell of a lot to do,' I said.

The very next moment he picked up all eighty kilograms of me and shouted the living daylights out of me. Needless to say, he was happy. Very happy indeed.

I left the office early that day. I had promised to make a gift for Astha. Something that he could give her when they went out for the first time. More than for him, I wanted to do that for myself. The gift I was to make for her was the one I had planned to make for Avantika, but never got a chance.

The gift didn't take that long. I had already made it a thousand times in my head and because I didn't make it myself.

I had a designer friend who used to design packets for bakeries. So he hardly took an hour to put everything together. It was a beautiful small square paperweight made out of paper Mache. Its five of the six faces had the initials of Astha and a paragraph written about the good things in her that started with those.

As Avantika and Astha shared three initials, the writing part wasn't that tough. It turned out beautifully. It was big enough not to get lost and small enough to be used as a paperweight. Something that she could keep with her at all times. How I wish I could have gifted it to Avantika. Her name even had six letters.

'Deb, this is beautiful. I didn't know you could make such a thing,' Amit said. I realized it was not just the girls who had a reflex *sorry*, even Amit had a reflexive *thank you*.

'It's okay. But will you please sit down now? We are not leaving before eight.' It was 6:30.

'Eight? But they live so far off. It would take at least one and half hour to reach there?' he said.

'Half an hour Amit, just half an hour. Sit down and relax. Don't tire yourself out. And I would be thankful if you start with the work till the time we aren't leaving,' I said.

'What if there is a traffic jam? What if we get late? A flat tyre? Anything can happen.' I was about to kill him.

'Late? It's three hours to go. We are already dressed up and I have the car keys in my hand. And you think we will get late? Have you totally lost it?' I shouted.

'Okay, I am sorry. Don't get angry now. Please,' he said and silence took over. Only for while, though. 'Does that mean I still have time to change my shirt?'

'Okay, that's it. Now I *do* have to kill you,' I said and darted towards him. He ran and bolted himself in his room. 'Good for me, Amit. I am not letting you out before nine. I am sorry, I lied.' I bolted the door from outside.

The next few hours were the noisiest ever. Amit kept on

shouting for an hour or so and then shut up. He must have slept off, I thought. Or maybe he hadn't. Maybe he was doing the sheets. That's what I'd hoped for, at least.

'Deb, can't you drive a little faster?' Amit said as he tugged *constantly at my shirt as he always did whenever he was nervous.*

'Don't you worry, buddy. We will be there by ten.'

'*By ten?* That's an *hour* late. Deb, why don't you ever listen to me? I am elder to you. I got late in the morning too. Why *do you do this to me? Don't you like me or what? Okay, leave* that. I have a whitener with me. Can we just erase the love you part from this paragraph? I mean, isn't it too early? What if she doesn't like it?'

'This is my favourite song. One word more and I will throw you off.' It was my favourite song. The first one Avantika had dedicated to me. *Accidentally In Love – Counting Crows.*

I never could figure out why you remember these things *when they don't matter anymore. The funny part – you never* remembered them when they mattered. Okay, I just lied; Avantika and I celebrated every monthly anniversary, our 50th *date, the 100th date, our first kiss, absolutely everything.* I was looking forward to the 20th of May, the day our relationship started; our one-year anniversary, but Avantika had other plans. She had left me by then. She saved me a lot of money, though.

'Sorry,' Amit said and looked away.

He was such a kid, fifteen not twenty four. I wished to be him. I wished to be me. I wished to be Avantika's toothbrush.

The Girls Were Waiting

'Where are we going?' Neeti shrieked in my ear. I was on my knees until they were scraped but Amit refused to sit in the back seat with Astha. As a result, I had to turn the rear view mirror to an awkward angle *so that Amit could see her and vice versa.* Everyone was blushing. It was a pink world out there.

'I don't know. You tell me,' I said.

'India Gate! India Gate! India Gate!' Neeti jumped up and down. *The transformation was complete.* I was a babysitter, now stuck with two shy kids and one over-zealous one. I didn't drink or dance. But I loved going to nightclubs… a thing that I had picked up from Avantika.

Now, it had been two months since I had started earning and I hadn't spent a single penny. All my expenses were taken care of either by my parents or Amit. Still, I thanked the moment I hadn't suggested a nightclub to them. They were still seven.

I waited for quite some time for somebody else to speak but nobody did. Amit and Astha were too busy playing hide and seek in the rear view mirror. Shrey would have been blowing kisses by now, or kissing her real good had he been in the back seat.

'India Gate is fine by me. Amit? Astha?' I asked.

'Hmm... fine,' Amit said.

We reached India Gate at around 11:30 p.m. I had taken a very long route, as I didn't want too many people hanging around. There weren't. It wasn't that bad a choice. In addition, that meant more time with the three of them. Neeti, I am not sure, but I simply loved the other two.

The imposing India Gate was looking like it always did - *imposing*. I had often thought of reading the names written on it and counting them, but never got the time to do so. Clubbing took that time away.

The few people that were in the huge lawns were winding up their picnic stuff to leave. I also used to come there often with mom and dad as a kid. The rag pickers had already started picking up the pieces families had left behind. I too was doing the same. *Picking up the pieces.*

We crossed the arched metal ropes that marked the boundary of the lawns and walked towards the lake. I quite liked this place as a kid.

'So, Neeti. We are here. Want some ice cream?' I asked, as I wanted to leave them alone for a while.

'Yes sure. Let's go. Let's go! I did see them somewhere. Where did they go? Where? Where? Let's go. Where is that?' she asked.

'Over there,' I motioned.

'Let's go,' Amit said.

'Amit, you don't have to accompany us. We just want some time alone. Do you mind?' I asked. And expectedly, he didn't get it. He started giving me the *naughty-you* look. But till the time he didn't come with us, I was fine.

'Okay, we will just wait here,' he said. Astha seemed to have found something really interesting about the earthworms crawling about, as she never bothered to look up.

'They love each other, don't they?' Neeti asked nudging me rhythmically with her elbow.

'Yeah, I think so. But they never talk. They never meet up. I hope they do this time.'

'That's why you came alone with me here. Very smart, you are. I knew always,' she said.

'Yes, very smart,' I said. I tried not to further the eardrum risking conversation. I looked back to how Amit was doing. They were facing each other, all right. But I was sure they hadn't exchanged a single word. He was fiddling with the paperweight that jutted out from his back pocket.

'They are not talking, still? I know. She is always like that. She never speaks in front of him. You know what? I wasn't ill yesterday. She didn't want to come. She is old fashioned, you know? I am not like that. I wanted to come. But she said it's not right to go out like this. I am always ready. I am very modern.'

I had gotten used to such nonsensical blabbering from her. When I first met her, I thought she was a lunatic. Though she wasn't, but she came pretty close to it.

'I hope they do talk,' I said as we dragged our feet to the ice cream vendor. 'Hey, I am getting a call. Just hold on,' I said.

It was Shrey.

'Hey dude! What's up?' he had already picked up an accent. An American one from Germany.

'Your accent is up for one,' I said.

'Sorry *yaar*! You know, having an accent here helps. With the girls, you know!'

'I don't want to know. By the way, where are you calling from this time? Military headquarters?'

'Nope. I am at a German friend's place. And she is *so* hot and has a great ass, man! I am staying at her place for a while.'

'So life is great, huh?' I said mockingly.

'Great? It's awesome, man. The project is going great. We have finally managed to incorporate a special electronically controlled gearing mechanism that divides the fuel...'

'Why do you think I care? Just cut out that part.'

'Okay, never mind.' Amit would have said sorry after this, I thought. Even Astha.

He continued, 'But the sex is great, man. You should come over sometime.'

'Sorry, but I am not interested.'

'You still haven't got over her, have you? Go out man, have some fun.'

'I am having fun, Shrey,' I said irritably.

'Is it so? Where are you?'

'Am out with friends... and I am having fun,' I said as I walked away from her.

'Guys or chicks?'

'Two couples. Happy?'

'How's your chick?' he asked. I looked at Neeti, who smiled. She wasn't bad if not for her badly buckled jeans, frilly top and the eighties make up. And the way she spoke. Or behaved.

'She is good.'

'Did you sleep with her?'

'Why are you sounding like Virender?'

'No, seriously. Go out there and give her the time of her life. You are Deb, after all. She is waiting, man. All the girls are waiting. By the way, I called up Virender too. Yoginder was there too. They still share a room. They said they miss you.'

I didn't care. They almost didn't exist for me. But it did make me feel better. I made a mental note of calling them, though I never did.

'Have to hang up now. Bye.'

'Bye, Shrey.'

'Do sleep with her. Do it for me. And yes, saw Suhel's profile. He has put up his picture with Vandana up there. Bloody asshole. Anyway, bye.' Click. He was sex-ing himself to death. But I still didn't wish to be him, I wished to be Amit. I wished to be Avantika's mirror. Or even doormat wouldn't be bad. Ceiling fan would have been better. At least I would be able to look at better things.

Shrey still loved Vandana, I thought as I walked back to Neeti.

'Deb, I think they talked. I saw them. He gave her something when you were talking. So sweet, no? What was that?' her excitement level not dipping a teeny-weeny bit.

'Nothing. Let them see.' I couldn't actually tell whether they were talking but she was alternating between looking at the gift and him. Eye contact was a huge step forward. And that meant I had to stay away from them for a lot longer.

'Deb? Deb! Tell me! How many girls have you gone out with? How many?'

'There have been a few,' I answered, not striving for any real conversation.

'I expected this. Never mind, how many have you kissed? What does it feel like? Do you think they will do that today? Tell, tell, tell.'

It came back. *The girls are waiting.* I was trying to keep this away from my mind. But Neeti was as easy as they come. I could have got her to do anything within days. It had been months since I even talked to anybody else than these two girls.

'It feels good. Why do you think everybody keeps doing it all the time?'

'You are *so* lucky. You must have done it so many times. Tell me no, how do you do it?' This was going to be a long evening.

'It's pretty easy if you ask, and doesn't matter how you do it as long as you are in love.' *Pointless slobbering of tongues.*

'Okay, tell me more! When did you do it the first time? Where did you do it? You are not telling me anything. This is not fair. Tell, please no, please no, please no,' she screeched.

'I don't remember,' I said.

'What do you mean you don't *remember*? Try Deb, try! Okay,

when was your first kiss. Where did you do it? How was it? I am so sure you remember that. Now don't lie, you have to tell me something. I am your friend, no? Pleeeease!'

I remembered every second of it. If my memory allowed a little more, I could have told how many times I exhaled that night. 'I don't know. That's too personal,' I said as I stretched out on the lawns. The starless sky wasn't as enamouring as it had been on my Farewell night. *Nothing was.*

'I am sorry to have asked.' That happened to be her shortest shrill that day.

'Don't be.'

I turned to see how Amit was doing. They were doing better. They still won't talk to each other but their eyes were locked for sure. They sat on the bench close to the lake under a big tree. There couldn't have been a more ideal place. Smriti and I once had sex there, at five in the morning. We had driven all night to find a place where we could park and make out. We didn't find any. My car windows weren't tinted, so that didn't help us either. Eventually, we came to that place in a dire need for a walk after the long drive. We had no intentions of doing anything out there as it was almost morning. But our fate, horny as it was, had other plans. As we sat on the bench, the hug gave way to groping and within a few moments I had my jeans zipped down till my knees while she was literally naked, breathing heavily and moaning as I pushed myself into her, clawing in deep at her thighs. I had bundled her skirt in a lump near her waist and pulled her top right up to her neck. A few morning walkers were close by, but we carried on. Maybe we didn't know they were there or the risk of somebody spotting us egged me on. It had started raining then. We carried on until the rain became a little hard to handle. We had to rush back to the car parked alongside the railing. Half naked. The car had fogged up from the inside due to the rain. And we finished the unfinished business.

Her thongs were still on that bench. We decided to leave

them behind. That day was right up there in my list of make outs. Any such list is incomplete without one in the open.

'Deb, why are you so lost? I know I am not interesting enough. I am sorry for boring you. Okay, you tell me what we should do now? Anything that you want. Okay, I will tell you something. You know that Kumar from the equipment department? You know, no?'

'Yes I know. Everybody knows him. The one who hits on everybody, I know.'

'No, you don't know then. He doesn't hit on everybody. I think he likes me. He comes to my desk at least twenty times a day. He likes me no then? What do you think? He likes me?'

'Yes, I really think he does.' It still wasn't helping.

I looked at Amit. His eyes were still set on Astha. I wondered if he was blinking. Or if Astha was blinking any less than a million times a second. Anyway it didn't seem real. Every second that Amit spent staring at Astha meant an extra second of humiliation from Mr.Goyal. *Twenty five sheets.*

'Yes, Astha. He is good. I think you should go around with him.'

'But I don't want to, I don't love him. I know he is good, but maybe he is not lucky enough,' she gave out a punctuated he-he giggle.

'Maybe you will start loving him. Go out and try him at least,' I said.

'But Deb, I don't love him. I love somebody else,' she said. For the first time I saw a hint of sadness in her eyes. It wasn't actually sadness. It just lost its twinkle and wasn't wide open like it always was. That is, she seemed normal in those moments.

'Who is it?' I asked. Although I said this, I knew what the answer would be. I started hoping she wouldn't come out with it. But knowing her, I knew she would even have told me what colour panties she was wearing had I asked.

'It's you, Deb.' *What a surprise.* I should have stayed shut.

'Won't you say anything? At least say something. Something. Please say something, no?'

'Neeti, I am not ready for this. And for you right now. I am sorry. This can't happen.'

'Deb, we can at least try. You just told me, go out with Kumar maybe you will start loving him. Please at least give a try, no? Deb? If it is not good, we would break up. I promise.'

Did I just have to make life tougher for myself? It was probably the first time I was turning down a girl. Life had been strange. When I loved break ups and crushes, I had to fight for them. Now that I didn't need them, they were in plenty.

'No, Neeti. I have been through all this and I just know that it will not work out. I am not the guy for you. It is just an infatuation. It will go away. Don't you worry. It will be over in a while. Like this.' I snapped my fingers to try to be funny. It didn't work. She stared at me as if I just aborted our love child.

'Deb, how can you say that? You don't even know me that well. Give it a try. I will be a good girlfriend, I promise. Please, Deb. Don't do this to me,' she said. I knew her well enough. She was an ear shattering, dumb clingy girl with absolutely no sense of style. Inner beauty is eternal. But not when they are packaged like Neeti was.

'I am sorry.' I did feel sorry for her. But more than anything, she seemed to be pleading more for an ice cream rather than a relationship.

'Deb, have you decided? Please think about it. Please do. *Think about it again. Okay, I will not say anything, you think.*'

'I am sorry,' I said.

'Deb, don't be sorry, just think. Close your eyes and think.'

'But—'

'Just think, Deb. Close your eyes.' She covered my eyes with her hand.

I closed my eyes and all I could see was Avantika. Yes, she

looked extremely sexy in formals, as she lugged a laptop.

'Nothing, Neeti. There can be nothing,' I said. I feared that she might kiss me when she closed my eyes. But she didn't.

'You didn't think! You opened your eyes too soon. I couldn't even kiss you,' she shrieked.

'What?' I exclaimed. I felt like a genius. Though, I missed out on a kiss. Did I want it? Maybe. Maybe not. I missed Avantika, but a kiss is just a kiss, nothing more.

'Yes, I would have kissed you and then had it felt good... that would mean you love me. That's easy, no?' she asked. She *was* a lunatic, after all.

'It doesn't happen that way. You have to be in love to kiss. I am not in love right now.' I didn't believe what I just said. Maybe I had gone insane too. *You have to be in love to kiss?*

The girls are waiting.

'You will love me someday, Deb. I know you will. You just have to,' she said and lay down beside me. We didn't share a word for the next hour or so. Amit and Astha were still in the same state. I wondered if they had died and rigor mortis had set in, cementing them in their place. I wondered what it would be like to kiss Neeti, if I were to forget Avantika for a few seconds. It wouldn't be too good, I knew. *But, what the heck, she isn't coming back to see what I had been up to. She doesn't even care. Maybe in some twisted way, I am getting back her.*

Another fifteen seconds and I decided against it. There were other considerations. I had lost Vernita to a kiss, though earned myself love, but I couldn't afford an Amit. Or an Astha.

It was already 2 a.m. Just seven hours to the rendezvous with Mr.Goyal. I finally decided to call it a night.

'Neeti, I think we should go home now.'

'As you say, Deb.' She still had the deadpan expression on her face.

'I presume nobody needs ice cream here.' I broke their stare.

'Err... no Deb,' Amit said as he woke up from his stupor.

'Shall we leave now? It's getting late. And we have work to do,' I said.

'Shit! It's two? Let's leave. I am sorry, Astha. We will have to go.' I had never seen him exchange a sentence so fucking comfortably. So I was a genius. We walked to the car and Astha and Amit climbed into the back seat.

'What happened, Amit? Don't want to see me drive?' I laughed at them.

'No,' he said shyly.

We dropped them at their flat and all the way, nobody spoke. In the back seat, they moved their lips continuously as if to say love you, but not actually making a sound. Amit tracked Astha right until the time she switched on her flat's light.

'Shall we go now?' I asked him.

'Hmm...' he said.

We drove off.

'Amit? Are you *crying*? Oh damn! *You are crying*? What the hell?'

He was sniffing lightly before, but just after I said these words, he burst out crying. I had seen this happen a million times, you ask a close to tears person if he or she is crying and they would definitely be crying after that.

'No...' he said, as he notched up his crying pitch.

'I thought everything was fine. You seemed fine. I thought everything went great. What happened?'

He kept on crying. *Wailing*, to be precise.

'For God's sake, tell me what happened? And stop crying,' I shouted.

'I am sorry Deb, I can't help it. But, but...' he trailed off.

'What? Tell me this very second or I will push you off.'

'I love her so much, but...'

'But *what*?' I sensed something was wrong.

'But I want to marry her.' He started crying again.

I feared the worst. What Amit had feared the day before.

Maybe her marriage was already fixed with somebody. I dreaded the answer but I gathered the courage to ask him.

'So, what's the problem?'

'Huh? Nothing, I want to marry her. I want to marry her. I want to marry her.' Another Neeti. He stopped crying and started looking at me perplexed.

'So, what's the catch? Why are you crying? Have her parents already seen someone?'

'No! What are you talking about? NO!' He wiped his tears off with his shirt. He wasn't old enough to use tissues.

'Then why the hell are you crying?' I shouted out of irritation.

'*What if she says no?* I really want to marry her,' he shook my hand off the gear stick.

'Is that all? You nearly had me *dead* there.'

'You think that's not a big deal?' he asked.

'Shut up, Amit. I got you till here. Trust me, I will get you there. Forget all that, tell me how many sheets have you done?'

'Sheets? None, till now. I haven't started.'

'You haven't started? What the hell were you doing when I locked you up in the room?'

'I wasn't doing the sheets, I was just thinking about Astha.'

'Are you crazy or what? It's almost three and I have just six hours to go. What the fuck, man! You promised.'

'I am sorry, Deb. Don't be so angry now. I swear I will do it. Don't you worry about it; it will be ready by morning. I am sorry.'

'You should be, man. Please do something at least when we get back home.'

'By the way, she loved the gift. Thanks, Deb. I wonder what would have happened if you were not with me,' Amit said as he sank into his seat and dreams.

'Whatever.'

We reached my place and I crashed moments later.

Sheets and Dates. Two Dates

I chose a very opportune time to save Avantika from the goons, let go of Avantika's leg and fall off the cliff so that she could hang on and live. I had insurance and she had cheated me to get it.

I woke up with a startle. It was 8 a.m.

I couldn't see Amit around. Though we had different rooms, we slept in one because it had the air conditioner. I walked out, rubbed my eyes to scoop the last of the yellowish viscous thing out, and entered into his room. He was awake.

'Good morning, Deb,' he shouted excitedly.

'Easy, Amit. Good morning.' I forgot that I had to be angry with him for the work he hadn't done for me.

'Guess what? I have done all the sheets. The third was a little tricky, its material was still posing a problem as there is a transition from mild steel to gray cast iron here, so I just used the composite material formula to...'

'Cut out the crap. Just tell me how much you have complet...' I was still groggy. I stared more intently at the gooey stuff with one eye. So it hadn't quite registered what he had just said. It finally did.

'WHAT? Did you say *all*? What? Don't tell me you just said all? *All*? Amit, you did it all?' I asked and cleaned my hand on my tracks.

'Yes, Deb, I have done it all.'

I was living with a God. I jumped on to his bed and bear hugged the life out of him. I felt the skeleton crumble to pieces.

'You really did this? How is this humanly possible? How on earth did you do it?' I still wasn't out of shock.

'It wasn't that tough. You see, there is symmetry between the rack pipes and the overhead pipes. The pipes have been designed in such a way that they are interchangeable, only the stresses and bending moments change, that too negligibly. So the calculations have to be just extrapolated with the equation I formulated that I have written in the eighth sheet. After you do that, it's just the displacements that have to be taken care of. That's when the computer takes over. Wherever the displacement gives a red mark on the data sheet, you just have to provide a dummy support and it's done. And the hanger part was easy too. There is set pattern of changes in strains in every part of the pipe. So it wasn't tough. It was the least I could I do... and Astha and Neeti helped me. They didn't sleep the whole night. It wouldn't have been possible without them...' he said, and I didn't want to interrupt him. He loved those incomprehensible shitty sheets. I envied him. He had a passion. I did not. *Except a certain Avantika.*

'Amit. I don't need to know any of that.' I still stared at him just as Astha had been doing, the previous day. 'I really love you guys... and you really love this bullshit, don't you?'

'Yes, Deb, very much,' he said and balled himself up shyly. I wouldn't have admitted it even over my dead body, even if I loved those pipes.

'So let's go out there and kick the hell out of Goyal's ass!'

'Sure, Deb. I would love to see you do that,' he said. Just as I turned to look for my underwear, he said, 'I have never had a friend like you.'

'Same here, Amit.'

I hadn't. I was glad that I had told him. Reciprocated is

equal to told. *Of course I loved him.*

'Deb, I just called up at his office. He is having a meeting with Mr. Malhotra, Planning department HOD and some other Piping people. He won't be back before 11. Seems like I had a lot of time. We could have slept for two hours last night,' he said.

'I am sorry, man! You all had to stay up all night for this bullshit.' He wouldn't have slept; he would have done it better.

'It's okay, Deb. Just go out there and show that you are as good as your dad. I know why you took this up. Although your dad would have jumped off this building had he seen you work. But it's okay, no two people are alike. He probably couldn't have got me Astha,' he said.

'I can bet on that.' I got up from my seat.

'Where do you think you are going? It's just 9:30,' he said.

'That's why I am going.' I turned to leave and left five pipe sheets behind.

'Deb! You left these?' he said.

'Seems like you had a lot of time in hand beyond those two hours too,' I said aloud as I walked towards the meeting room.

'May I come in, sir?' I said as I knocked and opened the door.

'Can't you see that I am busy? This is a meeting; your unimportant things can wait,' Mr. Goyal barked. I could see the fear in his eyes. I loved it. I moved in for the kill.

'Sir, I thought the twenty five pipes of BINA refinery that you gave me yesterday to do were important. I thought that's why you asked me to do it in a day. Sorry sir, I could just do twenty. Sir, if you say, I will complete the rest five in an hour or two if you need them today.' I tried to be as explicit as possible. As I finished, Goyal's head shrunk to the size of a pea. All the people alternated between staring at him and me.

Malhotra broke the silence. ' Mr. Goyal? Twenty five sheets? These are of the BINA refinery project? One day?' he looked at me. 'You did all of it in *one day?*'

A senior manager, Mr. Bhatli, looked at Malhotra and spoke, 'Sir, I am not sure about this. But this part was to be done at senior manager level. Definitely not at trainee level. Deb, aren't you? How did you do it? Can I have a look at the sheets, please?'

I walked up to him and handed out the sheets. Malhotra and the three senior managers started to peruse the sheets in sheer disbelief. Goyal looked as if he was choking, I could tell.

'What do you have to say about this?' Mr. Bhatli said as he handed over a sheet to Malhotra.

'This is pure genius. *One day?* Mr. Bhatli, how long would your team have taken to do this?' Malhotra asked.

'Five to six weeks at minimum, sir,' he said.

'How did you do it, Deb?' Malhotra asked. I hadn't realized till then that it was really *such* a big deal. My ex-girlfriend was a porn star and my roommate was a God. Sweet life.

'Sir, isn't as tough as it seems to be. You see, there is symmetry between the rack pipes and the overhead pipes. The pipes have been designed in such a way that they are interchangeable, only the stresses and bending moments change, that too negligibly. So the calculations have to be just extrapolated with the equation I formulated and that I have written in the eighth sheet. After you do that, it's just the displacements, which have to be taken care of. That's where the computer takes over. Wherever the displacement gives a red mark on the data sheet, you just have to provide a dummy support and it's done. And the hanger part was easy too. There is set pattern of changes in strains in every part of the pipe. So it wasn't tough. But sir, this wouldn't have been possible if it wasn't for Amit. He is the genius behind this.'

I felt like I was back in college where during vivas I used to speak the most nonsensical things with the sky-high confidence and the professors used to see me with the same disbelief these people had written all over their faces. Only this time, it was because I was right. *Or Amit was right.*

'Did you hear that, Mr. Bhatli? Mr. Goyal? This is great work, Deb,' Malhotra said.

'Thank you, sir. But it was Amit who helped me with all of this,' I said.

'Mr. Bhatli, I need to see Amit after this meeting,' he said.

'Okay sir. I always thought Amit had the brains. I will do that sir,' Mr. Bhatli said.

'Deb, both of you have done a good job. You can go now. Keep up the good work,' Malhotra said.

I turned and just as I walked away towards the door, I heard Malhotra say to the others, 'Like father, like son. This chap will go a long way.'

I walked just a little slower to the door to listen to what others had to say.

I moved out smiling.

Mr. Goyal could have taken credit for spotting my talent, but I guess he was a dumbass after all. *Not a patch on my dad.* I was proud of my father. He would be too, the news would reach him, I thought. It did. But he knew me better than the Bhatlis and Malhotras. His message read –

Congratulations. Heard about you. I don't know what you are doing, but keep doing it. Because whatever it is, it's working. Miss you, son. Hope to see you soon.

That felt good, anyway. Amit was busy the whole day, as expected. He wouldn't get an out of turn promotion, as the system didn't allow that. But he wouldn't miss one for sure. The system doesn't account for geniuses, anyway.

'Hi Neeti. What's up?' I had nothing to do, so better than talking to a cell phone snap of Avantika, I thought it would be better to talk to Neeti. I hated to admit it, but it felt good talking to her. Or knowing that somebody cared. Some girl. Who incidentally could also go on and kiss me outside a relationship. I did start to think what Shrey said. Was it the best way to forget Avantika? Moreover, I feared my organ might turn vestigial out of sheer redundancy of the thing.

'Hi, Deb.' She looked and sounded miserable. I hadn't expected that. I thought she would go on mauling my ear with her stupid relationship thing even the next day.

'Are you busy? Can we talk? Actually, I have nothing to do with Amit all busy and stuff. And I am tired of sharpening pencils. I hope you are not still upset. I hope you understand. We can work this out.'

'You think so?' she said, raising her eyebrows up to her hairline. She did sound sexy in short sentences. Well... kind of. It was a welcome change.

'Yes, I do. Date sorts? You mind?' I lied.

'Okay, whatever you say, Deb... I don't have much work to do, anyway. I never do, you know. Okay, let's see. Let's go to Vasant Vihar, I have heard a lot about it, you know? But I've never gone there. Can we please go there? Of course, if you don't mind.' She was getting back to her usual self. Long sentences, often unnecessary.

'Sure, why not!' We left the office.

I quite loved it that way. Unlike the private firms, you can move in move out anytime you want to, especially if you don't give a shit about the work. Nobody can ever kick you out. And age turns out to be the biggest qualification.

We went to Vasant Vihar, which was a twenty-minute drive from my office. In its days, it used to be the most happening place in the city. But with its overwhelming popularity, wannabes had started to flock the place. But the regulars still kept coming to this place. It was still a sexy place to be in.

I couldn't say that I had a great evening, but after a long time, I'd gone out to a place, if you leave the India Gate outing out. Even Neeti, after the previous night's ordeal, was not saying as much as she was used to. She was a little depressed and that was the first time I felt she was not that hard to bear. But she was definitely likeable. Not that I had many people to compare her with.

'Bye, Neeti. Thanks for the lunch. If you see Amit, just tell him I have left. And do think about the night out. Please?'

'Okay Deb, will do that. Don't worry. Even I am excited about it. Thank you.'

'My pleasure,' I said as I walked away.

'Deb,' she called out. 'I am so glad we came out today. Thank you. If you need anything, just remember, I will always be there for you.' She turned back, with glazed eyes. She ran off. She was so much in love with me. I felt sorry for her. That day, she had acted and spoken like a grown up. She wasn't that bad, after all.

I went back home early that day and spent the rest of the afternoon sleeping after wrapping up some things I had to wrap up. I waited for Amit to come back. After months, I would be out on a night out. It was quite an unsettling feeling; nervousness was taking over some of my senses.

'Hi, Deb! You know what?' Amit said as I opened the door for him.

'No, I don't. Do I have a choice of not listening? I am just a little bit sleepy. We were out on a night out last night, remember?' I said. I didn't realize that when I was saving Avantika's life from villains in my dreams, it was Amit who had stayed up the whole night.

'Shut up and listen, Deb. I was given the responsibility of heading the whole piping job for the new refinery project that's going to start in December. And it's going to be so exciting. And you are working with me, so you should start working now. It is so amazing,' he said as he arranged the shoes in a perfect line and pulled his jeans another notch higher.

'Amit! No extra pay and extra work? Who does that? Okay, I am sorry, *you* do that. I am happy for you but I will stick to getting coffee for you,' I said. More work also meant more pencils to sharpen for me. I didn't quite relish that.

'Deb, there is something I want to talk to you about. Don't mind, but it is serious. Can we do it right now?' I had never seen such an expression on his face except once, when I caught him shagging. I thought he never masturbated until that day.

'Yes sure. Let's go and sit in your room. I have just used a mosquito spray in mine.' We moved to his room.

'Deb, I want to talk about Neeti. You know much more about relationships than I do. But Astha told me about what happened between the two of you. Neeti cried the whole night. And Astha didn't like it. And all of a sudden you went out with her today. Why Deb? You never did that before. I do not doubt you. I really like you. But I also really like Astha and I can't see her cry. I am sorry if I am wrong. But I thought it would be wrong not to tell you about this. I am very sorry.'

'Don't be. I can understand.' I did. I wasn't hearing this for the first time. I was so thankful I didn't kiss her previous night. Even when she was looking quite kissable by fifth grade standards, I did not do it. It was like a second shot, and I had done well at that. It wasn't tough, I thought.

'So, why did you go out with her today?' he asked.

'You will know soon,' I said. In those moments, I felt I had grown. I didn't kiss her, not because she wasn't my type or because I suspected she had dropped a few screws as a child. It was because I loved the little man and let him know that. I had learnt. I had made a friend and valued it. It was strange to actually look beyond the obvious. I felt like a sage. I had been so wrong. I missed Vernita, even Tanmay... and Avantika. One changes with time, from fighting for a window seat to the time when you are old and prefer an aisle seat closer to the washroom. I had chosen the aisle closer to Amit, letting go of the window to Neeti's life.

'Deb, there is also something else I wanted to tell you. Please don't be angry about it. I am sorry I did that. But that day when you locked me up in your room, I read your personal diary. There was a link you had bookmarked. I am sorry, but I couldn't help it.' He was more apologetic than I would have been after raping Neeti. I don't think I would have been apologetic at all. My insensate tool desperately needed to get in somewhere.

'I would have been very angry...'

'Deb, I am really sorry. I didn't mean to see it. You just kept...' he had hit the heights of paranoia.

'Amit! Will you let me finish? I don't have a diary. What you must have read was a blog I once maintained. I forgot its password so I stopped writing.' I did not forget it. Its password was – *Ilovedeb*. I hated it enough not to type it and loved it enough not to change it.

'You forgot your own password? You are kidding me. I am sorry, I told you. You don't have to lie to me.'

'Shut up, man. You know Gitanjali I told you about? She was the only reader I had. She kept trashing it, so I stopped writing. That's about it. Now chill.' I said.

'Whose story is it?'

'My,' I said, trying to recollect what all I had written. I remember Gitanjali refusing to read it any further. *Do not depress me Deb and for God's sake, get over her.*

'You really loved M, didn't you?' M was Avantika.

'I still do.' I said.

The doorbell rang.

'I will get that,' I said as I jumped out of his bed to get it.

'Who is that?' he shouted.

'I have something for you. Quick!' I called out to him and he came out shouting.

'Deb, I told you not to order from outside today. I had

called up the tiffin service… shit… what? What are you doing here? Deb, did you know they will come? What a surprise, Astha! Deb!' He looked at me and seeing me unmoved by all what was happening, continued, 'Oh so you knew. Why didn't you tell me? It is such a big surprise. Hi Astha! Sorry. I didn't expect this.'

'Hi Amit! Hi Deb! I didn't know about this too. Neeti dragged me here,' she said.

Seeing them talk felt like a better achievement than seeing Mr. Goyal lose his balls. After all, it was my doing.

'Okay, before we waste any more time. We have planned something for the two of you. We now know something about the two of you that you would take ages to tell each other. So, we thought we would just speed up the process for you. Welcome to your room for tonight.'

And I swung open the supposedly mosquito-infested room and for a few seconds I admired my creation. The room was filled with white and red balloons bobbing in it with a huge cake bang in the middle of the bed. Two massive teddies on each side of the cake with a bunch of roses in their hands completed the picture. There were frills criss-crossing every visible space on the walls. Half of my salary was gone. It was my first expense since I started earning. And it was worth it. I had kept the television light on and under the light from it; the whole setting couldn't have been more romantic. Piping sheets were much easier.

Amit and Astha waded into the room through all those balloons, awestruck at what they saw. I just loved it. Neeti winked at me in appreciation. The wink completed it. I had set this room for HER, just that she wasn't here. But her wink was. And I was.

I switched on the light. A gigantic poster awaited them, done beautifully in sparkling blue over a huge red sheet. It read:

The day Astha and Amit decide to marry each other.
Cheers to you guys.
—Neeti and Deb

'Takes care of your dad's worries, doesn't it?' I whispered into Astha's ear. Apparently, she too had been crying the last night for the same reason that Amit was. Only a lot harder. Her parents were pressing her to get married for quite some time now. Turned out, I was the happiest person last night out of all present in that room.

It seemed like their vocal chords had given way.

'Okay, I am bolting the door from outside. You are not going home tonight. And we won't open the door till the time you justify the cake and the balloons. Bye now. And don't you worry. Dinner is served. It's in the microwave right there,' I said and before they could shake themselves enough to say anything to me, Neeti rushed out and bolted them in. *No sounds this time around. He won't struggle to come out of that room now.*

Neeti and I pinned our ears to the door for the next half an hour or so, to catch any kind of sound. There wasn't any. We hadn't quite expected them to make out, but these guys weren't even talking. We both ate, sitting on the floor, right outside their door, just in case. Neeti drifted off before I could thank her for the cutest dinner I had ever had. I picked her up, placed her on Amit's bed, and saw her ensconce comfortably there. She looked beautiful sleeping. I was glad I kept my hands off her. Or was I? I missed being in a relationship. It sucked to be single.

I tried to read the newspaper after a very long time and didn't know when I fell asleep.

This time, I came in the way of a bullet that pierced right through my heart and saved Avantika. *Yet again.*

I woke up and walked up to their door. I saw more through prior knowledge than my still not fully opened eyes.

I creaked open the door.

'Good morning, Deb!' they said in unison. Quite clearly, they had not slept the night before. The balloons were still in their places. They were sitting on the floor facing each other. Like Neeti and I were, last night.

'Good morning, people. And why the hell do you think my parents invested in that huge bed?'

'Deb, we didn't want to disturb it. It is so beautiful. Moreover we had no camera in this room and we didn't want to let the most memorable moment of our lives go uncaptured. Thank you, Deb. Thank you very much. And I am sorry for doubting your intention about Neeti,' Amit said.

'I am sorry too, Deb. I was the one who started it. I am really sorry,' Astha added.

'It's fine, guys! So tell me. What did you decide? I hope we won't be disappointed by whatever you have decided,' I said.

'I hope not. We are leaving for Bihar tonight to talk to her father. Can you believe that, Deb? We are *actually* going tonight. I think I beat you there; I am meeting the girl's father within two days of my first date. *Deb, I am actually going*! Don't look at me like that,' Amit shrieked and burst with a heady concoction of pride, happiness, elation and a hell of a lot of other things.

'Is this true, Astha?' He had actually beaten me to it. I was so happy he did so. Anyway, I wouldn't have dreamt of doing anything like that, maybe except in Avantika's case.

'Yes, Deb.' She was stripped naked in front of me. That's how she made me feel, at least.

We hugged and shouted our tops off and woke up Neeti in the ensuing commotion. When she heard the news, she gave a shriek so loud that a couple of hyenas turned up at my door.

It was hard to believe that they were actually getting married. One date and that is all they took. It was just in the nick of time, or Astha's father would have selected one for her.

And two broken hearts in one house was the last thing I wanted.

They were at my place the whole day. They clicked pictures and discussed what they had to do when they reach Bhagalpur, her village in Bihar. Neeti and I, in the meanwhile, packed Amit's stuff up.

'You know what, Deb? I have never seen a guy like you. You are such a good friend. You are so caring, so sweet. I am obviously sad that we couldn't be what they are. But we are still more than good friends, no? And I am so happy about that. You are perfect, Deb,' Neeti said. 'Now what is that? You are stuffing the undergarments in the same compartment as the toothbrush? Give them to me. Let me do it.'

So much for being perfect.

Finally, the time came for them to leave. Just as they reached the main gate, they all shouted out in unison. 'Three cheers for our best friend, Deb.'

And they went on to the hip-hip thing which I always felt shouldn't be done more than twice; it becomes a drag the third time. But I loved it. I finally had friends, those who stayed up all night for me, that too for some damned sheets.

We all hugged and thanked each other for being wonderful friends and they left.

I was alone again. They were not to come back before a week, I was sure. So I had decided I would skip office for a week. I had been a good man for the last three days and I wanted to soak in my own goodness.

'I will pay you back someday for you are my best friend ever,' Amit told me and left.

Quite embarrassingly, he left me feeling loved, missed and in tears.

Amit's Gift

I spent the next few days lazing around at my place. Six days and fourteen hours to be exact. But without Amit, I didn't feel like going to office. Anyway, with the guard doing his duty, I didn't need to. I tried to rearrange my things, but gave up soon after realizing that I couldn't be doing any better to the room after what Amit had done.

I called up Neeti more than a few times to lend an ear to her shrieks, but even she wasn't that free anymore. I had watched all the porn I had. I snooped on Amit's computer. There wasn't any. I wondered if I had had sex more that he had masturbated.

Pipes were his only love, after Astha. I regretted not to have learnt anything about piping. At least I would have had something to do. It was supposedly the ideal life I had always imagined myself in. I had no expenses, I was doing nothing and I was as responsible for nothing. All I needed was Avantika.

I hadn't quite gotten over her. It wasn't that I was exercising my tear glands every day, but I still thought about her all the time. I daydreamed for hours at an end and imagined us being together in the future. At times, I did feel like contacting her, but I knew that would only add to the pain.

I always believed that one fine day she would return in my life... with a new boyfriend in tow and eventually drive me to suicide. That would be perfect. Two ex-boyfriends in jails and one dead. Sri Guru would be right too, then. She would then be the cause of all our sorrows.

But that was just one aspect. I day-dreamed about a million times during those months about the zillion ways in which we could cross each other's paths again sometime, anytime in the next many decades. And that we would walk into the sunset hand in hand, boyfriends, husbands, teenage kids, cancer notwithstanding.

I desperately needed to move on.

Tired from doing nothing the whole day, I finally decided to step out of the house to release the mouse from his trap. I had been feeding it for the last week or more. Feeding him required less effort than going out and letting him go.

As I entered my place, I spotted a big brown packet lying outside the gate. It was a courier. I checked for a Hyderabad address on it. There was none. It wasn't from mom. It was too big to be a prospectus of some college dying to take me in.

I opened it to find a big spiral bound document, which was about two hundred pages thick. I dreaded it to be some pipes or something I had done in the BINA refinery project and someone needed some clarification on it. Now that Amit was not reachable, I had no idea how I'd answer them.

'Deb, the dummy support you have provided here, do you think it will take the stress?'

'Deb, we ran it on Ceaser 2 and it is showing some major deviations, would you kindly check it and tell us?'

I reached for the cell phone to switch it off. As I switched it off, I flicked the first page open and expected semi circles and 3-D cylinders to jump on my face.

It was nothing like that!

Our Story
It screamed in big Times New Roman letters. *To Deb*, it said below.

I flicked through the page to reach the index. I read it. Twenty-one chapters. Twenty-one titles jumped out it.

Deb and Smriti, Deb and Fifth Semester, Deb and Splash, Deb and His Sister's Marriage, Deb and Yamini... Deb and Amit.

It was I. It was my story. They were *my* incidents. Everything that had happened was right there, in my hands. Somebody had recorded it. It was my life. On paper. The titles had me by the collar and transported me to the times they were set in. Everything started happening again. I watched everything go by. Smriti and walking in India Gate, Shrey having a smoke, I standing naked in *Splash*, kissing Avantika on the stairs, mom and dad leaving for Hyderabad... everything. It all came back. I was dumbstruck.

I started to flip through the pages, not to read, just to see what all was there in there.

Everything. Every *goddamned* thing.

The words came out and struck me. They were all either said or written by me. Some time or the other. Each one of them. The blog. Everything on the blog was right there in front of me. I skipped to the last chapter.

Deb and Amit.

It was Amit! I couldn't believe it. This is how he paid me back! He had strung it all together. I *so* loved the little man. I switched on my phone to call him up. He didn't receive.

I was trembling as I turned the first page to read. *Deb and Smriti.* I still hadn't come out from the shock it had sent me in. It was the best thing anyone had ever done for me.

My eyes welled up as I started reading it. Everything I had ever told him was in it. He remembered everything, every word, and every sentence. I started living every moment again. He had hung on to every word, everything that I told him. Everything that I ever loved, ever wanted, ever hated, ever felt. It was right there, in front of me. Amit was beyond pipes. He was my best friend. I would not give him up for a thousand jobs and a million girlfriends.

I was on the last chapter. It had been seven hours since I was reading it, never looking up unless it was for sniffing my fluids in. I was reading everything thrice and often even more than that. A lot of things were blog posts I had written on my own, but everything was so beautifully knit together that every new sentence deserved a tear. However strange it had been to listen to my stories with my girlfriends, he didn't miss a single thing I had told him. It often reminded me of things I didn't remember myself. He gave me the good times back.

I finished the last chapter. *Deb and Amit.*

I read the last line of it. *Deb, thanks for everything. You are the best.*

I cried a little more and thought about Amit a little more. I thanked God once more to have given me him and somewhere in between all that, I went off to sleep... *Our Story* scattered all around me on my bed.

I was woken up by the swinging open of the door of my place.

The Full Circle

There was nobody.

I went with groggy eyes to close the door.

As I locked the door from inside, she called out.

Think Deb, think. What does she want? What do you want? What does she want? Why is she here?

She had moved in and was standing right in front of me. 'Deb, come here,' she said.

She stood there in a black shirt and deep blue jeans, both of which clung to her body. I could have fed on her for days. Just when I started walking towards her, she ran up to me and ploughed into me, as she pinned me against the wall. She stapled me to the wall, my hands outstretched and pinned to the wall palm up. She stared deep and hard, came close and licked my lips once. She bit my lips and tilted her backwards until the first drops of blood seeped out from my outstretched lips. She then thrust her lips, tongue in my mouth, and hurt me with every bite of hers. We fought for dominance, sucked and bit wherever we could. She slipped her hand down and grabbed hold of my thing, and tried to push her hand back along it. It sent me into throes of ecstasy.

'Like it?' she asked as I pulled back from the kiss, grimacing in pain. She let go of me and stepped back. She unbuttoned her shirt but didn't take it off. She unzipped her jeans until something peeked out but didn't take it off either.

'Strip,' she commanded. 'I want you out of those clothes right now.'

I stripped. Out of my shirt and out of my shorts. And everything else. She moved further away as I moved towards her. Her smirk said it all. She had me naked and looking for cover. She didn't need any. She was looking gorgeous.

'What do you want?' she asked in the wickedest sense possible. She was staring where I was the hardest as if mocking at its size, presence and helplessness.

'I want you.' I was breathing heavily by then.

'I don't think you will be up to it.'

'I definitely will.' I grabbed her and she dug her teeth deep into my neck, pushed herself into me and grabbed hold of my ass, digging her nails in and clenched it. She climbed on to me, her legs wrapped around my waist and I carried her to my room. I dropped her on the bed amongst the scattered sheets of *Our Story*. She invited me with a naughty smirk all over her face. I slipped off her T-shirt. I kept her against the bed and kept her from grabbing hold of what was erect and rendering me paralyzed till the time she was naked. I pulled off her jeans.

'Like it?' she said again. It was a hot pink satin lacy panty. I was too frenzied to appreciate it.

'I don't think so. Doesn't suit you.' I grabbed it by my teeth and pulled it off slowly, never taking my eyes off her. She looked down on me, her eyes half closed and asking for it. I pulled it off slowly and bent over her.

She tried covering her breasts naughtily as I pulled out her hands to have one hard look at her. She was naked. I went down on her.

We crashed the television, we rolled over my laptop. I fought, I grabbed, I moaned. I was in. She bit, she clawed, she moaned. The more we became one, the harder she moaned, the more I groaned. This continued till the time I was dead with exhaustion.

I rolled away from her, leaving her body blue and battered. I was spent. We had our first sex... and I realized there were a lot of things a girl can do than just lie there while guy pumps away to glory. It was awesome.

'I was scared,' she said.

'About what?' as I outlined her breasts with my fingers. They looked gorgeous with my love bites on them. We had been barbaric.

'It thought you won't be this good,' she said as she grimaced as I pressed the biggest love bite I had ever given her. It was a huge bluish mark on the inside of her left breast.

'I was always this good,' I said and squeezed her right breast hard enough to get a shriek out of her.

'I don't think so, Deb,' she said, clenching her teeth.

'What made you come back, Avantika?' I asked.

'What we just did.'

'*This?* Which means you missed it. Proves my point. I was good.' I had expected something else.

'Maybe. Or that I found no one better.' She laughed out. She was still so gorgeous. She sat up and tied hair into a neat bun. Girls look better after sex, Shrey once told me. *So true.*

'I don't need anything of that,' I said and kissed her thigh, ready for another go.

'Easy, Deb. Just sit beside me,' she said as she fished something from her bag.

'Here goes, Deb.' She handed out some sheets to me.

It said - *Chapter 22. Deb and Avantika. Again.*
What?

'Deb, this is our story,' she said.

'Wh... at? Fuck. It was you? *It was you?* What for? Oh Avantika, I love you. But why?' For the third time, the flapping of the tongue. *How does she know about Amit? She is a witch.*

'Listen me out, Deb. Someone from Bramha Publications read your blog and mailed me. They wanted your story. I wrote it for them. This is what it is. The last chapter of our story. The end of our story. The end of me,' she said and started to look the other way. She had tears in her eyes.

The last part shook me to the roots. The pages fell out of my hands, trembling, shaking reaching out to her.

'*The end of... you?*' I asked as I fixed my stare at her and choked on my own words.

'I am dying, Deb. I am dying.' She broke down, turning away from my stare; she dug her face in my lap.

'What do you mean? What... What are you saying? Tell me you are kidding. Wh...' I went blank as I grabbed hold of her and made her look at me.

She looked up, her eyes filled up with all the sadness in the world, held my face with her hands and said, 'I have cancer, Deb. The drugs killed me. They killed me. Doctors say I have just a few months to live. That is why I am back. To spend my last few days with you. Please don't leave me, Deb. I want to live. With you. Please Deb. Don't let me die. I don't want to die. Please Deb... please...' she broke down and sunk inside my lap.

'Huh?'

I lost my senses. I felt numb. I looked at her. She was dying. *Avantika was dying.* The person I had dreamt of spending my life with, was right there in front of me. *Dying.* In my lap, begging me save her. Give her the life I promised I would. She was right there, asking for what she deserved. She wanted me to keep her, save her, love her. She was back with me, just as I wanted. But only to go forever, leaving me behind, forever... with the guilt that I couldn't save her. She would be gone, in a matter of days and all I would do was look at her die. In front of me. But I was helpless. I felt failed. I felt cheated. I felt punished. For all I had done before Avantika came in to my life. But why *her?* Why not *me?*

I mustered up courage to look at her again. She hugged me

as if to never leave. I never wanted to let her. She was beautiful. But I spotted things I was too lost in her to spot before. Her eyes were tired. Those eyes had lost the twinkle, those eyes in which I used to get lost in for hours, the eyes that said more than her lips, the eyes that winked naughtily, the eyes that saw a great guy in me. She had gone weak, her muscles were wasted, and her wrists barely had any flesh on them. She was all bones, her collarbones were prominent, her thighs were thin and scrawny... she looked terrible.

The love bites, which stood out, were on pale yellow skin, not on the glowing skin I used to touch on one pretext or the other. She barely had any strength when we made love, I remembered. I held her face, wet with my tears and hers, and noticed the change. Those pink lips had gone pale, that complexion lost its radiance. She was sick, and it showed. There was hair lying everywhere I saw. Chemotherapy makes you lose them, I had heard. I looked around to see *Our Story* scattered, beneath her hair, beneath her dying body. Beneath a dying me. Beneath a dying *us*.

I wanted to die. I wanted to die before her. I wanted to die with her.

'Avantika... What did the doctors say?' I asked as tears flooded my eyes.

'A few months. Last stage, Deb. A few months is all that is left for me now...'

I grabbed her and we cried out aloud. She broke out of me and started kissing away my tears. Just as I had done on the first night out.

It had been hours. I lay there looking at her, still in denial that she would be gone. I had lived these three months of separation, hoping that someday, some damned day, she will come back to me and we will be what we were again. She was back. But...

She spoke. I hung on to every word she said. If I survived

this, I would need every bit of her memory to carry on. I wanted to tell her how much I loved her. I wanted to hear the same from her. As many times as life would allow her. I would need her to say that she loved me with every breath she took. I would need whatever was left of her.

She locked my eyes in a gaze and said, 'Deb, they said... I will die in a few months... if I...'

'If...?'

'If I don't get enough of you, my sweetheart!'

'*WHAT?*' I let out, shocked.

And there it was, then. Her wink! She winked. And burst out laughing!

'What the fuck? What the bloody... *Are you crazy?*' I shouted at her as I jumped on the bed. How could I forget, this was Avantika!

'Aww... I am not going to leave your worthless life so soon, Deb.'

'You are an ass, you know that? Damn you, man! Were you out of your mind? I could have died, you bloody witch!' I shouted and swore happily.

'Why? You have cancer or what?' she stood up and hugged me.

'No, I don't. But I have great fucking girlfriend without whom I cannot live. And if she ever dies, I will go with her,' I said, looked at her and kissed her nose. Then, we cried a little more.

'Okay, Avantika. Does cancer spread through sex? Because I am ready to do it again, baby.'

'I don't think so,' she smiled and winked. I pushed her on the bed. I forgot about *Chapter 22*, whatever it was, it couldn't be better than this.

We spent the whole day on the bed making out whenever I was capable of it. It got wilder with each time and that's where the hair on the bed came from. Apparently, her weight loss was because of her aim to reduce to size zero. I categorically told her that it was absolutely unnecessary. She couldn't hold her laughter once I told her what I had imagined. *Deb and the Cancer Story*, it will forever stay.

'Deb, you have twenty missed calls on your phone. Pick it up.' I picked it up and she put me up on loudspeaker. It was the guard.

'Deb sahab? Deb sahab! I have been calling you since the evening. They caught me punching the cards today. They have taken both your cards. What do I do, Deb sahab? The vigilance team wants to talk to me tomorrow. What do I say, Deb sahab?' he asked frantically. There was a reason to be frantic. Suspension was a given. I knew Goyal was behind it. Nobody otherwise gave a shit about who punches your card. He wouldn't let this one go, I thought.

'Arjun ji, it's nothing to worry about. Tell them you just punched my card. Not a word about Amit ji. Get that? Just my card and tell them I asked you to hand over Amit's card to him as he forgot it on his desk. Just tell them I asked you do so, I will handle the rest,' I said.

'Okay, Deb sahab. Thank you.' He hung up.

'Avantika, can I have the laptop? If there is anything left of it, I mean!' I said.

'Why? Seems like you pretty much lost the job, didn't you? What are you going to do now?' she asked.

'Nothing much, drop some shit on people before I leave. That won't save my job, but will save my face, I guess.'

I didn't care about the job. I had Avantika. Jobs would follow. Although we hadn't exchanged a word about our relationship, I just knew she was there to stay. And there were plenty of jobs out there.

I typed out a long resignation letter addressed to Mr. Malhotra. I accused Mr. Goyal for mental harassment and all Amit's not-so-loved colleagues for making life hell for me, as they couldn't see me being so smart. Therefore, I had no choice but to start working from home.

'So what do you think? Will it work?' she asked.

'It has to. If not, dad will pull me out of this mess. So, it's not a big deal. I have you now.' I hugged her.

It got to me later that I had done a pretty good job with the letter. The vigilance was off me and I still had the job. But I resigned. I would have sounded guilty if I had not. I couldn't have possibly disappointed dad. I wanted him and everyone else to feel that I was a victim of office politics and I didn't want to continue anymore. Amit wasn't touched and that was all I cared about. Astha's parents wouldn't accept an *out-of-job* suitor. Goyal missed another promotion.

'So Avantika, I still didn't ask you something. What brings you back?' I asked.

'Sri Guru,' she said.

'Not again. He was the reason we were in this shit.'

'Shut up, Deb. At least now, I know that I cannot live without you. And for sure that you love me as much as I do.'

'Big deal. I could have told you that. Anyway, continue,' I said, happily irritated.

'I was back to my alcohol habit. The only time I didn't drink was when I was writing this book. I was fucking myself over all over again. It was then that I met Sri Guru again and realized I was running away from something that is truly mine. I was running away from my responsibility. *You.* I am ready to take that now. If something happens to you, I will make sure I set it right. If it is because of me that you see the bad times, it will be because of me, that you will see the good ones,' she finished. Thankfully.

'You bet! Whatever. I generally don't get this bullshit philosophy of yours. What I do get though, is that you are great kisser. Can we do it again?' I leant forward to get what was *truly mine.* She leant away.

'Before everything else, you should thank Amit. He read your blog and mailed me a comment, days after I met Sri Guru. He seemed to know a lot about me. That is when it all started to fall in place. He told me about you guys, and everything you did for them. I thought if these guys get treated so well, I should be in for super special treatment!'

'Ohh! Yup, I missed that. That is how those chapters came up. I will call him. But can we kiss first?' I leant forward and she leant away again. 'Now what? You still have something else? AIDS? Hepatitis? Whatever it is, I don't mind. Can we kiss?'

She again fished something out from her bag.

'Yes, there is something else too. Here goes. The first cheque from Bramha Publications. *Our Story* is being published this year. Like that?' She smiled and handed over the cheque to me. I read it aloud.

'What the...? Shit, this is unreal, man! I so fucking love you! I so, so, so, so, so damn love you! Can we please kiss now?' I jumped on to her, pinning her on the bed.

'We have to. *Chapter 22* ends with a kiss.'

We kissed.

Epilogue

And that, folks, is where my story ends. There was a lot of kissing, jumping on the bed, partying out, eating out and everything that followed when Amit and Astha came back, but let us keep it for some other time.

Avantika had her posting shifted to Delhi and I was still looking for a job.

Shrey was to come to Delhi in December, with his German girlfriend in tow.

When they came, (I have to admit I spent a lot of time staring at her ass), they wrecked my place, which Amit had so lovingly decorated now that Astha was a regular visitor. Shrey, among other things, made them kiss. Their first kiss, a month before they got married.

Virender and Yogender came visiting too and promptly asked them for a treat.

Amit, Astha, Neeti, Avantika... and of course, Shrey. I loved them all, they loved me back. Deb was back. Good times were back!

Life had turned a full circle. A screwed one, but a complete one.

Just in case you are interested in what happens two years down the line. Here is it...

Shrey too bought a copy of my book. *Pirated*. But he made quite some money in Germany and ordered the legal one. He was doing well too. He married the German and was disinherited from his family. He just became the youngest donator to the National Physical Laboratory. He hacked Suhel's account and somehow got him fired.

Tanmay and Vernita got married too after Vernita got pregnant. Vernita still works in that investment bank and rakes in quite some money. Tanmay, meanwhile, got through the IIMs and is travelling around the world on internships. Vernita talks to me now, occasionally. We never discuss the kiss. No matter how much I try to.

Virender and Yogender worked their way up right to the top before they were fired. For sleeping with their boss's wife. Together. It was her birthday party that got out a little of hand. They are now setting up their own auto-manufacturing unit. Together. The treat for that is still due.

And my best buddy now, Amit, has just shifted to the Middle East with their one-year-old son, Dev. His kid is already doing math sums. They are doing quite well too. We mail each other every day. In his last mail, he sent me the snap of his latest asset. An Audi. Last heard, his company was firing half his colleagues for inefficiency.

And yes, Neeti. She got married to Kumar last year.

Shawar is out. Paritosh is still rotting.

And for me - Avantika and I are still together. Avantika got me a job at her office and I was doing well. As her junior. The last place we made out at was our boss's cabin. Her idea. Avantika now though complains that I spend way too much time with my friends. Now that her Bengali classes are over, I am taking her to my mom today.

My book did hit the stands. I became a known face. Almost all those who knew me, now knew me better. Nothing more.

And of course... I love you!

Imagination seldom runs wild, but when it does, you have a book.